A PUZZLEMENT INDEED

"You're quite sure you're not the least in love with Andrew," Harry queried.

"Quite, *quite* sure," Becky confirmed.

"This is a puzzlement," Harry told the girl. "For he can see me and only true lovers can see and hear me."

"But Ally has seen you," Becky interjected.

"Yes," Harry the Ghost agreed. "That's part of the puzzlement. The wrong people—and too many of them—seem to be seeing me. I don't know what's to come of all this."

Becky's eyes lit up. "Do you think perhaps you might be able to haunt Papa until he gives up the idea of making me a titled lady?"

"I would hope we could find a quicker solution than one that involves changing your parent's mind since it seems to be something he does most infrequently. And, my girl, there are worse things you could be than a lady, I can tell you that." Sir Harry looked a mite affronted.

"Oh, I'm sure I've nothing against nobs—I suppose that's what you were—are—were—"

"Whatever," the ghost interjected in a testy tone.

Diamond Books by
Sheila Rosalynd Allen

THE RELUCTANT GHOST
THE MEDDLESOME GHOST
THE HELPFUL GHOST

The Helpful Ghost

Sheila Rosalynd Allen

DIAMOND BOOKS, NEW YORK

All the characters and events portrayed in
this work are fictitious.

This Diamond Book contains the complete text of the original
hardcover edition. It has been completely reset in a typeface
designed for easy reading, and was printed from new film.

THE HELPFUL GHOST

A Diamond Book / published by arrangement with
Walker and Company

PRINTING HISTORY
Walker and Company edition published 1990
Diamond edition / June 1993

ISBN: 1-55773-908-0

Diamond Books are published by The Berkley Publishing Group,
200 Madison Avenue, New York, NY 10016.
The name "DIAMOND" and its logo
are trademarks belonging to Charter Communications, Inc.

PRINTED IN THE UNITED STATES OF AMERICA

10 9 8 7 6 5 4 3 2 1

- *1* -

IF ANY OF the Wooster villagers had been on the top of the abbey hill that windswept April morning their worst impressions of the mercantile family who had descended upon Steadford Abbey three years before would have been confirmed.

"You must not, you cannot! I implore you—"

"Implore away but I must, I can and I *will*!" Thus saying the very spoiled Miss Becky Beal dismissed her interlocutor and ran down the wide front steps of Steadford Abbey's entrance.

Her sister Alice hovered on the brink of turning back into the house but duty overrode her fit of pique. She hurried in Becky's wake across the gravel drive, calling out for Becky to stop. Morning sunlight fell through the leaves of the copper beeches that lined the carriage road, dappling shadows across the swiftly moving girls.

Becky gave every indication of not having heard her sister's calls until she glanced back peevishly. "There is no need to get yourself into such a pelter. Go on back to your books."

"And leave you to roam the countryside with no chaperone and against Papa's express wishes? He said any more scrapes and you were for it, he'd overset his feelings and thrust you into a convent school to learn obedience and discipline."

"Stuff and nonsense," Becky replied as they passed the gatehouse rose gardens. "He'd never do anything so gothic. He couldn't bear the thought of sending me away."

Try as she might Alice could find no way to argue with her sister's words. Their papa had allowed Becky every leniency since they were in leading-strings and their mama had long ago given up trying to bring the girl to task. No matter how grave her offence, Becky simply ran to her father with tearful eyes and woebegone expression and all was forgiven.

Alice felt quite firmly it was due to Becky's abundant beauty. Her mother told Alice she was quite as pretty as her sister, although her beauty was of a gentler sort, the plain truth was people did not give Alice a second glance. Both Becky and their mother shared peaches and cream beauty, with honey-coloured locks and sky-blue eyes. Becky turned heads, her mother still earning smiles from the opposite sex upon her approach while Alice went unnoticed.

Alice had inherited her dark auburn looks and hazel eyes from her father. If one looked closely there were flecks of gold and amber in eyes that were much larger than her sister's. Her nose, while not Becky's petite, upturned button, was slender and straight and suited the classic lines of her face and figure. She had been told since babyhood that she would grow into her looks, but Alice longed for the baby-faced beauty that was her sister's.

Living in the shadow of compliments heaped upon her sister Alice had retreated to a world of books, living most of her hours in ancient Greece and Rome and long-gone British history. But at this particular moment she was racing headlong after her sister through muddy puddles which were quickly ruining her blue-kid slippers. As the sisters neared the thick stone walls that outlined the bottom of the abbey hill they crossed the wide driveway edged by oaks and copper beeches heading towards the stone buildings and arched gateway at which the walls ended. Stables flanked one side of the gateway, the other side flanked by the gate-house. The girls raced by a smaller gate which led from the gravelled drive through thick hedges to the gatehouse rose gardens and the abbey gatehouse itself.

Fannie Burns made a grimace at the sound of the girls' voices as she helped her mistress, Lady Agatha Steadford-Smyth, prune a bush near the kitchen doorway.

"That Beal girl should be taken well in hand about her hoydenish ways," Fannie declared.

Lady Agatha glanced up in time to see Alice disappearing from view into the stableyard across the drive. "She's such a quiet girl."

"Quiet?" The abigail was taken aback for a moment before she realised they were talking at cross-purposes. "If you mean Alice, I quite agree. And how that rackety family ever spawned such a meek little thing, I shall never understand. But that sister of hers is already notorious and just barely nineteen. How the abbey could have fallen to such philistines I cannot fathom."

"It fell these three years past and I, for one, am quite done up with the subject." Lady Agatha informed her servant. She had no intention of allowing Fannie to wax eloquent upon the subject of the Beals. Lady Agatha returned to her task with the roses. She reached to inspect the growing buds, the thick dark hair upon her bent head shot through with regal strands of purest silver. Large dark eyes and the figure of a woman thirty years younger belied her almost seventy years. But in truth her beauty came from a deeper source. It was the candor within her eyes, the calmness of her manner, that continued to attract to her the countryside's loyalty and love.

Lady Agatha was honest to the point of bluntness, given to speaking her mind forcibly and not without her own little crochets, including a healthy distrust of the opposite sex. But time and her granddaughter's husband had helped to mellow the bitterness she felt towards the male of the species.

Forced by her father into a loveless marriage, her husband gambling away her family home, her own now-dead brother Nigel tricking the drunken Homer Smyth into selling him the abbey in return for those gambling debts, she found little use for the male of the species. The sorrow of her son running away to be killed in the French war, of her daughter dying in childbirth, had hardened the bitterness she felt, until her granddaughter Jane brought warmth and love back to her heart.

The countryside which had always respected Lady Agatha, had grown to love her and so, although she herself had long-since reconciled herself to the abbey passing out of Steadford hands, the rest of the county—and her own abigail—had not.

"You may not care one whit, since you were so determined to cast it away, but others feel very strongly about a tradesman owning Steadford Abbey!"

"Since *you* are *determined* to natter on, please keep to the facts," Lady Agatha instructed her long-time abigail. "I didn't cast the abbey away—it was no longer mine and was sold by Sir Giles' solicitors."

"He asked you to take it back and you refused."

Lady Agatha continued pruning. Giles had been the second man she had seen good in after all her years of harsh treatment at male hands. Thoughts of her young cousin Giles softened her expression, her voice mild when next she spoke. "I am perfectly content living in the gatehouse."

"And before that the duke tried to give the abbey back to you before he and Jane left for the Americas," Fannie said, warming to her subject.

"You and I would rattle about all alone in that huge house," Agatha pointed out. "Besides, if I had taken the house back from Charles, Giles would never have come here to recuperate. He and Elizabeth would never have married. Did you read her last letter? The baby's growing by leaps and bounds."

"Botheration to all babies, you're just trying to change the subject," Fannie told her.

"I don't seem to be greeting much success at the attempt," Lady Agatha replied dryly.

"The point is that awful Londoner and his impossible wife and that bevy of girls would not have overrun the abbey!"

"Does two count as a bevy?"

Fannie gave her mistress a glowering look. "Mark my words, that Londoner and his family will bring disgrace down upon the abbey." She spoke the word Londoner as if mentioning a foreign disease. "I heard tell in the village that Letty Merriweather told Molly Beecher that George Beal's father was a common dustman! She said George Beal started out as a London street-hawker!" She waxed more and more incensed as she delivered that information.

Lady Agatha did not share Fannie's sensibilities. "It would seem he is one of these modern self-made men."

"Is that all you can say?" cried Fannie. "Steadford Abbey—the home of the Steadfords since the days of Henry Tudor—was sold to a dustman's family!"

Lady Agatha straightened up slowly, one hand pressed to the small of her back. "Since you ask, there is more I can say. Never in all these years did I realise that you were a snob, Fannie Burns."

"A snob! Me?" The abigail was put out. "Well, if you don't care about your heritage, I'm sure I shan't say another word."

"Hardly likely," Lady Agatha responded.

Miffed, Fannie pursed her lips and suiting action to words, saying nothing. However, her reproach hung heavy on the air between them.

While Fannie silently reproached Lady Agatha, on the other side of the drive Alice Beal was remonstrating with her sister. Alice tried to find persuasive arguments as Becky divested herself of a green-sprigged muslin gown.

"What if one of the stablemen come in? Papa will surely disown us both."

"Papa," Becky declared bracingly, "will never know. If you don't hurry, I shall leave you behind."

Alice fumbled with her own buttons, hooks and eyes, slowly following her sister's example. "They will never fit," she said of the second batch of rough male clothing Becky pulled out from beneath a mound of hay.

"They're not meant to fit properly," Becky replied as she tugged at wool trousers. "They are meant to disguise us as boys."

"This is a terrible idea!"

"Ally, if you're going to be such a droopy-drawers you might just as well hie yourself back to the house and play Patience—there is no need for you to come along."

"No need!" Alice reached for the rough woolen shirt Becky was handing her. "And leave you to go racketing

about the countryside alone? What if someone should recognise you?"

"In this?" Becky replied incredulously.

Alice had to admit that she herself would never have
given the young boy in rough country woolens a second
glance, let alone realise it was in reality her sister. Becky's
blonde curls were captured and tucked up under a dark
grey cap, her tiny feet encased in well-worn laborers boots
several sizes too large.

Tugging on rough breeches, Alice straightened up, her
face a mirror of her worries and fears. Her height fitted the
boy's clothing better than did her sister's petite figure. She
reached to pile her auburn locks under a brown woolen cap.
"This is your worst adventure yet!" Alice told her sister.

Becky smiled, the smile curving her full lips and lighting
her sky-blue eyes. "Oh, I hope so!" came the unrepentant
answer. "If you don't hurry I shall leave you behind."

Alice was scandalised. "You can't meet Paul alone!"

"I already have," Becky replied. "And you might as well
know I love him excessively and one day we shall wed."

"Papa's already told you he doesn't want you to even
see Paul." Becky made a face. "You sound exactly like
Papa."

"Papa is right," Alice defended.

"He may be right but you know as well as I he follows
his own pleasures gambling at White's and Crockford's."

"It's not the same for he's not a marriageable female,"
Alice said primly.

"Botheration!" Becky replied.

"Rebecca Marie!" Alice expostulated. "Good girls don't
swear."

"Bloody hell," Becky answered, adding insult to injury.
"Papa has his gambling hells and mama has her card games
and you have your books and I have my adventures and
that's that." So saying, she turned her back on her sister
and started for the stable doors.

"Becky, these boots are much too big!" Alice called out.

"Then stay where you are," came the ungracious reply.
"I shall roam the countryside free and happy whilst you sit

and read about some ninny-hammer medieval female!"

"I do not—"

But Becky was heading out the door. Unfortunately, before she had pushed the thick wooden door open Homer, the head stableman, thrust it inward and checked at the sight of an unknown visitor.

"What's this now? What are you doing in my stable?" he asked. "Jake? Tim?" Homer called out, all the while glowering at what looked to be a very young lad standing in front of him.

Alice, a little way away and unseen, ducked back amidst the tack, her heart hammering against her breastbone.

"I'm here to see Tim," Becky said in the deepest voice she could muster. She used his name since only Jake came through the door at Homer's command.

"Yes and why, might I ask?" Homer demanded. He was old and gaunt but his eyes blazed with the strength of his youth. The stableman took an aggressive step forward towards the unknown boy.

"None of your business," Becky snapped, her voice rising and then lowering as she realised Homer was staring at her more keenly. "It is family business," she added more quietly.

"I didn't know he had family," Jake said into the ensuing silence.

Homer's eye caught movement beyond the young stranger. Becky saw his eye go towards where Alice was hiding. "It's not his family, it's mine," Becky said quickly, trying to turn Homer's attention back to herself.

Homer came towards the thin young boy, ready to catch him and force the truth out of him. Becky waited until the latest possible moment and then lunged forward, striking out at the head stableman. Alice stifled her involuntary cry of horror at the sounds, stuffing her hands against her mouth, her eyes squeezed shut as if somehow this could help hide her.

The startled Homer fell back against Jake. "Damn and blast you to Hades, I'll give you what for when I catch you, you young jackanapes!" And so saying the stableman went after the scamp, Jake close at his heels.

Alice scrambled to her feet and lost her borrowed cap in the process, her long hair cascading in dark auburn waves down the back of the rough servant-boy's jacket. She reached to hike up her skirts and realised she had none on. Checking her headlong flight after her sister, Alice looked back towards the pile of green-sprigged dimity and went back for it.

By the time she peeked out the stable doors neither her sister nor the stablemen were anywhere to be seen. Alice plucked up her courage and went forward into the sunlight, telling herself repeatedly that she would never again try to restrain her headstrong sister. If Alice had not given herself the self-same lecture a hundred other times, it might have comforted her more.

"Alice?" Lady Agatha was just coming out of the gate-house across the drive. She looked thunderstruck. "Alice Beal, is it possible that it is you?" she demanded, thus belying Becky's claims that none would recognise them.

Startled, Alice blushed crimson and turned and ran as fast as her legs would carry her, the gowns and chemises held against her chest.

Lady Agatha watched in complete bewilderment as the girl raced up the hill towards the abbey. Then, turning back towards the gatehouse, Agatha went in search of Fannie.

"Fetch me my blue pelisse, Fannie. And a bonnet. I must pay a visit to the abbey at once."

Fannie came away from the dining room where she was folding fresh-washed linens, her eyes wide with surprise. "You haven't been up to the abbey in over a year."

"Yes, well, close neighbours do better the more distance they keep. But I cannot countenance girls dressed in rags careening across the countryside alone."

"I told you that Becky Beal was a hoyden pure and simple. She's bound for trouble, that one. I'll warrant she's seeing some boy on the quiet, like as not."

"That's as may be but it was Alice I just saw racing away. And she was dressed as a man."

BECKY HID IN the spinney, her drab brown clothing blending in with the underbrush as Homer charged through and on beyond, Jake trailing in his wake.

Beyond the spinney the hill curved down towards the river Stour in the far distance.

"He's headed for the river," Homer said as he stopped to catch his breath. Leaning forward, he took great lungfuls. "I'm not as young as I used to be," he informed Jake. "But by Jupiter, we'll nab that urchin if we have to swim to do it!"

"Perhaps if we called Tim from the pasture—" Jake offered, but Homer waved away the words as he straightened up.

"And waste more time? Come along. We'll nab the sorry little blighter and then we'll find Tim and get to the bottom of all this! Ho, there, is that him?" Homer cried out as he caught sight of a youth in the distance ahead.

"No," Jake replied, "it must be Tim." Then, shielding his eyes from the sun, he corrected himself. "No, it's Paul Beecher from the village."

Becky gave a little gasp and raised her head. She watched as the stablemen moved off down the hill, calling to Paul to wait and help. If he thought quickly he would realise she must have been caught out, Becky reasoned, but her heart was beating faster and faster. Paul was tall, with the nicest, most honest, countenance and locks of thick curly black hair, quite the most handsome young man in the county. But it was undeniable that he neither moved nor thought fast. His was a solid, dependable sort of intelligence and strength of purpose that was most reassuring and comforting even though it could be described as slow-witted by those of less charitable temperament. Becky's own impatient wit often chafed against his patient and trustworthy perspective in which he thought all things out before proceeding upon a course of action.

Paul's only excursions into light-headedness were when Becky managed to twist him about her slender fingers, as she did her father and every male she had come across in her nineteen years. Paul did not know how to say no to the adorable Becky and so became caught up in her schemes even while giving her grave lectures about his misgivings.

Now Becky waited until the voices faded in the distance before venturing to uncurl herself and sit up straight. The tops of their heads could just be seen disappearing over the rim of the hill towards the river, Paul now joining the search.

She waited until she could see them no more before moving out of the spinney and away towards the side of the abbey. In the distance around the abbey hill all was serene, fat brown-speckled cows grazing in the pastures, fields full of green-growing vegetables punctuated by hedgerows and low stone walls. Wild spring hyacinths and crocuses, bleeding hearts and woodland mosses were sheltered beneath the ancient live oaks as the freshening wind whipped at wisps of Becky's golden curls that escaped the boy's cap she wore.

Out of breath, she ran as fast as her legs would carry her to the shelter of the rose bushes that lined the near side of the huge abbey. The house sat sentinel at the top of the hill, overlooking the surrounding countryside from its high vantage point, and rising three storeys above the crest of the hill, its building stones each two feet square.

But it was not the abbey's stone walls that Becky watched, it was its long narrow and open windows. Sneaking near rose bushes just beginning to bloom pink and peach and ruby-red, she crouched over, heading towards a hidden doorway near the front. Built in Tudor times as an escape route for the Catholic monks who originally owned the abbey, Becky Beal found the tiny doorway and its narrow hidden stairwell within a fortnight of her arrival.

She ducked inside the dark passage and felt a hand reach out to stop her. Becky Beal gasped, ready to strike out until she heard her sister's urgent whisper.

"Becky, it's me! We must change back into our own clothes and leave these here—Lady Agatha saw me!"

Becky could not see her sister's anxious face in the darkness. "We can't very well repair our clothes or our hair in the dark, now can we? They're bound to be dirty and wrinkled. It's a little late to become practical," Alice said with more than a little asperity.

"Oh, do stop worrying, nothing's going to happen now." Becky sounded disappointed. "We got caught much too early. But next time it will be easier as we've already taken the clothes."

"Next time?" Alice expostulated. Then came another thought, "They'll all think I'm the one running to secret trysts!"

"Nonsense," Becky said bracingly, "they never would."

Alice followed her sister up the tiny pitch-black stairwell, unsure whether she should take umbrage at her sister's dismissive words. As she thought about it, Becky continued: "Lady Steadford has barely spoken to Papa since we arrived. There's no reason for her to begin now."

"You did not see the look upon her face." Alice told Becky. "And it's Lady Agatha, not Lady Steadford, she was born a Steadford and married a Smyth."

"I never did get straight all those curlicues of when one is a Lady with her first name or her last and all the honorables and titles and such our governess spent so much time over."

"Which governess?" Alice retorted. "You chased them off as soon as they arrived."

Becky laughed, then whispered, "We're getting near Papa's room, so do be quiet. If you don't intend to have fun, I don't know why you came along in the first place."

"I came along to keep you from going completely beyond the bounds," Alice told her sister in a loud whisper.

"Shush," Becky replied.

The narrow stairwell opened into a huge built-in closet-clothespress that filled the inner wall of the capacious master suite bedroom. Becky listened but heard no movement in the room beyond.

"I think it's all right," Becky said as she stepped into the wardrobe and opened its door. The bedroom and the sitting room beyond were wainscotted with oak and papered in dark blue flecked with tiny golden crescents. The spring sunlight splashed brightness across the silent room, warming a patch of the oriental carpet and the wing-back chair by the west windows.

Becky stepped out, heading swiftly for the sitting room. Alice followed, holding her crumpled dress against the borrowed shirt she wore. Blinking in the sudden brightness, she stumbled on the edge of the oak wardrobe and lost her balance, crashing to the floor in a swirl of white dimity and tangled auburn hair.

"What the devil—?" a man's voice expostulated from across the room.

"Oh, Papa!" Alice brushed her hair out of her eyes and looked towards the carved walnut bed expecting to see her father reclining for an early afternoon nap.

What she saw took her breath away. At first she thought her father was floating a foot above the thick dark-blue velvet coverlet. Then she realised he was not her father, but another man. Or what looked to be almost a man. Dressed in tattered-looking antique velvet, he was dark-haired and rather big. And he was luminous. And he floated.

"Who—what—are you?" Alice asked, her eyes rounded.

The translucent figure shimmered upward. He was even bigger than she had thought and he looked aggressive. Alice shrank back as he came towards her.

"I am Sir Henry Aldworth, Bart." He sketched a slight bow. "Or at least I once was. And I am deuced glad that at last someone in this house can see me—the dearth of sensitivity amongst your family has been dashed boring."

Voices came from the sitting room. "I tell you, I heard someone fall." Mary Beal's high-pitched voice came from the hallway beyond.

Sir Harry the Ghost studied the girl who was squinting at him. "You can't hear me," he realised glumly. "I don't know what the modern generations are coming to, they have no sensibility whatsoever. You would think," he added peevishly, "that at least one of you would have some imagination. It gets blasted tiresome wandering around by myself in this house and never even able to scare up a bit of fun." He said this last with more than a little reproach. As he spoke he heard a familiar voice float up the stairwell, asking to see Mrs. Beal in distinctly regal accents. Harry cocked his head, a smile spreading slowly across his visage. "By Jove, I hear Aggie!"

Alice watched the ghostly apparition disappear before her eyes, quite sure her fall had addled her brain. Then she remembered Becky and ran through the connecting door to the sitting room and the hall beyond.

Lady Agatha's voice floated up the stairwell from the large entrance hall below. "I felt I must inform you, Mrs. Beal. I know not what to make of it, your Alice has always seemed a quiet, biddable girl, but there it is."

Standing in Lady Agatha Steadford-Smyth's presence, Mary Beal was obviously flustered. The former owner of the abbey was more than a little daunting to the daughter of a London washerwoman. "But—what can she have been doing?"

"I have no idea," Agatha replied. "Nor do I wish to conjecture on the subject or interject myself into your family concerns. It is a particular dislike of mine for people to meddle in where they're not asked. But in this case I felt it my duty since young girls can so easily lose their reputations once scandal-broth begins to brew."

"Aggie." Harry drifted in the air at the top of the stairwell. "Aggie, my girl, you've not come to the abbey in ages."

"I'm sorry if she upset you, Lady Agatha," Mary Beal apologised.

"You should concern yourself more with your girls' sense of propriety, Mrs. Beal, and less with my sensibilities. It is of no great matter to me but I felt it my duty to apprise you of what I saw. Alice has turned eighteen, I believe, and Rebecca nineteen. They should be well beyond childish pranks. It is time they settle down and stop kicking up larks.

You certainly don't want their reputations ruined before they've even come out."

"Oh dear, you don't think they're ruined do you, Lady Agatha?"

"I have no idea for I have no use for idle gossip," Agatha Steadford-Smyth replied. "However, I do not scruple to tell you that tongues wag at the least chance in such a small village. They always have and they always will."

"Yes, thank you, thank you, Lady Agatha." Mary Beal was wringing her hands. "I shall talk to the girls. Would you—could I offer you a cup of tea?"

"Thank you, no."

"A glass of sherry and a biscuit, perhaps?" Mary Beal cast about her for an appropriate suggestion.

"I am neither hungry nor thirsty. Thank you but I must get back to my chores."

"Your—yes, yes, of course. Your chores. One had no idea you did chores." Mary Beal saw Lady Agatha's quizzical expression and blanched. "I mean that people like you had chores. That is—thank you, thank you again."

"Aggie, you've hardly arrived girl, you'll not take off so soon," Harry remonstrated with the unhearing Lady Agatha. "Hell's bells, I don't know why you of all people can't at least see me!" Harry's tone grew more aggrieved but none could hear him.

The new butler, Peeves, closed the door after her ladyship and turned back to his mistress with barely concealed disdain. Peeves had been the Earl of Clare's valet before George Beal hired him away and promoted him. Wages and position notwithstanding, Peeves every gesture conveyed a faint tinge of distaste as he waited upon the merchant's brood. He corrected the Beal family whenever possible, the rest of the time suffering in silence at each gaucherie, reminding himself he had doubled his former salary by accepting George Beal's offer.

Mary Beal felt the butler's disdain and had complained to her husband that Peeves looked down his decidedly long nose at his employer's entire family. George Beal had given his wife a sound smack across her posterior, informing her in booming accents that that was exactly why he had hired the man.

Having been given this decidedly unuseful information and realising there was nothing to be gained from further petitioning her very positive husband, Mary Beal scraped along as best she could, mainly by seeing as little of Peeves as was possible. As soon as the door closed behind Lady Agatha, Mary hurried up the stairwell and away from the supercilious major domo. As she moved she walked straight through Harry's ghostly form.

Harry scowled at the small woman's receding back. "Must you add insult to injury, woman? By gad, I've never been treated with such disrespect in my entire death! Something had best be done around here," Harry said darkly. "And done soon!" he yelled at the household at large. Since none could hear him he ended more frustrated than he had begun. He strode up the stairs, stalking off in as high dudgeon as he could manage given his ghostly state.

- 3 -

GEORGE BEAL ARRIVED home from a day's hunting to find the household in an uproar and his wife remonstrating with him in high-pitched accents from the moment he walked in the door. She began a long tale of woe which followed him up the stairs and into their rooms as he changed his clothing, helped by Peeves. So upset that she totally ignored the butler's presence, Mary Beal told of Becky's latest escapade and then reminded her husband of every indiscretion Becky had committed over the past nineteen years until he finally cried halt.

"Enough," his deep voice boomed out. "Let me get my wits about me before I listen to you dish up all our girl's sins!"

In the long years of her marriage before Peeves arrived, Mary Beal would have ignored her husband's ejaculations and continued to stay her course. As it was, Peeves was standing in front of her husband with a very disapproving expression upon his face. "I shall be in the red drawing room," Mary informed her husband with as much dignity as she could muster.

Unfortunately her husband's attention was focused upon Peeves who was withdrawing from around George Beal's neck the cravat he had been attempting to tie. "Peeves, what the devil are you fussing over?" George asked as his wife left the room.

"The cravat does not suit, sir. There is a spot upon it."

"Damme, there is?" George squinted at the spotless-looking yellow silk.

"If I might suggest another colour, sir, I would think you might like to try the pale cream. It will look especially elegant with the deep purple of your coat."

"Do you really think so? It seems a bit tame."

Peeves kept his expression blank. "I have noticed, sir, that you often enjoy rather colourful combinations of dress."

"Why, thank you, Peeves," the hefty man said, taking the words as a compliment. "I'd best go find out what all the uproar is about."

Mary Beal and her two daughters waited in the small red drawing room. Three years previous, upon first seeing the grand mansion, she had declared the small room not only sweet but the only one in which she felt comfortable. She had furnished it with the few bits and pieces George had let her bring from their old house in London, and here she felt more at home than anywhere else in the drafty old abbey everyone made so much fuss over.

When her husband arrived downstairs Mary cast one swift glance behind him, reassuring herself Peeves was not about to make an entrance before she spoke.

"George, our girls must have teaching in deportment. They're growing as wild as red Indians and I don't know what's to become of them! Now they've even upset Lady Agatha!"

"Bother Lady Agatha," Becky said unrepentantly. She gave her sister a long look from under eyelashes, willing her to be silent on the subject of their current disgrace.

"You see how they address their own mother?" Mary asked their father.

George Beal was smiling. He was a big, bluff man, given to a hearty manner and loud-voiced comments. Sandy red hair was thinning atop his rounded head, his rounded figure sporting more than the beginning of a paunch. He stood by the fire, poking at the coals. He looked down at his elder girl with twinkling eyes. "So you've been up to more devilment, have you?"

"It's Alice who got caught by Lady A," Becky told her father with an unrepentant grin.

"They were dressed up as boys!" Mary Beal interjected.

"We were just having a bit of fun, Papa." Becky cast up at her father so roguish a look that he had to smile back at her. "It's dashed boring doing samplers and practising our piano lessons all day."

"Listen to her language," Mary Beal told her husband. "Lady Agatha has as much as said that none will ever marry them at the rate they are going."

"Well, there she's dead wrong," George Beal told his wife. "Becky will be married before the year is out and I'll find a likely one for Alice too."

The three women stared at the man who was husband, father and protector. "Father?" Becky quizzed.

"George?" Mary Beal added.

"Papa, what do you mean I'll be married too?" Alice spoke in a rush of words, her large hazel eyes filled with concern. "I never intend to marry."

"All girls marry," her father declared. "At least the good and proper ones do and none can say either of mine was a light frigate nor ever shall be!"

"George, why are you nattering on about nonsensical things when something important is being discussed? Of course the girls are good girls. But they are too wild by half and they must have instruction in the airs and graces if you expect them to marry well."

"They'll marry as well as any in the kingdom or my name's not George Beal." He continued with the air of a member of parliament about to give a stirring speech he was sure would be greeted with rousing approval. "I have long considered what you have said," he told his wife in stirring tones. "About Becky's pranks and mischief." He was rewarded with a startled glance from his elder daughter. "Yes, my girl, I am well aware you are a scamp and a hoyden."

"Oh, Papa," Becky smiled her most beautiful smile, "surely not a hoyden."

"Let's not mince words. Your mother's fears are justified—"

"*Thank* you!" Mary Beal interrupted.

"*However*," George continued, "I also realise the reason for Becky's high-spiritedness. And I have found the solution."

Becky looked dubious. The only solutions her mother and her many nannies had ever had for her tantrums and her petty rebellions were to send her to her room or dose her with vile-tasting medicines.

Mary Beal looked mystified, but Alice watched her father with a clear-eyed, curious gaze.

His next words startled them all.

"What Becky needs is a husband."

"Oh, Papa! Has Paul spoken to you?"

George scowled. "Don't start that nonsense again. What you need, my girl, is a husband that can tame you. Keep your high spirits under control."

"I shall hate him excessively!" Becky burst in upon her father's monologue.

"No, you will not," George Beal told his daughter. "I shall not allow it. Besides, you've not met him."

"So much the worse," Becky proclaimed in a highly dramatic tone. "How can my own father wish to send me into slavery with some unknown tyrant?"

George Beal was very nearly apoplectic. "Of all the ungrateful, slothful—" he searched for a word that would express his displeasure—"*girls* that ever drew breath, you are the worst. And to think to what pains I've gone to insure your future."

Mary Beal took a step towards her husband. "George, stop shouting and tell us what you are talking about."

"I'm NOT SHOUTING!" George Beal shouted.

"You shall bring Peeves in upon us!"

George looked intractable but he lowered his voice. "You shall all soon fall upon your knees asking for forgiveness! Rebecca—"

Becky found herself inwardly quaking for the first time in her short life. Her father never called her Rebecca. "Papa—?"

"You are a will-full and head-strong girl."

"Yes, Papa," she replied with proper meekness.

"I had considered giving you a London Season—"

"Oh, Papa," Becky's pleasure at the unexpected possibility was soon cut short.

"But I decided against it due to your overly boisterous nature." He did not add that he had also realised his

daughters would be treated as the progeny of a wealthy
cit—which meant they would be politely ostracized from
Almacks and the best parties and would have little chance
of making a worthy alliance.

Mary looked from Alice to Becky. She saw relief on her
younger daughter's serious face, disappointment shadowing
Becky's pretty features. "George, you have often said we
must find London husbands for the girls as there were no
truly eligible men in the county."

"I promise you I have the situation well in hand." George
Beal spoke in tones filled with wounded dignity.

"I have concluded an arrangement with the Earl of
Marleigh. His oldest son and heir, Lord Andrew Marleigh,
is not to be sneezed at, I can tell you. He is the prize of
the Marriage Mart and—" Becky's father paused for full
emphasis. "*And* he's going to marry Becky and make her
a lady. Lord Andrew and Lady Becky. Just think on it,
Mrs. Beal. And when the old earl dies, our Becky will be a
countess!" George Beal looked very proud of himself. "Not
that I'm wishing the earl, his father, into an early grave, mind
you, there's plenty of time for that. But wouldn't that just
make my old pa turn over in his grave. . . ." George sighed
at the thought, quite content with himself and waiting for
his family's praise.

"The Earl of Marleigh—?" Mary repeated faintly.

"But I've never even met him," Becky interrupted.
"Whyever should he want to marry me?"

"Perhaps he's nice," Alice put in.

Becky stamped her foot. "I shan't marry him!"

"Oh yes you shall," George thundered. "Of all the
ungrateful, disrespectful daughters that ever saw light of
day—Mrs. Beal—how could you spawn such an ungrateful chit?"

"I?" Mary Beal lost all words.

George Beal faced his daughter. "You *will* marry Andrew
because I wish it! And because his father wishes it and
that's flat! This is a civilised country, my girl, and you'll
do as you are bid."

Becky resorted to the most feminine of wiles, copious

tears. In betwixt her sobs she gently accused her father. "But Papa, how can you bid me to marry an odious stranger?"

"By Jove, you've no need to become such a watering-pot. I don't expect it."

"Oh, Papa," Becky breathed her words of relief.

"You shall meet him all right and tight, never fear. They'll be arriving the first of the week."

"They?" his wife interjected. She looked horrified.

"The earl, the countess and young Andrew."

"Mr. Beal!" Mary was flushed with distress. "Are you telling me you've invited nobs to this house and not even told your own wife!"

"Now there's no need for you to fly into a pelter, I've had enough nonsense with Becky and I'll not hear more. They're just people, after all."

"People!" Mary was stunned by her husband's want of understanding. "You know how I am about nobs—why I even cringe when Peeves is near-about cluck-clucking under his breath and forever telling us what we're doing wrong. And he's only a gentleman's gentleman!"

"And I've given him butler duties just because of that, Mrs. Beal. It's a mark of distinction, I can tell you. The more snobbish your butler is, the more you're looked up to amongst the nobs. Besides, it's the likes of us who are the stout stock England's truly made of, my girl."

"I don't mind being stout stock," Mary told her husband, "but I wish we were back in Southwark where we belong and never had to have truck with abbeys and earls."

"We belong anywhere we choose and can afford," George replied. "Without the likes of us just where would the likes of them be, after all?"

"Still in their castles and lording it over the countryside," Mary replied sharply. "Just as they always have done."

Becky could keep still no longer. "I'm sure you think all this odiously provoking Mother, but since I am the one most concerned and since it's Lombard Street to a China orange this Lord-Whatever and I shan't take to each other in the slightest, you've no need to worry about his family looking down their undoubtedly long noses at us. They may be coming but they shan't stay long enough to give you the fidgets."

George Beal was not about to have his perfectly laid plans upset by a whisp of a female. "You, my girl, had best not try any of your tricks and pranks on the earl and his kin or you'll have me to answer to. I've been an easy father—"

"Too easy by half," Mary put in with some little asperity.

"That's as may be, but you'd all best remember I am head of this household and you'll do well not to put me in a tweak about this. You, young Becky, will do as you're told." George delivered this pronouncement in booming tones.

Becky began to weep again but soon realised her tears were not having the proper effect. She sniffed them back, regaining her composure with remarkable alacrity and giving her father a saucy smile through the remnants of her tears. "I never have yet," she told him. "I have no intention of marrying some puffed-up conceited coxcomb. I don't mean to disoblige you, Papa, and I know how much your heart has always been set on having a title in the family, but that's flat!" So saying Rebecca Beal turned her back on her family and flounced out of the red salon.

There was silence in her wake, her father's complexion colouring as beet red as the walls. He fought for the proper words to vent his spleen. "Thunderation!" he finally bellowed.

Mary gave her husband a withering look. "You can swear the devil out of hell but it won't change the fact, you've been too gentle by half on that girl and this is the result."

"Gentle, is it? She needs a proper melting, she does, and I've a mind to give it! Here I offer her the biggest prize on the Matrimonial Mart and she turns him down before she's even seen him!"

"But Father," Alice cried out. "You can't have such a want of delicacy as to expect Becky to marry someone for whom she does not feel the slightest *tendre*."

George Beal glowered at his younger daughter. "If you wish to worry, my girl, you'd best worry not about my lack of delicacy but about your own and your sister's lack of manners. For marry you will *and* to whom I say, or my name's not George Beal!"

Mary Beal cast a reproachful look towards her husband. "You've let them have their way since they were tots and dumped porridge all over their nanny. I can't imagine how you can now hope to turn such sad romps into duchesses."

"It's countesses we're talking of and Becky will only be a lady at first. She'll have time to learn the rest before the old earl draws his last."

Mary Beal sighed. "George, any ninny-hammer can see that it won't fadge. This Lord What's-his-name will never come up to scratch. And she'll never like him since her mind's made up to hate him on sight. And even if he did and she didn't, she'd still need time to grow accustomed to the idea. You know what Becky is like."

"Damn and blast, woman, am I the ruler of this household or am I not? She'll have time enough to come to her senses and if she doesn't—if she doesn't"—he glared at his wife—"you shall make her come to them."

"Mr. Beal, mark my words, you are fast on to creating a high Cheltenham tragedy!"

- 4 -

TWO DAYS LATER Leticia Merriweather arrived at the abbey gatehouse, full of news. "Can you credit it? The Earl of Marleigh and his family about to visit the *Beals*?"

"No, I cannot," Fannie told the widow bluntly. "How could such a rough and tumble tradesman as George Beal know an earl in the first place, let alone invite him to stay? And in the second place, how do you know what they're about?"

"That's another story altogether," Leticia said delightedly. Never having been slim or silent, the widow Merriweather had become more rotund and more inclined to gossip as each year went by. The Beals had given her much pleasure these three years past, but now her excitement knew no bounds.

"Crockford's," Letty Merriweather breathed the word of the famous London gambling club. "I simply had to come tell Lady Agatha what was about to transpire at her abbey. And White's too, I'll warrant," she continued, going back to her original thought. "The earl is a gambler and he's in Dun Territory! Pockets practically to let, I'm told."

"And who's doing the telling, pray tell?" Fannie asked a trifle dryly.

"Peeves, their new butler overheard the parents discussing what all had transpired upon George Beal's last trip to London. And Margaret Summerville says—"

"Leticia—" Lady Agatha walked into the sunny kitchen where the widow Merriweather was being entertained by Fannie. "I thought I heard your voice."

"There will be visitors at the abbey—" Leticia began.

"Pockets to let!" Fannie scoffed. "The earl has holdings all over the north." She saw her mistress eyeing her with disapproval.

"Which earl are you talking of?" Lady Agatha asked.

"All entailed, he can't sell off one whit," Letty informed them both. "It seems the former earl realised what a rake his son was and made sure the lands would remain in the family. I tell you both, he's into the money-lenders. He's Quality, but he's fair on to drowning in the River Tick! Or he was until George Beal offered to pay his sums in return for a small favour."

"What favour?" Fannie asked.

"Don't encourage her," Lady Agatha remonstrated.

"Lord Andrew Marleigh, the eldest son and heir of the earl is coming to offer for Becky Beal's hand in marriage." Letty delivered her best news last and with the air of someone who had brought word of Napoleon's debacle and demise.

"The Earl of Marleigh visiting the Beals? Utterly impossible," Lady Agatha declared.

"They're quite impossible socially, I agree," Letty said placidly. "I mean can you just feature Becky Beal a countess? Peeves says they haven't a clue as to whether to use their forks or their knives."

Lady Agatha pulled a long face. "It would seem this Peeves says entirely too much."

"Peeves says it's more than a body can bear. What is the world coming to, I ask you, when cits not only invade the abbey but marry their daughters to the nobility!"

A knock at the door interrupted their conversation. Fannie disappeared through to the front of the gatehouse, coming back a few moments later, a strange expression on her face. "Miss Alice Beal," she announced, "is in the parlour."

"Oh, dear," Leticia spoke softly. "Do you suppose she heard me?"

Lady Agatha left Fannie to answer Leticia Merriweather and went to the front parlour. Alice Beal's bent head came up at the sound of Lady Agatha's approach. She quickly stood up and bobbed an awkward curtsey. "I've been sent, I mean, I've come, to apologise for—for disturbing you."

Agatha motioned the girl to a chair and seated herself across from the narrow Queen Anne chair young Alice chose.

"I was not disturbed," Lady Agatha replied. "I merely wished your mother to be aware of the possibility that your sister was treading dangerous ground. And compromising you in the process."

"But she hadn't. I mean, she didn't. She didn't even want me along, Lady Agatha."

"That's as may be but without Rebecca's penchant for rebellion you can't convince me you would have been racing across the countryside dressed as a boy. She could have gotten into extreme trouble, a girl alone traversing the land without chaperone or safety."

"Oh, no, Paul would have—" Alice trailed off.

"Who is Paul?"

" . . . Paul . . . Beecher." The name came unwillingly.

"The butcher's son?" Lady Agatha sounded more stern than surprised. "Are you saying she was going to meet a male? Alone?"

Alice swallowed hard. "Lady Agatha, I implore you, don't ask. I cannot tell you more, my word of honour is at stake!"

Steady dark eyes regarded the young woman. "I normally applaud loyalty, Miss Beal. But not at the cost of propriety and a young woman's reputation."

"There's nothing improper, I assure you."

"Wandering the countryside unbeknownst to your parents and dressed in urchin's rags is already the height of impropriety—meeting young men *alone* and on the sly is simply beyond the pale. Has your governess taught you nothing?"

"We've had so many—most of them gave up on us quite early on," came the honest reply.

"And your parents? Surely they must have instructed you in deportment."

"My mother used to say we were growing like wild flowers. Now she says we've become wild Indians and she's afraid of what's to come next."

"I quite agree," Lady Agatha told the girl.

Alice stood up, her face crimson. "I'm truly sorry if we've caused you any distress. We never meant to."

"You should worry more about your mother's distress, my girl." Lady Agatha's expression was much softer than her words. She saw in the young Alice glimpses of her own granddaughter Jane many years ago. Alice was nothing like Jane in colouring but her wide honest eyes reminded Agatha of the clear-headed intelligent honesty with which Jane had always met life. Agatha admitted to herself she hoped the younger Beal sister would be able to withstand the seduction of following in her older sister's rebellious and brazen footsteps.

Alice was at the door before she turned to face the elderly and very patrician dowager. She bobbed another curtsey and then looked into Lady Agatha's stern yet somehow friendly expression. Alice's voice was faint. "Lady Agatha, may I ask a question?"

"Of course," came the reply.

"Is it possible—I mean do you believe—that is—have you ever seen the Abbey Ghost?"

Agatha was startled. "What?" she demanded in rather louder tones than she intended. "What are you asking, child?"

"There's been—talk—of a ghost at the abbey. I was just wondering—"

Fannie appeared in the doorway behind Alice, drawn by the sound of Lady Agatha's exclamation. "Is something the matter?" Fannie asked. Alice turned at the sound and faced the grim-faced Fannie. "I'm sorry," the young girl exclaimed in a little rush of breath. "I'm so sorry—" She ran past Fannie and on outside.

Fannie watched her go and then turned back to see Lady Agatha's quizzical expression.

"More goes on with that one than meets the eye," Lady Agatha pronounced.

Leticia Merriweather came down the hall from the kitchen. "What did the girl want?" she asked, her eyes alight, her ears attuned to the hint of intrigue in the air.

"I'm sure I don't know," Fannie told the busybody.

Leticia Merriweather was not to be dissuaded. She turned to her old friend Agatha. "You must tell me all," she proclaimed.

Lady Agatha stood up, straightening her back to her full height and staring down at the dumpling of a woman who began to visibly shrink under Agatha's dark-eyed accusatory gaze. "I do not think the Beals are any concern of yours, Leticia. I know they are no concern of mine," she added in ever more repressive tones, leaving Fannie to see the diminutive widow to the door.

When they were alone, Fannie approached her mistress. "Why were you shouting at the poor girl?" Fannie queried with a perplexed brow.

"I never shout," Lady Agatha corrected and said no more.

Fannie watched her life-long employer. Lady Agatha looked decidedly uncomfortable. She was almost blushing.

While Fannie kept watch over the obviously preoccupied Lady Agatha, at the abbey Alice tapped on Becky's bedchamber door. Becky had been banished in disgrace to her own chambers, out of her father's sight until she learned to mend her ways. Since she had no intention of mending her ways, she was prepared for a very long stay.

"You can't really blame Papa," Alice began, trying to placate Becky who was pacing from window to bed to door and back. "He's only trying to do his best for us."

"I can blame him and I do," Becky replied tartly. "Papa intends to make a cake of himself—and of the rest of us—dangling us—and especially me—in front of some nob's family. Alice, you may think me dicked in the nob to go against Papa but I assure you, if I do not make a stand now as sure as rain you shall be the next victim led to the slaughter!"

Alice did not greet her sister's words with any great fear. "I don't think 'dicked in the nob' is quite proper language for a future countess."

Becky made a face at her sister. "You always were odious. I promise you, I shall *die* before I succumb to such a plan."

"You may have to," Alice said practically.

"Thank you very much for the support, dear sister."

"Becky, even you can see you can't continue to rattle about as you have been—we're both grown now—there are rules society insists upon."

"Fiddle!" Becky replied. "If Papa hadn't made so much profit from his woolens we wouldn't have to worry one whit about what *society* insists upon and I for one would be glad of the lack."

"Yes," Alice replied. "I can quite see you, scrubbing floors and chimneys in some London hovel, with none to wait on you hand and foot and never a new gown nor any to vent your spleen upon. Quite a picture, I'm sure."

Becky made a face. "If all you can talk about is Papa and his edicts this will be a short conversation and even less consolation to your poor put-up sister."

Alice bit at her lower lip. She contemplated Becky's rebellious expression and spoke slowly. "I've heard—somebody—speaking of the Abbey Ghost again."

"Tut, they're trying to make a cake of you," Becky said in very assured tones. "You can't believe in such romantical nonsense. All that hobgoblin talk was made up by someone so that Papa would pay more money for this old mausoleum than it was worth."

"What's this I hear?" Sir Harry the Ghost came through the wall while Becky continued speaking.

"It was probably Lady Agatha herself."

"How dare you cast aspersions on the finest woman who ever lived!" Sir Harry thundered.

"She would never stoop to such a thing!" Alice defended.

"And how would you know what she would or would not do?" Becky asked practically, having heard only her sister.

"I simply know," Alice replied. "For I know her character."

"Good for you, young miss," Sir Harry put in. "Any who stand up for Aggie are friends of mine."

"What's that?" Alice breathed the words, her eyes growing round with surprise as she stared at a point just past her sister where Sir Harry shimmered half-visible.

Becky gave her sister a quizzical stare. "What's what? Why do you look so odd?" Becky glanced over her shoulder at the cherrywood dressing table beyond and then looked back at her sister. "I've got to sneak a message to Paul and you must help me, Ally."

"Can you hear me?" Sir Harry queried the young Alice.

"But yes—I can hear you!" Alice was quite beside herself with mixed emotions.

"Well, I should hope so," Becky replied.

"What?" Alice said, her attention distracted between her sister and the apparition that stood beside her.

"What, what, what—" Becky gave her sister a searching glance. "*What* is so distracting you?"

"By Jove," Sir Harry said in delighted tones, "You can *hear* me! Damme, but things are finally looking up around her—good show girl!"

Alice desperately wanted not to see what she was seeing. "Oh, dear—" she managed to breathe as she spoke. "Why are you here?"

"Why am I here?" Becky repeated in surprised tones.

"I live here," Sir Harry replied.

"But you can't—" Alice said faintly.

Becky stared at her sister in total perplexity. "Are you sure you're feeling quite well?"

"I can live here, if such a state as this can be called living, and I do," Sir Harry asserted. "And so I shall until accounts are made right."

"Alice!" Becky stared into Alice's confused eyes. "You're mumbling. Are you having a fit of the vapours?"

"No!"

"She'll never understand," Harry said. "She hasn't the ghost of an idea I'm even here."

"What a strange choice of words," Alice told the ghost.

Harry smiled contentedly. "I rather liked it myself."

"What do you mean a strange choice of words?" Becky said to her sister. "You are staring at the wall and mumbling, what would you assume if you saw me in such a state?"

Alice swallowed and deliberately turned away from the luminous vision beyond her sister. "I am not talking to walls."

"Then who, pray tell, are you talking to?" Becky demanded. "There's no one else in the room."

Sir Harry drifted close to Alice's sister, peering straight into her eyes. "She not only suffers from a want of imagination, but she's got bad vision too. Besides bad manners and a horrible lack of tact."

"You can't say that, there's no way for you to know," Alice replied to the ghost but her sister answered her first.

"Ally, are you funning me?" Becky demanded. She stamped her foot in punctuation and in pique. "There's no one else in this room and you very well know it!"

"Spoiled," Harry said. "I rest my case," were his last words before he disappeared through the wall.

"Ally!" Becky exclaimed. "Are you listening to me?"

"Yes." Alice gave her full attention to her distressed sister. "Of course I am. Now what are you nattering on about?"

"Me? Me!" Becky was momentarily at a loss for words. "You have been talking at cross-purposes ever since you entered this room and you ask me what I am nattering on about? What are *you* nattering on about!"

Alice thought of a great many possible answers but none of them truly served. So she looked her sister square in the eye and spoke one word boldly. "Nothing."

"How good of you to agree," Becky said with some little asperity. "Then perhaps you will listen more carefully because I have a plan. But you must help me get a message to Paul."

The mention of Paul drained Alice's cheeks of all colour. "Oh, no," she managed to say.

Becky eyed her sister. "Are you saying you won't help us?"

"No—that is—no! I mean Papa says you are to be betrothed to the earl's son."

"That's as may be," Becky replied practically, "but in the meantime I shall do as I please." She thought about the words. "And in the future I will do as I please too."

Alice stared at her older sister. "You can't defy Papa."

"Can't I?" Becky asked back. "Perhaps I shall run away with Paul and never be heard from again!"

Alice continued to stare at her sister. "Oh, dear," she said, the hopeless inadequacy of her utterance leaving her silent in its wake.

Becky however looked quite pleased with herself.

- 5 -

AGATHA STEADFORD-SMYTH REREAD the urgent missive that had just been delivered to the gatehouse. When she looked up she met Fannie Burn's inquisitive expression and ended her serving woman's suspense.

"It's from Mary Beal," Agatha told her abigail. "Our most urgent attendance at the abbey on a matter of most personal importance will be most awfully appreciated. I am obviously quoting," Agatha ended.

Fannie took a moment to assimilate this information. "*Our* attendance?" she queried.

"She says she has taken the liberty of sending her carriage."

"*Our* attendance. I mean, whatever she might want to talk to you about, whatever could she want with me?"

"I misdoubt we shall ever know unless we heed the invitation," Agatha replied in practical tones.

Lady Agatha arrived within the hour at the abbey, a reluctant Fannie Burns in tow.

"It looks like rain," Mary Beal offered as Fannie and Lady Agatha came through the oak doorway into the cavernous and cold entry hall. Peeves closed the thick door with a thud which reverberated around the woman, rattling the marble busts of ancient Steadfords that still occupied positions of prominence in the huge stone-floored entryhall.

Mary Beal and Fannie rewarded the butler's *faux pas* with quick looks at the culprit, Mary Beal irritated, Fannie merely perplexed. Lady Agatha turned more slowly, meeting Peeve's hooded gaze with her own direct stare. A flicker of recognition, of obedience, passed between them, Peeves bowing low to Lady Agatha.

"So sorry, Lady Agatha—Mrs. Beal," he added before

Lady Agatha could reprimand him. "This way please—"
The butler was all consideration as he showed the way to
Mary Beal's red salon.

Agatha had not seen the room since Mary Beal had
transformed it. On the threshold Lady Agatha checked, for
one quick moment, her own sensibilities distressed at the
hodge-podge of cluttered furnishings surrounded by riotous
red velvet. Chairs, settees and even the walls were enclosed
in deep red.

"Is anything wrong?" Mary Beal asked in hesitant tones.
She stood behind Lady Agatha who blocked entrance to
the room.

Agatha moved forward. "No—I'm sorry, I was merely—
admiring—the changes you have made."

Mary visibly brightened. "Were you truly?"

Agatha was saved from having to answer by Fannie's
entrance behind them and the reentry of Peeves with a cart
of refreshments.

"Upon my word!" Fannie said as she entered the tiny
overstuffed room. Then she collected herself and fell silent.

"Yes?" Mary looked hopefully towards Lady Agatha's
serving woman. "Is there anything you might need? Want?
Besides the tea?"

Fannie smiled at the shorter and well-rounded woman who was continuing to chatter, trying to make herself
comfortable in the presence of Lady Agatha. "Thank you,"
Fannie answered, casting a reproachful glance towards her
mistress. "We are both quite famished," she added, gilding
the lily.

Lady Agatha gave her abigail a quelling glance but she
did not disavow Fannie's words. "Thank you," she added
quietly as Mary offered her a plate of cakes.

"Oh, no!" Mary Beal exclaimed. "It is I who am hon-
oured to have you here. Both of you. I can't tell you how
happy I am!" She delivered the words and then lapsed back
into uncomfortable silence.

"Indeed?" Lady Agatha's steady gaze disconcerted the
tradesman's wife who sat bolt upright, nearly spilling the
tea Peeves had just handed her.

"That is—I suppose you are a-wonder over what I have called you here for. Asked you here for."

"Invited," Fannie added quietly.

"Yes, invited, of course, *thank* you." Mary Beal smiled at Fannie, her worried eyes at odds with the rest of her face. "The plain truth is that we are—my husband and I—we are not used to some of the niceties of the, well, upper classes, as it were. If you follow me." Mary Beal's eyes beseeched Lady Agatha silently.

"And there is a reason—a purpose to these disclosures—" Agatha prompted.

"Oh my, yes!" Mary said and said no more.

Lady Agatha studied the woman before her. Mary Beal was dressed in the height of current London fashion, her gown of raspberry-coloured silk with high waist, low décolletage and short puffed sleeves. The unfortunate fact that Mary Beal's more than voluptuous curves pushed the simple dress past its best lines was not to be commented upon. Nor was the strange topknot of lop-sided red curls which threatened to come loose of its red ribbons at each shake of her head.

"You see," Mary Beal was saying, her curls swaying alarmingly, "my husband has invited some London nobs, er, I mean he's invited an earl to stay. The Earl of Marleigh." She suffered a tremour of intimidation as she said the words. "I think I could manage, if it weren't for the girls."

"You are worried for your daughters?" Fannie interjected.

Mary glanced towards Fannie, more at ease with Fannie's curiosity than with Lady Agatha's pleasant but decidedly noncommittal expression. "My poor girls," Mary said, shuddering at the thought of what was to come. "I've tried to bring them up proper but you see my husband has always spoiled them and, well, not to put too fine a point on it, our oldest, Becky—Rebecca actually, such a pretty name I always thought—well, she's to be engaged to the earl's son and she doesn't know how."

Agatha Steadford-Smyth eyed the woman. "I beg your pardon?"

"Yes, well and she'll have to beg his a lot too!" Mary said. A strangled cough escaped Fannie's lips. Mary Beal gave her a concerned look before turning back to face Lady Agatha squarely. "Nor can I teach her. Becky I mean. I know next to nothing about the ways of the nobs—nobility I mean—and, well, there it is."

"There is what?" Lady Agatha asked.

"Our problem in a nutshell."

Agatha took her time before next speaking. "I would imagine that being engaged is very much the same in any circle or social circumstance."

"But how?" Mary Beal's hand were clenched in her ample lap, her eyes beseeching first Lady Agatha and then Fannie.

"How what?" Fannie asked the nervous woman.

"How *everything*. What does one call an earl, to his face I mean, and his wife, and what do they talk about? How does one entertain them? Do you think they might play cards? Whist? Peeves says there are strict rules of etiquette about which spoons and forks and all—he says we'll be having fifteen or twenty of them for each of us." Mary looked horrified at the thought. "At every meal! I don't have a clue which is for what or even why it matters as long as you can eat your food, but there it is. What are my girls to talk about with the young lord?"

"Whatever they usually talk about, one would assume. Whatever interests them," Lady Agatha said.

"Oh, that's quite out," Mary Beal replied quickly, trying to keep her courage screwed up enough to ask the favour that seemed her only hope. "Alice is only interested in books and Becky is only interested in horses and devilment." As these words gave her guests pause, Mary went quickly on. "You are the only personages I know well enough to even broach the subject to who have experience in these kinds of things—my husband says your own granddaughter married a duke so-and-so," she faltered. "So I am throwing myself and my girls upon your mercy," she ended dramatically.

"What can you think that we could do to help?" Lady

Agatha asked in an incredulous tone.

"Teach my girls deportment. Just the little bits that can get them by this visit. At least some hints on what is and isn't done so they won't look foolish and disappoint their father. He is so looking forward to having a title or two in the family tree."

Fannie managed to keep a straight face. She kept her eyes on Mary Beal, afraid to look towards Lady Agatha for fear of laughing out loud. She could well imagine how Mary Beal's words had struck her mistress. "How long would there be for such an education?" Fannie asked for want of something else to say.

"Fannie," Lady Agatha began, "I really do not think there is any reason for discussion—"

"Oh, please, don't say no!" Mary Beal spoke quickly before Lady Agatha could finish her sentence. "I shall be forever in your debt, and you will be doing such a kindness and there's no one else to ask—"

There was something winningly honest about Mary Beal that Agatha Steadford-Smyth liked. As for Mrs. Beal's logic or how she ran her household or raised her daughters, these were other matters. The sum total was that although she liked the woman Lady Agatha had no wish to become a social arbiter for the Beals or any others.

Lady Agatha stood up, earning an alarmed look from Mary Beal. "We are hardly the ones to help in any event. We lead quiet lives far removed from the social whirl. We have little knowledge of, and less use for, the latest on-dits and such that constitute polite conversation. It would never serve."

"Please—hear me out—" Mary asked piteously.

Lady Agatha checked her march towards the door. She hesitated and then walked instead to the windows, reaching to push back one of the heavy red velvet drapes and look outside at the grey-tinged day.

"You are my only hope," Mary repeated as Lady Agatha looked out at the darkening skies. A promise of rain hung in the air, leaden clouds hovering low over the elms and beeches. A work cart clattered up

the abbey road, young Tim delivering fresh vegetables
to the abbey kitchen. Fannie was speaking to Mary Beal.
"Girls spend years learning the finer points of deportment
and etiquette."

"But we still have time." Mary pointed out. "They are
not here yet." Lady Agatha's voice came from across the
room. "A coach and four is pulling up the abbey drive. And
another behind it. Both bear what could be the Marleigh
crest and one seems to be piled high with baggage."

"Oh, dear." Mary stood up, moving towards the windows
with dragging steps. "Lady Agatha, I implore you!"

Beyond the imploring woman Lady Agatha could see
Fannie Burns watching her with a quizzical expression.

"It does seem a shame," Fannie said quietly.

They were interrupted by Peeves opening the door from
the hall and announcing the arrival of the Earl and Countess of Marleigh and Lord Andrew Marleigh and Lord
Hieronyius Hargrave.

Mary Beal seemed to wilt where she stood. "They're
multiplying—" she wailed in a soft little voice.

Lady Agatha spoke in calm but bracing tones. "You
shall *not* allow yourself to succumb to the vapours, you
are mistress of Steadford Abbey, Mrs. Beal, and you must
remember your station and do your duty."

"But what *is* my duty?"

"Naturally, you must greet your guests."

"I cannot do it naturally, of that I can assure you."
Mary Beal rose to her feet, her hands still clasped together. "I must try to do what must be done." Mary Beal
started towards the hall with the air of one being led to
the slaughter.

"Might I suggest," Agatha said quickly, "you tell Peeves
to show your guests into the main salon."

"The main salon?" Mary repeated.

"Very well, madam," Peeves said, turning away.

Mary started after him but Fannie stopped her. "There's
a connecting door. Here." Fannie pointed towards a small
side door to their left. "You want to already be there when
they come in."

"Oh, dear—" Mary followed Fannie towards the door and then hesitated on the threshold, as if ready to bolt back to the safety of her small red room. Fannie gave the woman a tiny push over the threshold and closed the door firmly leaving Mary Beal alone on the other side. Mary took two faltering steps into the huge main salon just as Peeves was throwing wide the double doors to the main hall and bowing the earl inside.

Peeves pronounced the visitors' names with obvious pleasure. "His lordship, the Earl of Marleigh, her ladyship, the Countess of Marleigh, Lord Andrew Marleigh and Lord Hieronyius Hargrave.

"How . . . how do you do," Mary managed to say as Peeves's announcements died away. "Your lordships, ladyship," she added hastily. "My husband is not at home but I shall send for him, shall I?"

Mary looked from one to another, finding no help in the gazes that quizzed her silently.

The Earl of Marleigh was of medium-build, with piercing blue eyes and a rather pronounced nose and receding chin. He gave the briefest of bows to the little woman across the room. "Please do not allow us to discommode you, Mrs. Beal."

"Oh, no. I mean you were to send word ahead, so we didn't quite expect you yet but—that is—" she tried her best to give the nob a smile. "All's well that ends well my papa used to say."

"Did he really?" Andrew asked.

"You're sure to think this ends well, Mrs. Beal," he continued with a twinkle in his blue eyes. "We're not about to camp with your family after all, it seems we're to stay at Hargrave House."

The bored-looking young man next to Lord Andrew roused himself enough to give Mary Beal the merest sketch of a bow. "Not had the pleasure before, but Hieronyius Hargrave, your servant, Mrs. Beal."

Mary Beal felt completely out of her depth. "My servant?" she responded faintly.

The countess gave her son's young friend a frosty smile.

"Hargrave House is so very dose to the abbey, Hero, I would have thought you already acquainted with the Beals." There was a tinge of sardonic humour beneath her innocent words.

"Family in London," Hero explained to the countess and to Mary Beal. He knew the countess was perfectly aware of the fact that his very high in the instep family would never have called upon the Beals in any event.

"Since you constantly complain about the tedium of the countryside, it would seem to have been your loss," Lord Andrew told his friend rather enigmatically.

Before any return comment could be made George Beal came through the door from the hall. "Marleigh, glad you've come but what's this I hear from Peeves about you not unpacking?" he asked in booming accents. Still dressed from his ride to the village, George smelled of horseflesh and leather as he greeted the room. "Thought I saw your coach so I hied myself back here just in time, I see. Of course, you'll stay."

The earl, faced with his wife's taut expression, spoke quickly. "The Hargraves have asked that we keep their son's company at their house, so it is settled. Have you met?"

Andrew spoke after the two men exchanged greetings. "Actually, we've been charged with keeping watch over Hero so that he falls into no more bad books."

"Bad books?" George Beal frowned.

"Don't spoil my reputation in the country at large, old man," Hero stopped Andrew. "It was all an unfortunate mistake."

Andrew's eyes were alive with mischief. "Yes and I'm sure Lady Sophie's parents would quite agree with you. Elopement, after all, is not something near and dear to the hearts of parents."

"Elopement?" George Beal interjected, his frown becoming a scowl. He turned toward the earl. "Marleigh, what's this talk of elopement?"

The earl gave his son silent rebuke. "A complete misunderstanding of intentions I assure you. Nothing more."

"Yes, but whose?" George persisted. "Has this to do with Andrew?" he asked suspiciously.

"No, no—a young lady simply misunderstood Hero's request for an audience and thought he was proposing a rather rash venture."

When George heard Andrew was not involved he lost interest in the subject. His countenance brightening, he looked towards his wife. "Why have you got them all standing about in here? It's bloody cold and there's naught to eat. Ring for Peeves to bring some cakes and sherry to my study where the fire's already laid."

"We cannot stay," the countess murmured.

George Beal turned towards the countess and flashed her a brilliant smile. "We've not had the pleasure until now but I can see I have been the one who has been sorely used. Marleigh, you never told me your better half was such a beauty." He reached for the countess's hand and delivered what he felt to be a very elegant kiss.

The Countess of Marleigh gave the impossible man a hint of a smile, determined to maintain the proprieties no matter what the personal cost. Unable to withdraw her hand from the florid man's grasp she looked helplessly towards her husband.

"I think," said the earl, "we should carry on immediately to Hargrave House and call again tomorrow."

"What a good idea," Mary Beal said even before the countess could acquiesce and earning a swift look from Lord Andrew.

George Beal came away from the countess, to the countess's unending gratitude, and planted himself in front of the earl. "No need to rush off, Marleigh," George said.

"Mr. Beal, you let the poor man alone," Mary Beal said with asperity. She didn't hear the slight intake of surprised breath from Lord Hero, nor see Lord Andrew's obvious amusement at her innocent familiarity.

"But the boy will want to see Becky—" George objected.

The boy in question lost his good humour, his eyes hooding over. "I am sure tomorrow will be quite soon enough," the earl's son responded.

"Well—if you've all decided—" George began unwillingly.

"Yes," the countess nearly snapped the word. "We have. Philip—" she said to her husband in ringingly imperious tones. "Shall we?" She turned towards the doors, nodding imperiously to Peeves.

Mary Beal stayed where she was. She allowed herself a great sigh of relief as the visitors left but her relief was short-lived as thoughts of the following day encroached.

- 6 -

LADY AGATHA SAT before her pier glass as Fannie dressed the thick silver-stranded nut-brown hair of which Agatha was more proud than she would willingly admit. At her age such luxuriant hair was a blessing not often granted and well she knew it.

"I tell you, this is the worst of courses and we shall sorely regret having interfered where we do not belong."

Fannie finished dressing her mistress's hair. "It's not interference when a body asks for help."

"Mark my words, Fannie Burns, your willingness to help the Beal girls has no hope of meeting with success. And when we fail we shall be in the middle of a complete debacle. Calumny will be heaped upon us by the parents and overly polite derision will still descend upon those defenceless girls."

"I never thought I'd live to see the day when Agatha Steadford was afraid to give a bit of charity for fear someone would cast aspersions at her for trying to help the defenceless."

"Fannie!" Agatha challenged her serving-woman. "You trespass beyond all bounds!"

"That's as may be," Fannie replied stoutly. "But the truth is the truth and it shall set us free!"

"I swear your tongue and your penchant for meddling shall ruin us both."

Fannie lost her troubled expression, a smile lighting her plain, handsome features. "Are we going then?" she asked.

Agatha Steadford-Smyth pulled a long face. "We are going to the Abbey but you had best lose that smile because soon enough you will repent of my being so addle-headed as to listen to your pleas."

Fannie's smile remained in place. "You like the girls."

"Don't look so smug, Fannie Burns. The results of your handiwork are yet to be seen. Well, we'd best be about it," Fannie's employer said with none too good grace. "Since we've accepted the invitation to tea there's nothing else to be done but hope for an unexceptional first meeting between these ill-suited parties."

The scene that greeted their arrival at the Abbey was one of only slightly-controlled confusion. The entryhall was clotted with visitors, the host and hostess nowhere to be seen, and Peeves bowing low to the earl but doing little else.

With an experienced eye, Lady Agatha took in the situation at a glance. She moved towards Peeves with a determined stride and fire in her dark eyes.

"Peeves." The imperious voice dripped politeness but there was a hint not only of authority but of reprimand. The butler turned towards Lady Agatha as she reached his side. "Please see to it that a fire is lit in the west salon—immediately." Her last word was underscored and the butler heard the nuances of contempt beneath her polite tone.

"I am frightfully sorry for my lateness," Agatha said to the other visitors. "Please allow me to introduce myself, I am Agatha Steadford-Smyth. Mrs. Beal asked me to see to your comfort until she could join us—urgent estate business has detained Mr. Beal and Mrs. Beal was called upon to help a tenant in sore distress—"

Fannie Burns heard her punctiliously honest employer prevaricating with the air of one accomplished at the sorry art. Fannie could not believe her ears. But one swift glance from Lady Agatha changed Fannie's expression from that of astonishment to one of a more noncommittal mien.

"If I might ask you to follow, I shall show the way. We shall pass the original abbey chapel along the west hallway—its architecture might provide a few minutes interest as it was built in early Tudor times and is completely unaltered."

Fannie Burns was astounded at her employer's words. Unaltered was not the most apt description since if truth were told the chapel had been neglected for at least a half-century. Lady Agatha was offering to view a decrepit part of the abbey, something she had never been wont to do, and Fannie was struck silent by the event. The earl, however, instantly responded to the demands of polite society, sensing in Lady Agatha a formidable grand dame.

"If I am correct, Lady Agatha, you are Ambrose Steadford's daughter—I met your father in London shortly before his death. He was quite advanced in years but he was the soul of politeness to a young scamp who had little to recommend himself other than a shared interest in prime horseflesh."

"How kind of you to tell me, your lordship," Agatha responded. Not a hint of her own problematical relationship with her father could be heard in her tone or seen in her eyes. "Here we are," Agatha continued, throwing open the doors to the long-unused chapel. "I'm sure you will enjoy it immensely."

The next quarter-hour was spent in discussing the origins and history of the musty and cobweb-ridden chapel the small group of abbey guests were discovering. Whilst the tea party were perusing the wooden pews and the vaulted apse above the choir loft and the intricately carved oak altar, Lady Agatha cast a swift aside to Fannie, bringing her serving-woman to her side and sending her in search of their hostess, charging Fannie with delivering Mary Beal as soon as possible to her guests below.

Mary Beal responded to the knock on her sitting room door with a distracted plea for whoever it was to stop making such noise. Fannie took this for invitation. She opened the familiar door but checked on the threshold. The onslaught of a hundred shades of red attacked her eyes. Mary Beal had redecorated Lady Agatha's rooms in what seemed her favourite colour.

Mary Beal herself was standing helplessly before a red settee across the sitting room, her husband by her side. On the settee Becky Beal sat, looking quite defiant as she glared up at her mother.

"I'll not go down, no matter if you bring an army to get me!" Becky told them all.

"Miss Burns, I don't know what to do with her." Mary Beal fairly wailed the words.

"You'll do as you're told," George Beal said over his wife's words and his daughter's continuing objections. "Or I'll cast you out upon the parish as an ungrateful wretch who won't obey her parents!"

Becky Beal's voice rose to match her father's, Fannie quickly closing the door. "I'd rather sink to an early grave than be forced into a loveless match with a horrid duke!"

"He's not a duke," Fannie corrected as she came forward. She spoke in a controlled tone several levels below the loudness with which Mr. Beal and his daughter had been declaring their crossed purposes. "And if you never meet him you cannot, in good conscience, call him horrid, now can you?"

This logic stopped Becky's passionate storm long enough for her to look towards Lady Agatha's abigail. Mary Beal urged her daughter to let her mother finish fastening the buttons that lined the back of her lovely gown. And in truth Fannie had to own the gown was lovely. Made of soft and frothy muslin sprigged with tiny sky-blue flowers and adorned with sky-blue ribbons at the high waist and on the puffed sleeves, it set off Becky's delicate blonde colouring and brought out the blue of her eyes.

"I don't even know what to say to an earl," Becky said, giving Fannie a hint that the girl's fit of temper was not altogether without reason.

"Upon entering the room," Fannie said, "you will be presented to the earl and you are to give him a very pretty curtsey and tell him you are pleased to make his acquaintance."

"That's all there is to it?" Becky asked disbelievingly.

"That's the sum of it," Fannie said with quiet authority. "You'll answer when spoken to and be as polite as ever you can and it will soon be over." Fannie saw that her last words were greeted with more warmth than her first.

"I won't go in alone," Becky said with a stubborn tilt to her chin that brooked no argument.

"You shan't have to," Fannie replied. "Your mother and father will be with you."

These words did not have the desired effect of calming the girl. "I want Ally," Becky said. "I want Ally with me or I shan't go at all." Nor would she allow her toilette to be finished until they had invaded Alice's room and Becky made sure that Alice was joining her sister, mother and father.

Agatha Steadford-Smyth entertained the earl's family and young Hero Hargrave in the west parlour, Peeves attempting to redeem himself in Lady Agatha's eyes by a flawless presentation of refreshments.

When Fannie opened the door all turned to look at the Beal family.

Alice, in a plain cotton gown the colour of green grapes, with high neck and long sleeves, looked shyly towards the thick Turkey carpet as she and her sister entered the room. Becky was more bold, defiantly glaring at the assemblage. Beal heaved a sigh of relief. His opinion, which he had vouchsafed all morning, was that once the young ones had met all would be well. His wife was less sanguine about the possibilities for catastrophe that still lay before her little brood.

Her thoughts upon her fears, Mary Beal glanced quickly towards Lady Agatha, her gratitude in her eyes.

"Ah, I see that you have discharged your duties to your tenants," Lady Agatha said.

Fannie had forewarned them of the excuses Lady Agatha had made for their unpardonable breech of etiquette, so neither of the elder Beals compounded their *faux pas* by outright confusion. But Mary Beal coloured in a most unbecoming manner as she stammered her apologies.

"The point is we're all here," George said practically. He smiled at Lord Andrew. "And you get to meet our Becky."

Our Becky was thrust a little forward and found herself staring into the countess's unwelcoming expression. Her gaze shifted to the earl's piercing eyes as she bobbed a curtsey and remembered to say how do you do. Alice followed her sister's example without meeting anyone's eyes.

The earl gave the younger girl a swift look and then turned his attention upon Becky. His smile was much warmer than his wife's had been as he assessed her charms. Relieved that her father had not been exaggerating the girl's beauty, the earl looked towards his son.

"Rebecca, Alice—this is my son Andrew and his friend Hieronyius Hargrave."

Becky was intent upon disliking Andrew and so saw little to recommend either of the two young men who stepped forward and bowed. It was Alice who spoke. "Hiero—?"

"Yes," came a reply in a slightly less bored voice than usual. The man who answered was fair and pale. "All call me Hero, you must do the same." As he spoke his eyes went past the quietly pretty Alice to the honey-tressed Becky. She was undeniably fetching. "Your servant," Hero said to Becky as he bowed.

"Your servant," Lord Andrew was saying at the same time. His dark blue eyes held no hint of his thoughts.

7

GEORGE BEAL WAS impatient to have Becky and Andrew become better acquainted. In his mind, proximity to the earl's son would overcome his daughter's unreasonable objections to being made a lady. Becky's father subscribed to the common wisdom that a female could come to care for any male she was left alone with—hence the need of society's protection of her virtue by keeping the female of the species safe from such association until the proper alliance was decided for her.

Now that George had found the right candidate for his elder daughter's affections he fidgeted at the necessity of making niminy-piminy conversation.

"Becky," George boomed, "show Andrew the Long Gallery and all those old Steadfords that used to own the place—"

George's suggestion was met with less than enthusiasm by his daughter but he was not prepared for the look of utter horror from the countess. Nor for Fannie Burns's fit of choking. Even Lady Agatha was a little taken aback although she tried to maintain a calm facade.

"What a way to put it, Mr. Beal," Mary rebuked. "I'm sure I don't know what I'm to do with you. He's as rough about the edges as he was when he was a boy."

"How—quaint," the countess commented dryly.

Lady Agatha took the situation in hand. "I would be most happy to accompany the young people through the Gallery, Mrs. Beal."

"Gad, they don't need a chaperone now, do they?" George asked the room, earning another incredulous glance from the countess. "I thought everything was decided."

Lord Andrew choked. "Terribly sorry," he managed to say in a strained voice.

"Philip," the countess said in a voice as cold as ice. "I don't understand the drift of this conversation."

"Ah, yes, well," the earl looked from his wife's anger to the mixture of perplexity, embarrassment and shock on the faces of the rest of the small group.

"Of course they need a chaperone," Mary said quickly. "Don't they?" she asked Lady Agatha.

"I'm quite sure they will enjoy hearing the history of the various portraits," Lady Agatha said.

"I, for one, should be glad for it," Hero said in a languid drawl.

George Beal scowled ferociously at the sandy-haired young Lord Hargrave.

"If Andy has no objections, of course," Hero added when he saw George Beal's expression.

"It sounds like a happy excursion," Andrew replied. "What say we all go?" he added, earning a quick look from Lady Agatha. She saw glints of barely suppressed laughter in his dark blue eyes although his expression was perfectly sober as he continued. "If it suits our elders' pleasure," Andrew concluded politely, sounding very much like an obsequious fop and earning Becky's total scorn.

Alice felt acutely embarrassed. Her cheeks blazed crimson as she spoke quietly into the deadly silence around her. "I should like very much to hear more about Lady Agatha's ancestors. That is, I'm sure we'd all enjoy it."

Andrew glanced at the blushing girl as her father spoke. "I don't see why."

"You certainly don't," his wife told him smartly before turning to smile at the countess. "Husbands, bless them. Whatever are we to do with them?" she asked in a conspiratorial tone.

The earl looked at his expertly polished black boots so as not to intercept his wife's frigid expression.

Mary Beal, however, was unaware of the countess's indignation since she was cajoling her elder daughter into joining the other young people.

"If Ally is coming too, then I suppose I must," Becky said ungraciously.

"I declare," her mother said. "You sound as if we were dosing you, instead of offering you a rare treat."

"Shall we?" Lady Agatha asked ushering the party towards the door. Andrew followed, casting a sidelong glance toward the shy Alice. Quiet and self-effacing she seemed destined to be one of life's background figures, often there but seldom really seen or heard.

As the parlour door shut, the countess turned to her husband. "How long must I endure this farce, Philip?"

Fannie Burns, well aware of what the gist of their conversation must be, asked about the intricately worked silk shawl Mary wore. George Beal lost all interest in the small talk around him. Barely restraining himself from a prodigious yawn, George sought help from the only masculine company available to him. "Marleigh," he said with a fine disregard for the difference in their stations and social positions, let alone that the countess was speaking, "what do you say to a look at my gun collection?" Aware of his wife's glaring irritation, the earl accepted with alacrity. "If the ladies will permit us, I would be most interested—"

"Philip, I am feeling poorly. I am sure it is the headache," Jane Marleigh said in louder tones.

Mary Beal was all solicitude. "Oh, my dear, I suffer from the most raging pain at times, myself, I quite sympathize. Would you care to partake of a short lie-down?"

"Wonderful suggestion, Mrs. Beal," the earl replied before his wife could frame a suitably spiteful rejoinder.

The countess, seeing no help was coming from her husband's quarter, turned towards Mary Beal with barely controlled ill-temper. "I believe I might benefit from a few moments *solitude*."

Mary offered to show her to a bed-chamber, but Fannie, anxious to spare Mrs. Beal and the countess more of each other's company, suggested that Peeves do so.

Left alone with Fannie, Mary Beal heaved a profound sigh of relief as she poured herself another cup of tea. "I must tell you this is the first cuppa I will have enjoyed all afternoon."

Fannie nodded. She was looking through the window at the lowering clouds. Rain had threatened for two days but as yet had not fallen. The weather inside the house seemed to be mirroring the weather outside. Storm clouds all about but the storm itself so far avoided.

If the earl were truly in George Beal's debt, it was understandable that he and his wife were forced into company they obviously cared little for, but their son was another matter. Fannie had no use for a young man who let himself be so thoroughly managed, filial duty or no. It showed a want of strength in his character. What a merry chase the strong-willed Becky would lead the boy if their fathers succeeded in their matchmaking.

"Just a touch more tea to hot it up?" Mary Beal asked as the comfortably silent minutes passed.

"Thank you," Fannie replied absently.

"And another of these lovely teacakes, I'll warrant they'll not do neither of us a bit of harm."

"I believe it's 'not do *either* of us' or 'will do neither of us'," Fannie corrected since they were alone in the room.

"Oh, *thank* you, Fannie," Mary said with all her heart. "That is *exactly* what I want you to do! You must explain all these little niceties for I don't want my daughters to be ashamed of me when I come to visit their grand establishments. I'm so very grateful for any help you can give. But you must concentrate your best efforts upon the girls. It is of the *first importance* that they hold their own with the nobs."

"Polite society," Fannie amended.

"What? Oh, yes," Mary smiled her gratitude. "Will you have a bit more tea Miss Burns?"

Fannie felt quite at home with the simple-mannered merchant's wife. Mary Beal reminded her of Hetty Mapes, the kindly village woman who had been cook at the abbey until it was sold to the Beals. "No need to worry, Mrs. Beal. Her ladyship can manage anything."

Alice walked next to Lady Agatha as they strolled down in the Long Gallery. Fascinated by Agatha's stories about her ancestors. Behind them the two young men bracketed

Becky with their attentions. Becky found she enjoyed Hero's address in spite of herself. Andrew was as silent as Hero was vocal, allowing his friend to monopolize the conversation and convincing Becky that Lord Andrew Marleigh was every bit as dull and boring as she had known he would be.

"Oh," Alice clapped her hands together, "this one is *you*, Lady Agatha, isn't it?"

The others flocked near to see the portrait. A young vibrant beauty looked back at them, wearing a low-cut dress of crimson and gold fit for a princess.

"Is that really you?" Becky asked.

"Of course it's Lady Agatha," Alice replied.

"Exactly so," Lord Andrew opined, coming closer to take a more thorough inspection of the oil painting.

Alice ventured a sidelong look towards the tall young man who now stood beside her examining the portrait. She topped five and a half feet but she found herself having to look a good deal upwards to glimpse his face. As she watched a lock of his wavy chestnut-coloured hair fell casually across his forehead as he leaned a little forward. His eyes were darkest blue and alive with intelligence, his features more squared than chiseled. A strong handsome face altogether in keeping with the masculinity of his body. He was at least six feet tall, his broad-shoulders outlined by an exquisitely tailored forest-green coat, his long legs clad in tan breeches and dark-brown riding boots polished to a mirror shine.

Andrew glanced back and down, catching Alice's gaze with his own. He saw her golden topaz eyes filled with an expression of lingering surprise, as if she had seen something in her perusal of him she had not expected. Her lips were full, and pink.

"Oh, I say," Hero was leaning near. "Lady Agatha, you were a prime article."

"Don't go doing it too brown, young man," Agatha said, earning a smile from Hero.

"Lady Agatha." Hero responded with sardonic glee. "I had no inkling you would be as adept at the current cant."

"I'm neither adept nor current," Agatha replied, "but I'm a dab hand at saying what I mean, thanks to close association in my long-gone girlhood with stablehands who were quite inventive in their expressions."

The laughter she earned from Hero and Becky brought Andrew's eyes away from Alice.

Lady Agatha continued. "If truth be told my abigail is not above a bit of colourful vocabulary at times herself."

"I'm afraid that is all my father knows," Becky offered artlessly.

"I can rather well imagine," Hero replied, remembering the earlier scene in the parlour. He saw Becky begin to take on a defensive posture and smiled winningly. "What fun you must have."

Becky watched the sandy-haired Hero's grey eyes. He was an inch or two shorter than Andrew and perhaps a bit too thin, but all in all, she liked him much more than the self-assured Marleigh heir.

"It is not always so wonderful, as even on short acquaintance, you already very well know," Becky replied honestly. She gave a sidelong glance towards Lady Agatha. "Especially not when the likes of you are about."

"Oh, I do say!" Hero stared outright at the girl.

"What Rebecca means," Lady Agatha interjected, "is that having lived a simple and industrious life, her father is not acquainted with all the niceties of formal conversation."

"I am sure Mr. Beal feels such attributes of polite society are no more than a waste of time and effort," Andrew put in, earning the attention of the others. Lady Agatha regarded the young man thoughtfully. Hero looked at his friend quizzically whilst the Beal sisters each reddened perceptibly. But where Alice's eyes went downwards, Becky's flared in anger.

"I'm sure politeness goes far beyond the voice of one's words," Rebecca Beal told the young lord. "If one could only be resourceful enough to find the true meaning beyond the sweet nothings many of the so-called polite society essay, I would venture to say one would often find them less than kind, let alone polite."

"I'll warrant you are probably correct," Andrew replied smoothly. "With a certain element of the ton, at any rate." For the first time the young couple were facing each other directly. "In fact I am quite persuaded, Miss Beal, upon our small acquaintance, that you are quite resourceful enough to ferret out any meanings, hidden or otherwise."

"I would hope so," Becky replied acidly. "It would seem if I am to travel in so-called polite circles I must become adept at ferreting out the true worth of those I associate with since they more often than not say one thing whilst meaning quite another."

"I think we've seen all that's to be seen," Lady Agatha interjected forcibly. "Shall we join the others?"

Sir Harry the Ghost came through the ceiling high above the small group. He drifted down towards the Long Gallery, peering intently at Lady Agatha. "I heard your voice again and I thought I was dreaming, Aggie-my-girl."

Alice gave a quick start at the sound of his words and looked upwards. One brief glance at the shimmering form, descending past the tall mullioned windows caused her to squeeze her eyes closed.

"Alice?" Lady Agatha questioned.

"Ally?" Rebecca turned towards her sister at the sound of Lady Agatha's concern. "Whatever's come over you? You look like you've seen a ghost."

Her sister's words made Alice gasp. She saw Lady Agatha staring at her intently and coloured. "No! I saw nothing—" she prevaricated.

"Alice Beal," Sir Harry said, "you'd best not tell such bouncers unless you want to suffer the same sorry fate as I."

"Oh, no," Alice replied in a tiny voice.

Becky recognised the faintly glazed expression in her sister's eyes. She had seen it once before in her own bed-chamber. "Ally," her sister insisted sharply, "don't go wool-gathering now. We have guests."

Alice turned away from Becky, avoiding Lady Agatha's eyes and finding herself once again staring into Lord Andrew's intent expression. "I'm sorry, I—I wasn't attend-ing . . ."

"Don't worry m'dear," Hero replied. "I do it all the time. Been caught at it myself many a time. No offence, Lady Agatha," he added, "but I've been wondering about some of these chaps, how they met their end and all."

"No offence taken," Agatha replied. But her attention was on Alice as the small group headed back towards the wide curved stairwell. When Alice could not help glancing back at Harry's shimmering form, Agatha saw the direction of the girl's gaze and turned clear around, staring intently.

The others had reached the head of the stairwell. Seeing Lady Agatha turned in the opposite direction, Andrew spoke. "Did you lose something, Lady Agatha?"

Agatha heard Andrew's words but did not immediately turn to face him. Something luminescent glowed at the far end of the Long Gallery beneath the tall, narrow, mullioned windows that let in what little light could be achieved from the fast darkening grey day. Agatha squinted, the better to make out the outline of—of something—

"Lady Agatha?"

"Yes. Forgive me. I am coming."

"Damn and blast that boy to hell and back," Sir Harry expostulated. "She almost saw me, I know she did!" Since neither the youth he blasted nor the woman he cared about could hear him his only small reward was Alice clasping her hands fast against her ears. "And well you should quake girl," Harry continued in thunderous accents. "And tell the rest what fury I shall pour forth if they keep interrupting me and my Aggie!" The ghost was angry at the young man for interrupting Aggie's concentration but he was more angry at the sorry state in which he himself now appeared. Or rather did not appear. "Aggie has to hear me and, by God, she shall or I shall—I shall *do* something!"

Unfortunately, Lady Agatha did not hear Sir Harry's dire prediction. She was shepherding her small flock down the wide stairs.

"Lady Agatha?" The Countess of Marleigh appeared at a chamber door at the foot of the staircase.

"Another interruption!" Harry groused. "Can't a ghost have a bit of *peace* about this house?"

"If you would please wait for me," the countess continued.

The others did as the countess bid, hearing her explanation of the headache and her need to be transported to Hargrave House forthwith.

"Aggie!" Sir Harry the Ghost called out. "Oh—Aggie, girl—" he said in a much quieter tone. "I would tempt the devil himself to have you at least see me."

"That's much better," Alice said from the bottom of the steps. She didn't look upward towards the ghost.

"I beg your pardon," the countess replied.

"Alice? Did you say something?" Lady Agatha asked.

Alice, mindful of Harry's warning, said only "I'm sorry," leaving the countess and the two gentlemen completely mystified.

Rebecca however came close to her sister, taking her hand and clasping it firmly. "I shall never let them take you away," she whispered. "Don't ever worry. No matter what happens to your faculties, I shall defend you to the end."

Alice's own doubts about her sanity were uppermost in her mind and her sister's words were met with true gratitude and a tremulous smile.

Within the half-hour Homer, the abbey coachman, deposited Lady Agatha and a very dispirited Fannie at their garden gate. They didn't speak until they were safe inside the tiny gatehouse, the thick oak door bolted against the outside world.

"I swear, I'm all to pieces," Fannie said truthfully but inelegantly.

"And I," Lady Agatha agreed. Sinking to a flowered chintz armchair in the small parlour, she untied her bonnet ribbons. "I am not the one to say I told you so, but Fannie surely you can see your plan will never suffice."

"I've learned the value of one old saw, I can tell you that," Fannie replied. "You can't make a silk purse out of a sow's ear and that's that."

"That may be that, but we are committed to the attempt," Lady Agatha reminded her long-time friend and serving woman. She did not deliver the next words, "Thanks to you," but Fannie felt them all the more keenly.

"I was wrong," Fannie said, "and when I'm wrong I'm willing to admit it."

"You may be willing to admit it but just what are we to do about it?" Agatha asked practically.

Fannie nibbled at her lower lip. "That's a bit more of a puzzlement, I'll admit. Perhaps I should tell Mrs. Beal there's no hope."

"I've already tried that," Agatha replied dryly. "With her and with you. It did no good."

"Well then," Fannie began but soon lapsed into silence. "There must be another way," she ended after careful thought.

"I sincerely hope you can think of it for I am at my wit's end with still no hope in sight. I must admit I would have simply washed my hands of the whole affair before this gruesome tea we just endured. But now I find I quite hesitate to leave such lambs to their inevitable slaughter at the hands of Countess Marleigh."

"What do you think of the son?" Fannie asked with the familiarity of long friendship.

Agatha pursed her lips in contemplation of the young man Fannie asked about. "I find him rather hard to read. He seems to be intelligent and I have seen glimpses of a lively humour within him but he has been, at best, tedious when he addresses Rebecca. And," the dowager spoke more slowly, "I am loath to say this but I have serious doubts about his strength of will. I am the last one to deny filial duty," she added quickly, "but in dealing with one such as Rebecca Beal, a husband must keep the upper hand or there will be no peace in the household. She lacks both restraint of tongue and patience of attitude."

"I quite agree. She is a holy terror," Fannie interjected, "and no gilding the lily about it. I'm sure I don't know what's to become of her, father's wealth or no father's wealth."

Lady Agatha was not attending. Her gaze mirrored the reflexion of her thoughts, her brow furrowing in concentration.

"Aggie, are you wool-gathering?"

"What?" Lady Agatha focused on her serving woman. "I suppose I am."

"You need a rest before supper," Fannie pronounced. "We're both quite fagged, I warrant."

"Yes, I think I will go on upstairs for a bit." Lady Agatha allowed herself a small sigh. "I think your prescription is just to the point, Fannie."

Agatha Steadford-Smyth climbed the short staircase towards her room while her abigail went to see about the evening meal. Inside her cozy room, with its bright curtains and chintz coverings, Lady Agatha reached to a low bureau drawer and brought out a collection of yellowed envelopes tied with a fading red ribbon. She stared down at them but did not untie the bundle. After a few moments she replaced them in the drawer and lay down on her bed, using her shawl for a blanket as she closed her eyes and let her mind wander towards sleep.

8

THE COUNTESS OF Marleigh kept to Hargrave House for the next sennight, the earl bringing her regrets that her continuing *malaise* would not allow any visits for the present. While Hero volunteered to entertain the countess with cards and gossip, the earl and his son rode to the abbey only once during that week, traversing the short distance between the estates and meeting George Beal after an early breakfast.

Later, all three men rode to Stoneybridge to look over the horses at the quarterly auction, for the earl had declared that owning prime cattle was one of the marks of a true gentleman. With the earl's expert help, George bought a two-year-old dappled grey with sleek lines, good rounded quarters and plenty of heart room. The earl promised it would be a real prime goer and Andrew opined that any gentleman would be slap up the echo holding his ribbons atop a high-perch phaeton on Rotten Row.

George was quite taken with the picture of himself as a London dandy and decided on the spot to buy a high-perch phaeton the following day if the earl and his son would lend their expertise once more.

George attempted to convince the men to stay to tea but the earl insisted they had been too long away from the countess and she would be expecting them. He did, however, invite George to Hargrave House for a day's shooting on Thursday.

While George was impatient for Lord Andrew to dance more attendance upon Becky, his wife was relieved at the thought of not yet having to entertain the countess.

"I declare I am so grateful they decided to stay at Hargrave House," Mary told Fannie. "My imagination fails when I try to picture what it would have been like, having the countess underfoot all day." She shuddered at the thought.

They were in her favourite red parlour, looking through an almost current London ladies' magazine in search of the perfect dress for Becky's engagement ball.

Fannie looked doubtful. "You are quite sure there is to be an engagement ball, still."

Mary nodded her head firmly, if not happily. "When my husband makes up his mind to something, none can change it. It is why he is so successful in business."

"Succeeding at business is a quite different matter than succeeding at affairs of the heart," Fannie opined.

"He's told cook to lay in the refreshments for the ball. George succeeds at anything he puts his hand to. He has the knack of turning things his way."

"I wish him luck with *this* venture," Fannie said dryly. The sound of dull thuds came periodically from above. At the latest resounding thump Mary Beal looked towards the ornately frescoed ceiling.

"I am rather more concerned with Lady Agatha's success with the girls," she confessed. "I hope they are paying close attention to her admonitions regarding proper conduct and all."

In the girls' sitting room on the floor above, Mary Beal's hopes seemed doomed to failure with at least one daughter. While Alice balanced a heavy book atop her auburn locks and attempted to keep it in place as she crossed the dark blue carpet, Becky sat curled up and glowering on a pink flower-patterned chaise longue.

Alice Beal managed to take three steps before the book fell on her seventh attempt and was ready to give up. "I'm quite, quite positive I can never manage this properly, Lady Agatha."

"Patience, child. Rome was not built in a day."

Alice bent to pick up the book and retraced her steps while Becky watched and pulled a face at her sister. "You look quite the ninny parading about like that."

Alice had the book back atop her curls. "I may look the ninny, but I shall master this," she said with resolve.

"Why?" Becky asked. "Whatever reason will we ever have in the course of our entire lives to carry books atop our heads?" She turned her attention upon Lady Agatha. "I, for one, have no intention of ever having use for such an accomplishment, I assure you."

"If you sit in such ungainly positions, I quite agree," that formidable lady responded sharply, her patience with the recalcitrant girl wearing dangerously thin. "And if you wish to be mistaken for one of your scullery maids, I again agree," she continued, earning a sullen pout from Becky.

"I will not allow anyone to treat me as if I were a common maid."

"I assure you, young lady, if you do not improve both your posture and your attitude you will never pass for ought else, and most certainly not as a member of polite society." Agatha Steadford-Smyth impaled the girl with her darkling gaze. "In point of fact, you could not at present even pass muster as a lady's maid. There is not an abigail in England that does not have better command of the King's English, better posture and better manners."

The book on Alice's head crashed to the floor, punctuating Lady Agatha's remarks.

"I'm sorry," Alice said into the ensuing frosty silence. She picked up the thick volume of Roman history and replaced it on her head. With a resolute step she started out, moving slowly, her arms rigid at her sides.

"Relax, Alice," Lady Agatha told her. "Think yourself into the top of your head, with each step think of nothing but the slight movement of the book and correct your stance . . ."

Alice did as she was bid, moving slowly still but with less rigidity. She walked the full length of the room and hesitated facing the far wall. With renewed confidence she held her breath and negotiated a slow turn, smiling as she returned towards Lady Agatha, the book wobbling a bit but still on her head.

When she at last reached Lady Agatha's side, she smiled hugely. Her words tumbling out a little breathlessly, Alice glowed as she spoke. "Have I mastered it?"

Lady Agatha was never one to give praise lightly. She

smiled back at the girl. "You have begun the process. Now we shall make it two books."

Alice groaned. "I shall never be able to manage *two*."

Becky sprang up from her couch, nettled by Lady Agatha's words and Alice's success. "I shall put *three* upon my head straight off—" she promised rashly.

Agatha Steadford-Smyth gave the girl a scolding glance. "I have found that braggarts are invariably hoist upon their own petards."

Becky, as rash as ever, did not listen to Lady Agatha's warning. She reached for the topmost three of the volumes Lady Agatha had commandeered from the library below and plopped them upon her head. Their unaccustomed weight surprised her but she was determined to show up all the nonsense that went with what she called "ladyhood." And so it was that Becky Beal began a march across the small sitting room floor with rather more confidence than was warranted by her performance. At her first step the books swayed, at her second they tumbled with a crescendo of thuds to the carpet around her feet.

Red-faced, Becky cast one glance towards Lady Agatha and, after seeing the older woman's sardonic expression, the younger woman reached to retrieve the books. Her pride committed her to mastering the feat.

At Hargrave House the shoot was ended and Andrew and Hero had left their elders sitting in the gun room drinking ale.

"What I am saying," George reiterated to the earl, "is that the children have to spend more time together."

"Yes, well, that is one possibility," the earl replied.

"One? Are you saying you disagree?"

"Not precisely disagree, you understand, but there are occasions whereupon it is best to allow the least proximity before the nuptials are announced."

"I don't understand," George Beal replied.

The earl took a moment to frame his next words. "As fathers," he said smoothly, "we have an obligation to insure our children's futures."

"And that is precisely what we're doing," George put in for good measure.

"But alas, that often means going against what our children think they might want."

"And that is the verified truth," George said with deep feeling.

The earl nodded. "Therefore, it behooves us to establish circumstances in such a way that the young people cannot refute our wishes thus insuring their acceptance of what they may not necessarily agree to upon first thought. Although," the earl added hastily, "they are sure to agree in the end, of course. But youth seldom has the wisdom of age and sometimes must be brought to heel."

"Rather like a good hunting dog," George Beal agreed.

"Precisely," the earl responded quickly. "How keen a perception you have of the study of human relations."

George Beal smiled magnanimously. "I've made my fortune by understanding what the public wants. You would be surprised, Marleigh, how many so-called businessmen pay no heed to such a simple fact. And live to rue the day."

"I think we agree, then," the earl told his friend. "The first order of business is to go forward with the engagement ball. At that point our children's futures will be assured."

"As soon as possible," George replied fervently.

"I agree," the earl said.

George's brow creased with worry. "I assume we must wait upon the countess's health," he appended.

"Not necessarily," the earl responded smoothly. "She is also anxious to see matters settled. In fact, I obtained a special licence so that we could dispense with the time needed for the usual reading of the banns."

George Beal smiled. Having found a kindred spirit his spirits expanded. "Capital! Let's set the date."

While the fathers decided their children's futures, Andrew and Hero rode into Wooster ready for a glass of stout in the village inn.

"I say, Andy, this whole situation seems awfully havey-cavey to me," Hero told his boyhood friend.

Andrew turned his horse over to the ostler before he turned towards his companion. "And if I agree?" he questioned.

Hero Hargrave smiled, his habitual sardonic expression lightening into boyish handsomeness. "If you say yes to me, it's neither here nor there but if you say yes to your father's plan, old son, you will be shackled for life to a rich termagant. Upon briefest association, you must surely be able to ascertain that Becky Beal, no matter her beauty, would never give you one moment's peace."

"And if I refuse my father how much peace shall I obtain?" Andrew asked.

"It's that bad, is it?" Hero asked.

"It's that bad," Andrew admitted with a deadening of his expression that told his friend all.

Hero gave Andrew an elaborate bow. "Then you must bow to the inevitable with as good grace as I now bow to you."

"Thank you," his friend replied with a tinge of bitterness. "I am glad you agree that my course has been well and truly set. I am to be sold quite the same as a stallion at auction," he said in bitter tones.

"You do not sound as resigned to your fate as I thought. In fact, I might develop the impression that you were planning on crying off," Hero replied. He earned a quick glance from his friend.

Lord Andrew turned away, heading into the small ivy-covered inn. "I hear they pour a handsome portion," was all he replied to his friend's suggestion.

Lord Hero Hargrave followed the Earl of Marleigh's heir inside the small inn, glancing about the large common room before finding a seat. The room was dominated by a long oaken trestle table with benches drawn up to either side. A few patrons sat at the table, others scattered at smaller tables in the corners. Hero staked out a small side table as Lord Andrew stood at the bar, ordering two glasses of stout.

"Why ever did you agree to this insane misalliance?" Hero asked when Andrew sank to the hard wood seat across from his.

Andrew's expression darkened. "My father wishes it," he replied.

Hero laughed. "And when have your parents' wishes ruled your choices?"

Andrew's eyes closed over, his expression opaque. "Let's be quit of the subject, shall we?"

Hero stared at his friend, his mouth very nearly dropping open. "Damme, you do truly intend to offer for the cit's daughter, don't you? I don't know what's happened to your parents's sensibilities but Andy she is entirely ineligible. 'Pon my word, Andrew, no matter how you met or how taken you are with her, you'll live to regret it, family fortune or no—"

"I never clapped eyes on her until the very moment you did," Andrew answered. "Nor am I 'taken' with her, as you so quaintly put it. I shall, in all probability, regret it for the rest of my days," Andrew agreed. "But marry her I shall," he said grimly.

Hero Hargrave took a moment to digest his friend's words. When next he spoke his words came slowly. "I do not understand."

Andrew grimaced. "Nor can I, in good conscience, explain. Just accept my word that it must be so."

Andrew spoke with such fatalism that his friend was unable to think of words that might help ease his obvious pain. Hero resorted to the only solution at hand and motioned to the barmaid to bring another round of drinks.

The next day George Beal confronted his recalcitrant daughter. "It's my firm belief you have rats in your upper storey, young miss."

Becky was silent but her mother spoke soothingly. "Now, Mr. Beal, don't get yourself into a state—"

Her husband's high colour reddened further. "Mrs. Beal, you'd best see to your daughter and her manners."

"And you'll see to your own," Mary answered with asperity. "Since the servants are tittering about the scenes you create."

"Let them titter as they will, I hire them and I pay them

and I can sack them! They do as I say, and so shall you, my girl," he added, turning on Becky.

She stamped her little foot. "I won't mind and none can make me. I'd as liefer run away to the wilds of America!" With this pronouncement she ran towards the French doors which led onto the terrace. Her father made a grab for her but she slipped past. The day was clear and windy, the gusty wind catching at Becky's honey-coloured curls as she ran outside and down the terrace steps. She hurtled forward as her father chased after her, shouting. She rounded the corner and raced straight into her intended's arms.

Shock stiffened every fibre in her being, her sky-blue eyes wide with it as he smiled down at her with perfect composure.

"My dear Miss Beal," Andrew said, "what an unexpected pleasure. And what a spirited greeting. You quite take my breath away."

"Unhand me," she shrieked.

George Beal checked just behind his daughter, his wife behind him on the terrace, peering around his shoulder. "Andrew, my boy—?" George said with some little surprise himself at the unexpected meeting.

Andrew stepped back from Becky, smiling easily at her father and then bowing towards Mary. "Your servant, Mrs. Beal. I was just arriving to pay my respects to your family, and to ask if you, Mr. Beal, and your daughters would do me the honour of accompanying Lord Hargrave and my family to church on the morrow. I was on my way to greet you but the abbey prospect was so lovely I gave myself the pleasure of taking a quick turn through your garden. It is such an invigorating day. As your daughter seems to agree," he ended dryly.

Mary tried to find the proper polite words of greeting but Becky raised her small chin in an attempt at a haughty air, her eyes stormy. "I've changed my mind," she announced as she retraced her steps. Her father stepped back, treading on his wife's foot.

"Yes," Andrew said easily, ignoring Mary Beal's little cry of pain as he followed Becky towards the open library doors. "I quite agree with you, Miss Beal. So sensible. There is after all a bit more of a chill to the wind than it first seems. Might I suggest a warm wrap if you decide upon another stroll in the garden?" He spoke with the utmost civility, the edge of irony more in his eyes than his voice.

She flounced through the doors, trying her best to ignore her noble companion. "I don't care what you suggest," she told him defiantly.

George Beal heard his daughter's words. "You, young miss, will keep a civil tongue in your head or you will get a proper melting, I can promise you that."

Mary Beal smiled timidly at the tall young aristocrat. "Would—would you care for some refreshment, my lord?"

"What a charming suggestion," Andrew replied.

"I'll just be a moment—"

"Mrs. Beal," Mr. Beal said. "Ring for Peeves."

Seeing her avenue of escape closing she gamely tried to forestall the event. "I don't quite like to bother him," she said honestly and earned a bemused expression from Andrew and a sound put-down from her husband.

"There's no use to prose on at me," Mary insisted with more stubbornness than was her normal wont. "I want to see to things myself."

"And where are you going, missy?" George ended as Becky headed for the hall door.

"I feel quite fagged," she fibbed.

"Yes." Lord Andrew said with all signs of commiseration. "You do look a bit under the weather."

"Does she?" her father asked, eyeing her worriedly. "Go on then, you'd best get to your bed. You don't want to go sick and miss church tomorrow."

Becky's head came up, her cheeks flaming. She looked ready to spit at the arrogant young man who smiled blandly back at her.

"Well, go on, then," George told his daughter. "Don't dawdle about gawking at your intended. You'll have the rest of your life to look at him."

This news was met with a strangled cry from his angered

daughter before she sailed through the door. For good measure she slammed it behind her, the sound reverberating
throughout the lower floors.

George Beal found himself staring at the earl's son.

Andrew smiled languidly. "A high-spirited girl."

In the sitting room beyond, the housemaid dropped her
feather duster and ran to the kitchens, sure she had heard
the Abbey Ghost. "I tell you I must have done, and he was
banging away something fierce, he was!"

"Don't be fanciful," the butler told her in quelling tones
but the kitchen maid was properly impressed, gasping at
the older maid with wide eyes and rounded mouth. "Either
of you," Peeves added when he saw the young maid's
expression. "Any of you." He looked towards Cook and
the scullery maids.

The cook had recently come to the abbey from one
of London's best clubs and she was at least as formidable as the redoubtable Peeves. With a steady gaze she
stared him down until the small man gave her a brief and
frosty smile.

"Your staff is your own responsibility," he admitted.

"Yes," she agreed. "It is."

With a little sniff of impatience, Peeves left her province
and went back down the hall towards his own in time to
see Mary Beal leaving the dining room carrying a tray of
sherry and biscuits.

"Madam," he called out in shocked accents, causing her
to nearly drop the tray.

"Oh, it's you," she said, looking for all the world like a
child caught at mischief.

Peeves took the tray from her. "This simply isn't done."
He opened the library door for the mistress of the house
and bowed ever so slightly as she passed on ahead of him
into the room.

While George and Mary entertained, Becky was curled
up upon her bed, uncaring for the damage she was doing
to her peach-coloured muslin round gown. With angry little
jabs of her feet she kicked off her matching kid slippers,
the light shoes flying across the bed-chamber.

"Becky?" Alice's voice came from the door. She opened
it and peered inside. "Are you unwell?"

"I won't marry that coxcomb, I would be as liefer to—to
drown." Becky waxed eloquent for several minutes about
all the punishments that would be lesser than marrying Lord
Marleigh. But as she spoke her voice became less and less
angry and more dispirited. "Oh, Ally, I don't know what
to do. You must help me."

Alice promised she would, a resolute expression hard-
ening her features. A few minutes later she left her sister,
slipping into her own bed-chamber to retrieve a heavy silk
shawl before descending to the lower floor. She let herself
out the front door and headed across the wide porticoe
towards the wide, shallow steps that led to the carriage-
drive.

"Jake," she called out to the stableman who was coming
around from the kitchens. "Has his lordship left yet?"

"No, miss, he's just called for his horse."

"Would you tell him I would appreciate a moment's
conversation? I shall be in the spinney."

"But, miss—"

"And don't tell my parents," she warned before she took
off across the lawn towards the thicket of close-growing
copper beeches and shrubs.

Jake took off his cap to scratch the back of his head, then
put it back upon his head before he went for the nob's horse.
It was no business of his if the younger girl were growing as
wild as the older one, he decided. Mayhap it was catching,
like measles.

Andrew however, upon hearing of the request, seemed
much more curious about Alice's intent. He mounted his
chestnut and walked the high-spirited animal towards the
spinney.

The roiling winds whipped dry leaves up from the ground,
swirling them around the horse's legs before they settled
back onto the grassy lawns which stretched down to the
stone walls that surrounded the base of the abbey hill.

The wind caught at Andrew's dark hair, ruffling through
it as he leaned forward to duck a low hanging branch

and entered the small wood. He saw Alice ahead and dismounted.

She stood at the base of the only oak in the small stand of trees, watching him approach with eyes that gave away nothing of her intentions. A dark green silk shawl was bundled over her raspberry-coloured round gown, reminding Andrew of a rose amongst thorns. A gust of wind startled the leaves at their feet and loosened her auburn curls.

"Miss Beal," he said with a slight bow. "To what do I owe this pleasure?"

The expression in Alice's eyes resolved itself into a stern rebuke of the smile he gave her. "This will hardly be a pleasure, your lordship, for either of us."

"I am afraid I am at a loss."

Alice took a deep breath. "You must not marry my sister."

Andrew Marleigh was startled into a look of blank surprise. "I beg your pardon?"

"You cannot possibly *wish* to marry Becky," Alice continued. "After all, you have barely met and upon such little acquaintance have not grown in any way close. If you do not accede to your father's wishes, then Papa can't make Becky accede to his."

Andrew Marleigh had never been spoken to so bluntly in his twenty-six years. The fact that it was a woman, a very young woman at that, who was speaking so plainly astounded him. He thought of a great many retorts, from condescending put-downs to laughing directly into her face but her earnest expression stopped him. That, and the fact that her eyes now seemed as green as the woods around him in the shadows under the trees. "Do you know your eyes change colour each time I see you?"

Alice had been prepared for a great many responses and had been trying, as she waited for him to speak, to form rebuttals to any of the demurs he might possibly make. She was not prepared for the words he actually spoke. She faltered. "I—I beg your pardon?"

"Yes, well, you should do that also, you know. You see, it is not polite to tell a gentleman he must cry off from marrying your sister when the gentleman in question has not yet proposed."

"But you will if I cannot convince you otherwise."

"My dear Miss Beal, I am afraid my own hands are as thoroughly tied as are your sister's."

"Are you saying you will not stand up to your father?"

Andrew took a step closer to the stiff-backed young woman. "I am saying I cannot disappoint my father's wishes."

"You would *marry* someone you do not love simply because your father wishes it?"

"Many have suffered that fate," Andrew replied enigmatically. "It is often done for reasons of estate or other pressing family concerns."

Alice stared up at his handsome face. "I think it a fate too horrible to contemplate."

"Which? Obeying your parent or marrying me?"

Alice bridled. "And I find your humour to be out of place when my sister's happiness hangs in the balance."

"Perhaps she could learn to care for me," Andrew offered. "Many have."

"And now you parade your conquests?" Alice could not believe her ears. "I can see I made a grave error in attempting to appeal to your better instincts. There is nothing more to be said."

Lord Andrew could not help smiling down at her grave little face. "Is there nothing else you wish to ask?"

"No."

"Then perhaps actions are called for."

"I beg your pardon?" Before she had finished speaking she found herself pulled forward by two strong hands. Alice was so bemused that she could only stare at his whipcord hacking jacket. Absurdly wondering if the brown velvet lapels were as soft as they looked.

He tipped her chin up and in one and the same fluid movement his lips descended to cover hers. His lips were warm, she thought through her shock and then she lost all coherent thought, something sweet and almost painful welling up within her heart and overcoming all else.

When he had reached to kiss her, he had no thought

about what he was doing until she was in his arms. His own actions took him by surprise but her response aroused him the more, his demanding lips searching out her secrets. Her lips opened of their own volition.

He held her tighter, lost in the moment as her body melted against his and her arms pressed him closer. They were breathless when they finally pulled apart, each of them experiencing unexpected emotions.

Andrew Marleigh fought against the onslaught, angry at himself. "I must apologise," he said, stepping back and speaking stiffly. He saw her confused expression and fought for control over the situation. He found it with a rather forced smile and languid words. "As you can see, marriage to me would not be the worst fate that could befall a fair young damsel."

At his words Alice blushed to the roots of her dark auburn hair. She turned and ran from him. Andrew watched her go, almost following her before he made himself stay where he was. If he followed her, he would kiss those lips again, that he knew. Instead, he reached for the chestnut's reins, mounting and heading down the carriage-drive at a furious pace.

Behind him, Alice Beal was racing too. She ran across the windy grounds, tears filling her eyes as she headed for the safety of her rooms.

9

THE ANNOUNCEMENT OF the abbey ball was greeted with mixed reactions amongst the recipients of invitations and villagers alike.

There were those who were glad to see the abbey once again taking its rightful place in county society. There were others who were happy to be invited to meet the Earl of Marleigh and hob nob with the London swells. There were some who said they were inquisitive about the changes the Beals had made in the abbey, but the majority by far were in a state of avid curiosity about the announced alliance of Rebecca Beal and Lord Andrew Marleigh.

None could credit such a fantastic *liaison* but none could bear to be among the missing if the event actually occurred. All of this meant there were no regrets sent and that Becky Beal's engagement ball was destined to be that best of all party epithets, a sad squeeze.

As the days stretched out the stories of the rich arrangements for the ball at the abbey were bruited about the entire countryside but never so much as in the village of Wooster. Everyone talked of it, from the county women in their gardens to the ploughmen taking a mug of ale at the Kings Crown, to Mr. Beecher, who cheerfully listed for each customer who entered his butcher's shop the entire order. "Fresh venison, beef, veal and salt-water fish. And when you've taken into account their pheasant, chicken, mutton and fresh-water fish—not to mention all the fruits and vegetables, some even coming from London—why they'll be dining like kings of old."

The butcher's son, Paul, listened to the talk. He was a straightforward young man, full of youth and strength and the milk of human kindness. He was also besotted with the beauty of Becky Beal, who having turned his head had left him bereft of his natural sense and innate wisdom.

The more Paul heard of the opulent arrangements for the abbey ball, the more he worried about his beloved Becky. He had always known that one day Becky would marry someone else for he had nothing to offer her. But he knew from the note she had smuggled to him, she did not want this marriage.

Paul made a promise on his private honour to deliver his precious Becky from the evil forces which surrounded her.

Becky herself was mired deep in the sloughs of despond, contemplating the pluses and minuses of life in a convent versus life as Lord Andrew's wife. Lord Andrew was not fairing well in the contrast. However, the alternatives were, to be truthful, bleak. Becky, even in her most conceited moments, had to admit she was not cut of the cloth to be a nun, nor did she have the patience and training to be a governess or even a lady's maid which took a great deal of training and knowledge let alone a silent tongue.

As the days went by Becky was more and more firmly convinced her father was set upon his course and that her words and deeds would have little sway over what he had decided. The vision of herself as a spinster, dependent upon her father's largess for her entire life did not appeal to young Becky. The idea of being a lady, with jewels and servants and riches to spare suited her down to the ground until she thought of all the boring people such as the countess to whom she would be forced to be polite. What she wanted was to marry Paul and still have the jewels and servants and riches. And she had always gotten what she wanted from her father. But how to convince her father to give in to her this time was more than she could yet figure out.

The night of the abbey ball was crisp with a late April nip to the air, the moon high above and almost full. Carriages moved in stately precision up the torch-lit abbey road, the abbey itself blazing with light and warmth at the top of the hill. Footmen, bowing low, put carriage steps in place and helped the gentry alight from their curricles, carriages and phaetons.

The sounds of music and revelry floated out on the early spring night air accompanied by music and mirth, Steadford Abbey was alive with laughter. Andrew and his parents were among the earliest arrivals, but he soon left the others below and sought the solitude of the dark upper gallery. He was so wrapped in dark thought that he noticed none but himself as he paced. Aware he must join the company below, he could not yet bring himself to meet the assemblage. Surely even the veriest nodcock amongst them must realise the true import of this engagement when it was announced. His friends in London would be torn between laughter and pity. He could bear neither.

"It will never work," Andrew muttered to himself.

"I'm glad you have the sense to see that, at any rate," Sir Harry the Ghost replied from behind the handsome young Corinthian.

Startled, Andrew turned on his heel. "Sir? Who are you? Why don't you show yourself?"

"I *am* showing myself," Harry replied in a testy tone. Sir Harry saw Andrew gaping at him and relented a bit. "You are talking to me, are you not?"

"Good grief, man, I can see right through you!" Andrew exclaimed.

"Count yourself fortunate. Most can't see me at all."

"But—but—" Andrew sputtered, "you seem to be a ghost."

"Yes, and why should I not, since that's what I am," Sir Harry confirmed.

Lord Andrew's eyes dilated in alarm. "I cannot be seeing this."

"And if you are?" Sir Harry asked with raised brow.

"If I am, sir, I swear I am ready for commitment to St. Mary of Bethlehem."

"Bedlam, is it? Well, if you think that is your due, you'd best find out before you marry and sire children. But I would venture to say that anyone who has the sense to employ such an impeccable valet cannot possibly be dicked in the nob. That mish you've got on is exquisite and those thumpers, polished to a mirror shine, my boy, but your cravat—now that's a work of art. Is that the latest style? What's it called?"

With a bemused expression, Lord Andrew listened to the ghost admire his shirt and boots. Struck dumb for the moment, he could only stare at the vision before him until he recalled himself to his manners and replied.

"It's—it's called the Mathematical. Sir—you speak in normal accents and you seem to have a fine sensibility but your own appearance is—to be blunt—not of the first water."

Harry's eyes went skyward, beseeching an entity he hoped would listen. "If there is any order to this universe, you will not allow this slight to go unanswered." When no thunderbolt descended and Andrew remained standing and looking perfectly fit, Sir Harry heaved a put-upon sigh. "I assure you," he told Lord Andrew. "No matter how Top-of-the-Trees you may fancy yourself to be in life, it is most wretchedly impossible to sustain such distinction of appearance when you've been dead for forty years. One can hardly advertise for a valet in this condition."

"Forty!" The startled word escaped before he could contain it. "Forgive me, I am sorry—"

"It's a few decades late for protestations of sympathy," Harry said dryly.

"I mean for my inexcusably impolite behaviour. I don't mean to gape at you so, nor quiz you, but you see I am not in the habit of conversing with—with, well I know no other words, *ghosts*, and I am not quite sure how to proceed."

Sir Harry grimaced. "You're doing as well as any. I myself am not slap up the echo these years. I keep forgetting to even introduce myself."

"You have a name then?" Andrew asked politely.

"God's teeth, doesn't everyone?"

"Most, in fact all, in my acquaintances, have, but I have never before conversed with—"

"A ghost," Sir Harry finished for the young man. "Yes, yes, you've already said. Henry Aldworth, Bart., at your service, sir."

Andrew found himself giving the apparition a bow as he introduced himself, all the while telling himself he must be dreaming or truly demented.

"All call me Harry," Sir Harry continued after the introductions were accomplished. "And precious few of them there are these days, I can tell you, what with all those that could see me taking French leave and decamping to Kent and the wilds of the Americas." Sir Harry seemed to lump both places together as beyond the pale of civilisation.

"They run off, do they?" Andrew asked weakly.

"Not from me, they don't," Harry defended himself. "I'm not such a dead bore as all that. Well, I may be dead," he corrected and then eyed the young lord balefully. "But I don't scruple to say that I have never been a bore."

"I can quite see that," Andrew replied. "And I would venture to say not many ghosts have your range of vocabulary, nor your mastery of the current cant either."

"I keep my ears open," Sir Harry agreed, somewhat mollified by the young man's words and beginning to see some merit in the boy. "Now what's to be done with you?"

Lord Andrew took a step back from the Abbey Ghost. "I beg your pardon?"

"This one is going to be the very devil to put to rights, make no bones about it. By rights, you shouldn't be able to see me." He stared into the younger man's perplexed expression. "It's a muddle."

"It is?"

"Well, damme, you don't want to marry the girl, do you?" Harry demanded.

The younger man stiffened. "Sir, it is not possible for a gentleman to answer such a question when—when—"

"Don't try to slumguzzle me, my lad. I've no patience with polite circumlocutions when talking plain and straight will get things done faster. You're not in love with Becky, are you?"

"I, that is to say, well, no."

"That's better. You'll get used to it in the end. Believe me, life's much simpler if you just say what you mean and hang what people think."

"Much simpler, I would imagine, since one would have few friends and no dealings with polite society."

"Well, do you want to get out of it or not?" Sir Harry demanded.

"Yes," came the immediate reply, devoid of all conventional sham. "But," Andrew added in the next breath, "It can't be done."

"Never say never, my boy. That's one thing I learned after I woke up in this state." Sir Harry gave Andrew a long shrewd calculating look before continuing. "The puzzlement is that you can see me. You shouldn't be able to, you know."

"You mentioned that before. I assure you, it's a complete surprise to me," Andrew told the ghost.

"Yes, well, are you by any chance in love?"

"Decidedly not!"

Sir Harry shook his ghostly head. "This is a new page in my book, I can tell you that. I shall have to think on it."

"If you could do something—" Andrew started, stopped and then began again. "That is to say, if there were a way to avoid this marriage—it would have to be done soon. In point of fact, now. Since this evening's announcement will commit us irrevocably—"

"Yes, yes, I know."

"Sir Harry, you are . . . fading. Sir Harry?" Andrew called again.

"Never fear," Sir Harry's voice said. "I shall be back."

Andrew looked towards where the ghost had stood. He shook his head a little and then passed his hand over his eyes. He walked to the tapestry-covered settee a few steps away and sat down.

The fact of a ghost's existence seemed impossible once the apparition vanished. And the conversation when remembered seemed decidedly whimsical, not to mention wishful when one considered the rash promise the ghost had made. Light footsteps sounded from nearby, coming closer. Andrew kept his eyes squeezed shut, afraid to open them and see another apparition.

And so it was that Alice did not see him until the light from the candle she held illuminated a booted foot stretched out on the carpet directly ahead of her.

"You," she said.

"So sorry," Andrew said, sitting up straight and then standing. "I didn't mean to startle you." He watched the surprise in her eyes change to distress and looked away himself, glancing in the direction she was headed. The Long Gallery stretched to the front of the house and there ended in mullioned windows with wide sofas set between them. "It would seem you were also looking for a bit of solitude before joining the party," he remarked in a neutral tone.

When she spoke her voice was tremulous and low. "I thought no one here."

"Or rather wished not to be alone with me again?" he said. "I must apologise for my actions when last we were alone."

Alice looked up into his dark blue eyes, seeing the unhappy glints behind his polite smile. "Oh, no, it is I who should apologise," she said, earning a surprised look. She rushed on before she lost her nerve. "I was most distressingly bold and I had no right to take you to task for any of this as it is my father who is the most to blame. I did not think to say it then but I hope you know I do realise all this must be quite as distressing for you as it is for Becky. In fact, the more so because of your social position and—friends."

Andrew was not accustomed to have young misses commiserate with him nor to having them be so direct in their meanings. Her words were as blunt as they had been in the spinney days before and yet they did not have the sting they would have had from other lips. He could see her very real compassion.

"I have no wish to cause your sister distress," he replied truthfully without truly replying. He watched her bite her lower lip and look down.

"I should not have spoken," Alice said, avoiding his eyes. "Then or now. Please forgive my impertinence."

Andrew touched her chin, lifting her face so that he could once again look into her golden topaz and green and hazel eyes. They seemed as dark as richest chocolate in the small light from her candle. Its flame sputtered in the drafts that swirled up the staircase and down the wide hall, carrying faint sounds of the music and conversation far away below them.

"This night your eyes are darkest brown, not golden as they were in the sunlight. But always beautiful," he told her softly.

As are yours, Alice almost told him, staring up into the inky blue of his questioning gaze. He seemed to be asking something with his eyes but she had no experience of men and could not read the meaning. All she knew was that he was the most handsome man she had ever seen and that the tip of his finger still touched her chin.

Andrew was supremely comfortable with the London debutantes who swirled through each Season wrapped in silks and pretty speeches and full of flirtatious coquetry. Becky Beal, although sadly lacking in town polish and polite conversation, was very like the young women he knew; beautiful and selfish. They were vain with the natural vanity of those who have no knowledge of the wider world and have even less curiosity about it.

But Alice was an enigma and each time he saw her Andrew was once again intrigued. She had been surprised when he touched her face, he had felt the little trill of shock that coursed through her. She did not offer pretty protestations against his gesture, she did not pull away.

His hand still tipped her chin upwards, his eyes warm in the candlelight. "I'll warrant that kiss in the spinney was your very first," Andrew said, his voice soft. He saw her gaze slide to his lips and then fly back up to meet his eyes, her innocence strangely compelling. He leaned forward, mesmerized by the soft lips that were slightly parted and bare inches away.

"Andy?" Hero called out from the head of the stairway, startling his listeners. "Is that you?"

Andrew's hand dropped from Alice's chin. He straightened and turned towards his friend, returning the greeting easily, which was well because Alice found herself unable to utter a word. She took a great gulp of air, still facing away from the others as Hero, accompanied by Mary and George Beal, came down the Long Gallery.

"I was admiring the artwork," Andrew told them all.

Hero saw Alice turning around to face them and grinned. "I'll warrant you were at that."

"Lovely pieces you have, ma'am." Andrew addressed Mary Beal.

Mary looked towards the vast collection. "They came with the house," she told him artlessly. "But I do enjoy them in the daylight. In this light, there's so little to be seen."

"Ah, but the presence of art is always a restorative to the soul."

"Quite," Hero said archly. "Much like that of pleasant companions." He made a small bow to Alice.

"Yes, yes," George Beal said. "Art's all well enough when you've time for it but we've been looking high and low for you, Andrew. The dancing's begun and Becky is pining away to dance with you." George delivered this most blatant of lies with a bland expression. In truth his daughter had warned him she might very well dance all over Andrew's feet, whereupon her father had told her she would not be able to use her backside for a week if she kept to her threat.

"Sorry," Andrew was now saying stiffly. "I must have lost track of the time."

"With such a charming companion, he can't be faulted, can he, Mrs. Beal?" Hero said gallantly.

Mary Beal was unused to the fine art of flirtatious small talk and was not sure whether to agree her daughter was charming would be gauche or not so kept her peace.

George took advantage of Herds pretty words and moved to put his arm around his youngest daughter. "She's a fine one, so quiet and biddable, she is. I've been telling young Hero here all about your bookish ways, Alice my girl, and he, for one, isn't put off at all. Imagine a man who likes a book-learned woman, isn't that a treat?" George had no use for book-learning in females or anyone else and merely tolerated Alice's peculiar habit. He found it amazing that such a young buck as Hero was not repulsed by the idea of an intelligent woman. After all, all men knew that an educated woman was bound to be stubborn and argumentative.

"I find a taste for literature charming."

"You see?" George asked his daughter. He gave Hero a broad wink. "One could do a lot worse than to marry such a sensible girl. And well dowered too."

At her father's words Alice's gaze flew to Andrew's. He saw her consternation and winked, earning a tremulous little smile in return.

"Come along then, Mr. Beal. You've got one engagement already to worry about this evening, let's not set your sights too high." Mary led the way to the party below.

Andrew fell into step beside Hero, and let the Beals walk a little in front as Hero spoke in low tones to his companion. "What do you think of her?"

"I beg your pardon?"

"Shy Alice," Hero explained. "She's not the beauty her sister is but she'd be a much more tractable wife and can be trained, I'm sure, in the social graces. By Gad, think of the dowry—it'll probably be larger than her sister's since she's not got the same looks."

"You were always one to go for flash over substance," Andrew said, nettled for some reason. "Honeyed curls do not make for a honeyed disposition, nor are they the first stare of beauty as far as I am concerned."

"Yes, but don't you think I might slip back into my parents good grace if I settled down and married into all that money?"

"I was not aware you had developed a tendre for her," Andrew replied in cool tones.

"Good grief, that hasn't stopped you, old man."

"You'd do well to consider the girl's feelings," Andrew said sharply.

"Gad, you'd best be careful, Andy. One would almost think you had designs upon the creature," Hero replied.

"Perish the thought," Andrew said quickly, trying to deny the feelings that rushed about within him.

"Precisely. After all, you are to marry the older sister so you cannot very well dally with the younger. Besides, it's just not done."

Andrew's voice was even colder. "I have never dallied with any other than experienced women and I would never compromise such a young innocent as Miss Alice Beal."

But Hero's attention was elsewhere and he did not notice the strength of his friend's reactions. "Yes," Hero said, almost to himself. "I think I shall chat her up a bit."

Their host turned back to address the two young men and so Andrew had no further chance to dissuade his lifelong friend. Andrew was very glad of the interruption. He had the most insane impulse to plant a facer directly onto Hero Hargrave's nattering mouth.

10

A QUADRILLE WAS just ending in the ballroom when Lady Agatha looked up to see the Beals enter with Hero and Andrew. At the beginning of the evening she had informed the Beals in quite forceful accents that she would not stand to greet their guests along with them. Mary Beal had particularly wanted Lady Agatha beside her, both for helpful instructions as well as because, as she put it, it wouldn't seem right for a Steadford to merely be invited to the party. The county would expect Lady Agatha to help receive the abbey's guests.

Agatha was not to be persuaded. She felt the best way to end the county's speculation about the Beals was for them to be accepted as the new owners of the abbey as quickly as possible. Three years was time enough for people to talk behind their fans. And so it was that Agatha Steadford-Smyth made herself comfortable on a gilt chair where she could see the entire ballroom and beyond into the huge parlour which had been opened and filled with tables heaped with delicacies and drinks. Beyond the enormous epergnes surmounted with mountains of cakes and fruits and marzipan, beyond the punch bowls and milling throngs, card tables had been set up in the blue parlour which led off the huge main parlour. A lively game of loo and a quieter one of backgammon were already being enjoyed by some of the older guests whilst the younger ones joined in the dancing.

Old friends came by, spending a few moments' conversation and wandering off, to be surrounded by yet more of the local gentry paying their respects.

"What a sad squeeze," said Fannie who stood by her mistress's side. "You dare not breathe deeply for fear of bumping into someone."

"Yes, it is quite a success," Lady Agatha agreed. She called to a footman, instructing him to open the terrace doors so that cool air could revive the company. He did as she bid, the huge candlebranches flickering in the breezes that refreshed the overheated room.

"I'm quite pleased with the way Mary's dress turned out," Fannie declared as she watched the little woman being introduced to Squire Lyme and his wife, Eleanor. Since Fannie had designed the dress she could be pardoned for taking pride in the high-waisted violet satin gown with its edging of creamy embroidered lace and the creamy underskirt with its deep violet border.

Fannie looked from Mary to the other ladies that graced the room. None had finer gowns nor more up to the minute ones, Fannie prided herself. She smoothed the skirt of her own jonquil crepe gown and glanced at the sea green silk Lady Agatha wore with pride. Fannie had refurbished the gowns herself with gold braid trim for her mistress and new nile green ribbons for her own. Perhaps the countess's silver and tulle dress was the height of elegance in London but Fannie felt is was the outside of enough and much too grand for country wear.

Becky and Andrew came down the line of a country dance, moving gracefully past the narrow gilt chairs.

"She looks lovely in that gold peau-de-soie," Fannie commented.

"Too gaudy," was Agatha's opinion. "Alice is the better dressed."

Fannie glanced towards Alice at the other end of the country set with Hero. "Pale pink and pearls are very proper but they're not eye-catching."

"Proper young girls do not wish to be eye-catching. They wish to be modest, decorous and unexceptional," Lady Agatha said firmly. "Eye-catching indeed," she sniffed.

"All the same, Becky looks a proper treat," Fannie continued, unrepentant.

While Fannie admired Becky the girl herself was just coming off the dance floor. She had allowed Andrew a dance with as much good grace as she could manage but once on the floor she had been so exhilarated by the music she had quite forgotten to be upset.

"Would you care for some refreshment?" Andrew asked politely.

"I would adore some lemonade," she replied.

He returned her to her mother and then went to fetch the lemonade. Mary was engrossed in a very dull conversation, so Becky looked around at the room full of people. Most of them she had been introduced to only this evening, their names swimming about in her head and then forgotten in the midst of even more introductions.

She saw a smiling young woman heading towards her and smiled back.

"Hello, again, I'm Charlotte Summerville," the woman said. She had dark hair and eyes and looked almost Spanish except for the red highlights that burnished her smooth curls. "Lady Agatha introduced us. Do you mind if I sit with you a moment? I am escaping a most dull conversation concerning Squire Lyme's pigs."

Becky's nose wrinkled. "Is that the best he can manage as party conversation?"

"Oh, my dear, he has three subjects of conversation. The first and dearest to his heart is his livestock. The second is the state of the trout in his streams and the third is the collapsing state of the modern world, thanks to Boney and various politicians he calls fat-headed and too liberal by half."

"Whatever does he mean?" Becky asked mystified.

"I'm quite sure I neither know nor care," Charlotte responded and both girls laughed. "I think the countess has the best solution for getting away from bores. She has closeted herself with her husband over a game of backgammon in the small parlour beyond and pretends to hear nothing around her. She's not truly deaf as some contend, is she?"

"I don't think so," Becky replied, grinning. "I think she's just above us all."

The girls laughed the more as they discussed the countess's condescension.

"Here, here," Lord Hargrave said as he arrived beside them. "Two such lovely visions sitting out a dance?"

"Lord Andrew is finding some lemonade," Becky explained and then introduced the dark-haired beauty to the fair, blonde lord.

"I beg your pardon, did you say Hieronyius?" Charlotte asked in dulcet tones. There was just the right touch of intimacy in her tone, not so much as to be forward but enough for the gentleman hearing it to look closer into her dark eyes. She had reached her late twenties and was still unmarried thanks to the poverty of her widowed mother's purse and the lack of what both mother and daughter felt were truly suitable matches in the countryside, Charlotte was adept at flirtation.

"My mother was of a poetical bent," he explained, smiling. "Rather like your sister," he told Becky who made a face and dismissed Alice's literary interests with a quick shrug.

"She'll get over it," Becky declared.

"My mother doesn't seem to have," Lord Hargrave continued to Becky but his eyes were on Charlotte. "Actually all call me Hero, it's so much shorter."

"And so appropriate?" Charlotte asked with a smile and arched brows.

"That you will have to judge for yourself, Miss Summerville."

"I am quite sure of it," she told him, flashing another lovely smile at him. "And if I am to have a Hero, he must call me Charlotte—"

"And may he have the honour of this dance?" Hero asked.

"The pleasure is truly mine," she murmured as Andrew arrived back with Becky's lemonade.

Introductions were made before Hero escorted Charlotte to the dance floor. Andrew's eyes went round the assemblage. "I have not seen your sister in some little time."

"She escapes parties as if they were the plague," Becky replied. "Why do you seek her?"

Andrew was at a loss to answer the innocent question. "I was merely wondering if—if she might like a glass of lemonade," he finished lamely.

George Beal came towards them. "Aren't you young people going to dance?"

"We have been dancing," Becky told her father, a little pout coming back to mar her features. The pout deepened when Andrew jumped to his feet and offered his arm. With shockingly bad grace Becky stood up. "I suppose this means I must."

George leaned in towards Andrew's ear. "I'll have them play a waltz, that'll keep her close and do the trick."

Andrew flushed but Becky's father did not see the younger man's reaction.

"What did he say?" Becky demanded.

Andrew looked down at the diminutive beauty. "He said he most especially is calling up a waltz."

"Oh, good, I've just learnt the steps," Becky said ingenuously. Her escort's expression was wry as they walked onto the floor and began to dance. Becky concentrated carefully on her steps, so engrossed with her movements she barely noticed who she was moving with, much to Andrew's continuing ironic amusement.

There was a bit of commotion behind them in the parlour, the sounds finally growing loud enough to be heard over the music and gain their attention. Becky gasped as she saw Paul Beecher coming directly towards her. A footman was telling him he had to stop, George Beal was coming from across the length of the room, and still Paul came forward.

He was dressed in his best wool coat and white cotton shirt but the butcher's son was sorely out of place in the midst of the silk and satin finery around him.

"Becky, I've come to talk to your father," Paul said.

"Young man," George Beal came barrelling up behind the villager. "Just what do you think you're doing?"

"I've come to offer for Becky, Mr. Beal," Paul said into the sudden silence as the musicians trailed off and all else listened with baited breath to the angry exchange.

"You'll get out of my house before I forget your father is a friend of mine and give you the what-for you deserve for barging in here," George bellowed.

"You let him alone," Becky yelled at her father, making matters worse.

"Stay out of it, missy, or you'll get the melting that's long overdue you."

"George—" Mary came rushing up beside her husband. "Don't make a scene in front of all our guests."

"I'm not making a scene, he's making the scene and I'm ending it," her husband answered.

"Shush—"

"Woman, don't shush me," George looked past his stunned guests and shouted at the musicians. "Play—that's what I'm paying you for!"

The music began again, guests turned away and pretending to converse. A few even began to dance around the small group in the middle of the floor.

"I'll not let my Becky be married off to someone she hates," Paul Beecher told George Beal without even a glance at the young man who stood beside Becky. As tall as Paul himself and just as muscular, Lord Andrew Marleigh could easily hold his own in a fight. At the moment however, he was staring at the young villager with a bemused expression, as if watching a play instead of being one of the participants in the drama.

"Your Becky? *Your* Becky! And just what's been going on behind my back?" George demanded.

Lady Agatha could stand the display no longer. "Mr. Beal this is not the place."

"I know that," he snapped.

Agatha overrode the man's angry words. "Paul, if you have something to discuss you may wait in the library. Lord Andrew, I suggest you accompany Rebecca to get a breath of fresh air on the terrace. Fannie, you can act as chaperone. Mr. Beal," she added in tones that brooked no denial, "I shall accompany you and Paul to the privacy of the library."

"I don't want to go outside," Becky interrupted. "Papa will surely murder Paul and I won't let him!"

"I assure you there will be no bloodshed in the abbey while I am present," Lady Agatha told the girl in polite but sharp accents. "Andrew?"

Andrew took Becky's arm and very nearly pulled her to the terrace doors as George Beal stalked off beside Lady Agatha and his wife.

Hero saw Alice come running back into the ballroom and intercepted both her and her questions.

"I heard shouting—has something happened to Andrew? And Becky?"

"Your father is in the study with someone named Paul something or other."

Alice's face went white. "Paul came here? Tonight? Where is Becky?" she asked, alarmed.

Hero's brow bunched into confused lines. "Your sister is with Andy on the terrace."

"Are you positive?" Alice asked and then seeing Hero's expression, she tried for a trembling little laugh. "Of course she is, no doubt."

"What in blue blazes is going on with your sister and this chap?" Hero demanded. "He looked to be a cowherder or some such."

"He lives in the village," she informed her inquisitor. "But I cannot conceive of what he could be thinking of to come here tonight of all nights."

Hero Hargrave was not at all sure what the young villager had been thinking of but he was very sure it concerned Becky Beal. "Perhaps your sister knows," Hero offered.

Charlotte Summerville arrived in time to hear Alice's quick defensive reply. "My sister's done nothing wrong!"

"Has someone said she did?" Charlotte murmured. But her lifted eyebrow spoke volumes to Hero who remained silent.

"Hero?" the earl called him a little away from the girls. "What's this I hear about some young ruffian and Becky? Where's Andrew?"

"Andrew is on the terrace with Becky, at least so I believe, sir." Hero described the scene that had transpired as best he could to the earl while outside on the terrace. Andrew stood at the far end of the wide expanse, trying to keep Becky from going back inside. Fannie kept watch on the young couple but she stayed near the open doors allowing them to converse in private.

"You'll just make it worse for him, don't you see?" Andrew told her for the tenth time.

"I don't care, I don't want Papa hurting him!"

"Even upon such short acquaintanceship I can promise you I am positive Lady Agatha will not let anyone come to blows in her presence."

"My father is a brute!" Becky burst out.

"He merely wishes to protect you," Andrew said mildly.

"If he wanted to protect me, he wouldn't ask me to marry against my heart!" she replied passionately.

In any other circumstances Lord Andrew would have retorted to the chit with a devastatingly cutting put-down. However, at the moment, he could not work up sufficient ire.

"I'm sorry you are so disappointed in me," he said rather stiffly.

Becky Beal waved away his words with an impatient gesture. "Actually, you're not nearly as bad a coxcomb as I thought you'd be."

"High praise indeed," Andrew muttered.

"It's just that you're much too sophisticated and you always seem to be laughing up your sleeve at something and I have always loved Paul most awfully and I don't want to marry anyone else."

Andrew was torn between laughter and rue. Every mother and daughter on the London Marriage Mart had used every trick at their disposal to bring him to the point. And here was a cit's daughter who wished to throw him over for a man who seemed to be little more than a laborer.

"Is this—Paul—a farmer?"

"No, he's a butcher's assistant."

Having been given this startling intelligence, Andrew took his time replying. "I see," he said, although he truly did not. "And you have a lively interest in meat products?"

"Of course not," Becky stamped her little foot. "What on earth do I care what he does? All men must do something, it seems. If they don't farm or work in trade they rush off with guns and fishing rods and things. It's all one to me."

Andrew studied her. "I truly believe you mean that."

"And what's so surprising about that?" she asked.

"Many young ladies wish to better themselves through marriage."

"Pish and tosh," she replied inelegantly. "I imagine if one was poor, one would want to marry a rich man but I'm not poor. And as to bettering myself, I shall surely never be accepted as of the first consequence no matter how many titles Papa tries to buy for me, so why should I care what others think? I want to be happy and I don't understand why you don't want to be."

"What makes you assume I have no wish for happiness?"

"Well, you are willing to marry me, for one thing."

Andrew choked. "Sorry," he said when he could manage speech. "I applaud your candor."

"Why did you ever agree to all this?"

"I assure you, Miss Beal, I had no more choice than did you."

"But we both have," she exclaimed. "Don't you see? If you do not come up to scratch then we both shall be free and I can marry Paul."

"Free and penniless," he amended.

"Oh. Papa won't stay out of sorts with me forever. Being poor won't be so bad if you know you don't have to be and that it'll soon go away. You yourself could always earn some money or join the army or something," she cajoled. "Couldn't you, please?"

"I am afraid I can do neither," Andrew replied, his anger at the position his father had placed him in turning his words bitter.

"I think it's altogether too bad if you're so afraid of being poor that you won't help us get out of this mess."

Andrew started to defend himself and then stopped, allowing her to think the worst of him, rather than his father. "We should go back inside so that we do not occasion further talk."

"Fannie is here so they cannot accuse of dalliance, which I'll wager is what their tongues are wagging about Paul and me."

"All the same, you have guests to attend to since the rest of your family is—otherwise engaged. Besides, there is a chill in the air."

"I suppose so," she replied with bad grace and a deep sigh. She turned back towards Fannie and the people beyond inside the candlelit ballroom. "I also suppose I shall be quizzed by one and all."

"Hold your head high and ignore them. And of course, avoid any further rash acts such as whatever you said or did that occasioned your young butchers to come racing pell-mell into the middle of your ball," Andrew advised solemnly as they reached Fannie's side.

Becky thought about what he had said. "Further rash acts," she repeated slowly.

"Unless you want your father to disown you once and for all, I would suggest you heed my advice."

"Oh, I shall," she promised with a gleam beginning to dawn in her blue eyes.

"Shall we go in before we all catch our death?" Fannie asked, her shawl wrapped tight around her shoulders.

"Yes," Becky responded. She came forward past Fannie willingly, a tiny bit disconcerted at the stillness that swept the room when she entered. But she held her head high as Andrew had advised and swept through the crowded room towards her sister and Hero as if nothing had happened.

"Are you all right?" Alice asked when they came close.

"I'm fine but it's Paul who's closeted with Papa."

"Whatever can he have been thinking of, coming here tonight of all nights?" Alice asked.

"He was thinking of me," Becky replied. "And he had to come tonight since everyone knows Papa plans on announcing my engagement." She cast a swift glance towards Andrew. "And I can find no way to persuade Andrew to cry off."

Andrew turned as Becky spoke, Alice meeting his gaze and blanching at her sister's words. "Becky," Alice said sharply.

"Well, it's true enough," Becky said unrepentantly. "He doesn't want to be cut off by the earl and left without a competence." An idea dawned in Becky's head. "Unless possibly you would trust me now and break it off and I could pay you something later, after I've my own money—"

"Becky Beal!" Alice grabbed her sister's arm, her face crimson. Unable to look up at Andrew's angry countenance, she glared at her sister. "How can you be so unfeeling, so tactless, so *cruel*?"

Lord Andrew spoke coldly. "I appreciate your concern, Miss Alice, but it is totally unnecessary. Your father has arranged a bargain to which my father agreed and your sister is merely refining upon their work. However, I must disabuse you, Miss Rebecca, of any hope of paying me off later. I shall do as my parent wishes no matter the personal cost. Now, since my presence is obviously unwanted I am sure you will both excuse me if I attend upon my mother."

Andrew Marleigh walked away from the Beal sisters. His back straight, his expression polite, he walked across the room as if unaware of the curious stares he received.

11

LADY AGATHA WAS never precisely sure how she convinced Paul Beecher to leave the abbey library without serious harm coming to him from Becky Beal's father. Mary helped restrain her husband, Lady Agatha appealed to the common sense of the boy she'd known since birth and finally Paul agreed to leave and George Beal agreed not to bash in the boy's head. Yet.

Lady Agatha went back to the party as if nothing had happened and gave nothing but blank stares and repressive answers to all questions regarding the *contretemps*.

Andrew danced attendance upon his parents, bringing them to sit with Lady Agatha and Fannie, the only two in the room he could be sure would manage themselves with propriety. Lady Agatha called Rebecca and Alice over and told Andrew that it would be wise to dance with each whilst all the guests were still there in order to put an end to the tongue-wagging that could be felt all around them.

Andrew did as he was bid, dancing a country figure with Becky which required no conversation and very little proximity. He stayed beside Becky and the others throughout the next set, fetching lemonade and being properly attentive.

But when the music for another waltz was struck up he bowed to Alice, asking for the favour of a dance.

"Go on, child," Lady Agatha pressed the hesitant girl and soon Alice found herself in Andrew's arms.

They danced in silence for several moments until Andrew finally spoke. "If you never look up at me and we do not converse all shall see you were coerced into dancing and I shall be all the more censured."

"All the more censured? What do you mean?"

"There are many in this room who heard or saw enough to know young Paul came demanding your sister's hand and cannot credit why I have not called him out."

"A duel with Paul?" Alice replied incredulously. "What utter nonsense."

"It is the accepted way to defend a woman's honour. And of course a man's priviledge. However in this situation I agree that it would look—unconventional—at best."

"It would look absolutely ludicrous," Alice burst out and then blushed as she saw others glancing her way.

"If you continue to blush so often and so furiously whenever we are together I am afraid you may do your nerves damage and never again regain your glorious pale complexion. Or that people will begin to talk," he added in a sardonic tone.

He thought her complexion glorious, Alice heard the words spinning round and round inside her head. She searched for conversation to break the spell. "H-have you met the Regent?" she asked.

"Now wherever did that come from?" he asked. Seeing her confusion he continued, "Yes. He is rather difficult to miss if one moves in London society. Which I might add is not nearly so distasteful as your sister seems to imagine."

"Oh, I am sure you are quite wrong," Alice breathed.

"I am?" he quizzed, studying the topaz eyes until she looked away, quite out of breath.

"I'm sure it would be ever so much different for us than it is for you. We should probably be laughed at by one and all for trying to overstep the bounds."

"There are no bounds you need ever worry overstepping," Andrew replied gallantly. But he found himself meaning the words and saying more. "There are none I have ever met who are finer, more honest, than you. And I'll warrant there are none who would be more true," he said, thinking of the jaded beauties who thought nothing of dangling men on strings. Once an innocent young miss had married and brought forth her husband's heirs it was thought not only natural but socially *de rigueur* to take a lover. Or lovers, Andrew reminded himself bitterly as he thought of the heartbreak he had once felt at twenty when he learned he was not the first, nor would he be the last. Andrew caught himself. "Or more interesting," he added on safer ground.

Alice's brow furrowed. "I am hardly interesting."

"How can you say that? There are precious few young ladies who can speak of anything more than gossip and the current fashions. You, on the other hand, have the entire world of literature from which to converse."

"I think you are saying, in a very kind way, that I live closeted in my books," she said with a timid smile.

"No, I truly mean what I say," he told her. "I must own I am quite curious to know which authors, what subjects, appeal the most to you."

Alice watched his eyes. She could read no humour, no derision there. "Are you truly interested?" she asked and then, seeing his reply in his eyes, she went on. "I am positively addicted to history, I must confess. Ours and the Romans and the Greeks. There are such likenesses one begins to wonder if our race truly ever learns its lessons at all or whether we are doomed to repeat and repeat them." She hesitated before continuing in a lower tone. "And I dote on something truly dreadful."

"Your secrets shall be safe with me," Andrew assured her.

Her gaze drifted to his lips, remembering the secret kiss they shared in the spinney. And the touch of his fingertip to her chin earlier this night.

"A penny for your thoughts," Andrew said, earning another blush.

"I adore Shakespeare and Marlowe and I dote on Horace Walpole and Fannie Burney," she said in a little rush.

Andrew cast his eyes heavenward. "Alas, this cannot be true."

"I fear it is, sir."

"*The Castle of Otranto*?" he said, mock-horrified.

"And *Evelina*," Alice confessed.

The music ended while they discussed literature. Andrew led a smiling Alice back to her sister's side, both of them seeming to have forgotten the problems that surrounded them.

Becky leaned to whisper in her sister's ear as Andrew replied to a question of his father's. "You looked so engrossed, you seemed to actually enjoy yourselves."

"We did," Alice told her surprised sister. "We truly did. At least I did." She cast a shy glance towards Andrew.

"Then you must keep him occupied for a few minutes more, please, dear sister."

Alice looked wary. "Becky Beal, what are you up to now?"

"Nothing," Becky assured her sister. "I only want to run fetch something from my room."

Alice looked into her sister's guileless blue eyes. "Then why must anyone be kept occupied?"

"If you must know I want to write a note to Paul," Becky whispered. "And to get young Meg to give it to him so that he will not act so rashly again."

"This sounds too sensible to be true," Alice told Becky.

"Well, it's not. I mean, it's not too sensible to be true, because it is true. I don't want Papa to do something dreadful to him, so I want to warn him he must let me talk to Papa and not to come back until Papa says it is all right."

"Which will be the day after eternity," Alice told her sister tartly.

"Please, Ally, I don't want them looking about for me until I come back." And with that Becky stood up and left the room.

If her father had been in attendance in the ballroom he would have been sure to soon miss her and wonder why. But as he was still fuming in the library, he did not know until half an hour later that Becky had been missing for quite some time.

"Where is she?" he asked a group consisting of Alice, Andrew, his parents, Lady Agatha and Fannie.

Lady Agatha looked around the room. "She was here a little while ago, talking to Alice—"

Alice tried not to look guilty. "She wanted to get something from her room—"

George Beal's face darkened. He turned to his wife and glowered. "If this is more havey-cavey nonsense I shall not be responsible for what I do to that girl. Did that boy leave or not?"

Peeves was called and assured his employer the boy had been ejected from the abbey but George was not satisfied. He knew the wily ways of romantic fools and insisted footmen be sent to search the house. He wanted proof that Paul Beecher was gone and he wanted his daughter brought before him.

The news that was brought back to the master of the house was of mixed measure. While it was true that Paul Beecher was nowhere to be found it was also true that in searching high and low none could find the whereabouts of Becky Beal either.

Soon the search and the reason for it was making the rounds of the party in general and all were agog at the strange happenings in which they were privy. Those older and considered wiser amongst the abbey guests were heard to remark upon their earliest misgivings about trying to marry silk purse and sow's ear.

"She's gone," George Beal bellowed, apprising the entire assemblage, and insuring that any who might not have already known of Becky's defection were now fully aware of the situation. "Mrs. Beal, I shall disown her!" he shouted at his wife.

"Father!" Alice objected. "This is not the place to air your grievances."

"Don't tell me what I should and should not do, young miss or I'll do to you what I should have done to you and your sister long years since."

"Do with me what you will, the truth is still the truth."

George Beal stared at his younger daughter. "The truth is I have raised willfull brats!"

"The truth is you must stop ordering everyone about as if this were the dark ages. It is past time for people to be allowed to decide their own futures or we all shall end with only heartache and disaster," Alice said in stirring tones that rang across the assemblage.

The girl's words were such heresy, particularly from a female's lips, that even George Beal could not immediately respond. There was a moment of pregnant silence and into it the imposing figure of the Countess of Marleigh rose from her chair.

Standing up with regal dignity, she gave her host the briefest of glances. "Philip," she said to her husband in accents that demanded compliance. "It is past time we leave. Andrew," she continued to her son. "Please see to my cloak."

Andrew turned his attention away from the woebegone Alice. "Mother, perhaps we should wait upon the Beals—"

"My dear boy," the countess told her son. "As of this very moment you shall not have to concern yourself with these odious Beals to any further extent. We are *leaving*."

The earl heard the tone in his wife's voice and knew when defeat was upon him. "Yes, my dear."

"Your ladyship," Hero said promptly. "I shall order the carriage." Without waiting for a reply he walked away, stopping when he reached Charlotte Summerville and urging her to accompany him into the hall. Once there he beseeched her to allow him to call upon her mother the following day.

"But, your lordship," Charlotte said sweetly. "My mother and I live very simply. Although my maternal grandfather was Lord Summerville I have no title and no address such as you are used to."

"Nonsense," Hero said bracingly. "I won't hear a word of it. You are a diamond of the first water and I wonder that I've not seen it before. We've met at two dozen parties over the years."

"Ah, yes, but kind sir, you have never noticed me I fear because after your association with London ladies I could never hope to compete for your attention."

"Nonsense," Hero responded.

"I am sure to fail beside their polished facades."

"You have your own sophistication and beauty," Hero told her feelingly.

Charlotte smiled ever so prettily. "Do you truly think so? I've been so afraid you might think all country-bred girls the same."

"Never," he said with one swift glance back towards the ballroom and Alice Beal.

Charlotte saw the direction of his gaze. "The Beal girls are not quite country-bred having only moved from London these three years past. Which is all to the good since none after tonight can be blind to their faults and I know you must blush at this evening's antics."

Hero had to agree that he was quite beside himself with concern over his friend's future. But, that he would never tar Miss Charlotte with the same brush.

"I am so glad," Charlotte told the London beau. "I would be put to the blush to withstand association with either since one is a runaway and the other a shrew."

Hero could not disagree and so took hurried leave of Charlotte as the countess entered the hallway. Others were following the Earl of Marleigh's lead and leaving, calling for their carriages and going home to dine out for weeks to come on the story of the abbey ball.

Before the Marleighs left, Andrew took Alice's hand and kissed it lightly. He reassured her in quiet tones that all would be well but in her heart of hearts she knew this was the last the Beals would see of the Earl of Marleigh and his family.

Whilst her parents argued below, and Lady Agatha and Fannie returned to the gatehouse, Alice wandered into the Long Gallery, reliving the precious early moments of this evening.

The candles had guttered down in their holders, the gallery full of flickering shadows as Alice moved slowly towards Lady Agatha's portrait. She stared up at it, most of its dark colours lost from view in the dim light. Only the pale face and shoulders could be dearly discerned.

"She was a corker, I can tell you that," Sir Harry the Ghost said, giving Alice a start.

"Oh no, not again!" Alice exclaimed.

"I say, what a greeting," Harry replied. He saw Alice's gaze go back to the portrait. "I often come here myself," he admitted to the girl in gentler tones.

"Did you once know each other?" Alice asked.

Sir Harry stared at the oil painting, the expression in his eyes softening to one of great tenderness. "A very long time ago," he admitted.

"How sad she cannot see or hear you," Alice said.

"Yes," he replied sounding very sad. "Now," he continued, rousing himself from his reverie. "What's this I hear about your sister getting herself into more trouble?"

"She seems to have disappeared," Alice said. "And I'm afraid Paul Beecher from the village may be involved and I'm that worried for them. Papa has been pushed past all endurance and I am truly afraid for what will happen next."

"As am I," the ghost replied.

"It is very good of you to take so much concern over my family," Alice told him.

"It's not good of me, it's my job," Sir Harry replied. "And I must tell you I am in a deep quandary about what to do with you."

"With us?"

"No. With you."

Alice's hand reached for her throat. "I don't understand."

"Then there are two of us in the same quandary. The fact of the matter is the wrong people can see me."

"Wrong people?"

"It's a long story but I am bound to the abbey until I serve my penance for past wrongs by righting others' love affairs. Your sister's fiancé should be able to see me and he can. Which means your sister should be able to see me but she never has—but you do, which makes no sense at all. Unless you happen to be in love with this Paul person. You aren't by any chance, are you?" Sir Harry eyed Alice hopefully. "It would simplify matters tremendously."

"I'm terribly sorry, but I'm not in the least in love with Paul Beecher," Alice told the ghost. "You are talking about the man my sister loves."

Sir Harry sighed. "I knew this was a tangled brew. I don't know why I must keep solving ever more complicated situations," he fretted. "I should think it was bad enough to be in this state without having to constantly prove oneself and without even knowing how long I must suffer so."

"I think you are most terribly abused," Alice agreed.

"I agree," Sir Harry replied. "Now, how do we go about bringing this predicament to rights?"

"I don't know," Alice told the ghost. "But I should like to very much. Sir Harry, Andrew does not want to marry Becky in the least. Nor does Becky feel the slightest warmth for Andrew," she added in a little rush of words.

"That, my dear, is obvious to all," Sir Harry drawled. "The problem is simple. It's the solution that worries me."

"Since the countess learned my sister was missing she has told Lord Andrew he must wash his hands of us all, so I do not see how you can possibly help."

Sir Harry grimaced. "I admit it's hard to even tell where to start." He thought about it. "Where has your sister taken off to?"

"I have no idea, Sir Ghost," Alice said truthfully. "But I know she escaped down the secret stairwell. I can show you—"

"I know it well," Harry told her and was rewarded with a weak smile.

"Of course I suppose you would," Alice responded finally. "Oh, Sir Ghost, I am terribly afraid she has convinced Paul to take her to Gretna Green and Papa is bound to get there first and he will surely kill Paul dead!"

"That is usually the way of it," Sir Harry responded. At her confused look he continued. "Unless one becomes a ghost—which I must tell you is a very rare thing indeed—one who is killed is most assuredly dead."

Alice looked despondently at the apparition who shimmered beside her. "We must *do* something," she told him.

"On that score, we agree," Sir Harry replied. He continued to question Alice while below-stairs her parents waited for any report of Becky from the men who were searching the abbey grounds.

It had just gone dawn when the young Tim pounded on the gatehouse door. It was a few minutes before Fannie responded, unlatching the door and glaring at the boy.

"You'll wake the dead and do the devil a service if you don't stop that infernal racket," Fannie announced as she pulled her robe tight around her. She held a candle-branch in one hand and opened the door with the other, letting the young man in. "And if you wake Lady Agatha you shall wish you hadn't I can tell you. Now come inside and tell me what all this is about, bothering good Christians at such an hour."

"It's Miss Rebecca, Miss Fannie. We've searched high and low and she's not to be found."

"Still missing?" Fannie repeated. "Lord, that girl is a sad fribble and no mistake about it. She's truly gone beyond the pale with this madness."

"Her people are worried she's up and run off with Paul Beecher and her father is fit to be tied. Mr. Beal says he'll give her the biggest trimming of her life—"

"More like the only trimming," Fannie said caustically, closing the door on the windy yard. "I wish the rain would come instead of threatening for days on end. Has anyone gone to Molly Beecher and her husband and asked if Paul is home?"

Tim shook his head. "Not that I know of."

"I think that's the next step," Fannie said practically.

"But if he is to home, won't it make for more talk?"

"Which is worse," Fannie asked the boy. "A little more talk or the girl up and run off to Gretna Green?"

"Miss Fannie, it's too much for me to worrit over."

"Fannie." Lady Agatha appeared at the top of the short gatehouse stairwell. "What is all this infernal racket?"

"It's Tim come with news from the abbey. He says Miss Becky's never come back."

"Not back?" Lady Agatha repeated, her frown increasing. "Of all the cork-brained females ever born, that little scamp is the worst!"

Tim tugged at his forelock in an unconscious and ancient gesture of deference. "Mrs. Beal says as how if you should see Miss Becky you are to please send word straightaway."

"If I see that young chit she will get the lecture of her life," the dowager promised. "And be brought back to her parents upon the same moment."

"I don't know what's to come of it all," Tim said solemnly.

"It is unbecoming to speculate on your employer's lives," Lady Agatha told the young man in kindly but decidedly firm accents.

Tim tugged at his forelock. "Yes, m'lady."

Lady Agatha turned away from the top of the stairs. The young stableman looked expectantly towards Fannie who gave him a pert look before she turned towards the kitchens. "I'll warrant you've been wandering the countryside all night and chilled straight through. I've got a bit of stew left that you're welcome to if you want."

Tim pulled his cap from his tousled ginger locks. "I'd not say no," he answered happily.

"Nor have you ever when it came to my cooking," Fannie replied tartly. Secretly pleased that the boy who had grown up at the abbey still preferred her simple dishes to the elaborate ones the fancy new abbey cook made, Fannie looked upwards towards where Lady Agatha had been at the top of the stairs. "Would you like a bit of something hot?"

Lady Agatha responded from the hallway above. "No, thank you. It's much too early. I'll have my tea presently. And Timmy—you will be good enough to bring us word when the girl is found."

"Yes, Lady Agatha," Tim responded with alacrity. "If she ever is," he added darkly before he followed Fannie into the rosy warmth of the gatehouse kitchen. Tim sat down at the square oak table, the slate-floored room welcoming and homey. He watched Fannie reach up to the rough-hewn wood cabinets that held the china plates. Iron cooking pots hung on hooks above the fire which Fannie had already leaping in the grate. Large many-paned windows looked out across the rose gardens and the dark distances just beginning to be tinged with morning light.

"Becky Beal is sure to come to grief as sure as the sun rises and sets and that's a fact," Tim said as he watched Fannie pull a large iron kettle off the fire.

"She's bound to *bring* someone to grief, that I'll warrant," Fannie replied, ladling mutton stew into a large earthenware bowl. She placed it and a loaf of fresh bread before the young stableman and watched with satisfaction as he began to eat. "It's not what you should have for breakfast but it will fill your empty stomach and keep you warm when you go back outside so eat your fill."

"And don't I always?" Tim grinned between mouthfuls.

"I've never seen you go hungry," Fannie agreed yawning.

"You've not had much sleep yourself this night, Miss Fannie."

"And that's the truth of it. We didn't get home till past two." She sat down across the table, bringing herself a cup of hot strong tea. "Now tell me what all has happened since we left. Tell me every word," Fannie insisted, glad that Lady Agatha wasn't there to hear and disapprove.

"I've naught to tell you. They've scoured the abbey inside and out and called for Homer and Jake and me and I don't know who all else to scour the countryside. Mr. Beal is threatening to throw the baggage out—that's what he was saying when I left—and Mrs. Beal is wringing her hands and crying so hard her eyes are all red and Miss Alice trying to calm them down. None of them with a wink of sleep all night. Miss Fannie, do you think Miss Becky really has run off with Paul Beecher?"

"I doubt it most prodigiously," Fannie replied honestly. "But not because of any lack of Becky Beal trying. I think Paul Beecher is much too sensible to do something so foolish as to run away but it is the first place I would look for her since I think she will try to convince him to do her bidding."

12

IN A MEADOW that ran down to the edge of the river, Paul Beecher had first tried convincing Becky Beal what they were doing was wrong but soon succumbed to her charms. Deep green grass cushioned them, the overcast sky with its lowering clouds forgotten in the dark distance above their besotted heads. Their eyes were closed, their lips meeting tentatively, hearts beating furiously against their ribcages.

"Oh, Paul, I have thrown all to the winds—" Becky said a trifle breathlessly.

"To the winds," he repeated, taking in the words but not their meaning.

"To the winds!" Becky exclaimed. "My life is in your hands, my hero."

Paul Beecher blushed crimson. "I'm no hero, Becky Beal, and well you know it."

"You were like David in the Bible tonight, bearding Goliath in his den," she rhapsodised, looking expectantly towards her young swain. The moon came out from behind the clouds for a few brief instants and Paul Beecher saw sky-blue eyes gazing beseechingly up at him. "Promise me none shall ever keep us apart."

"I promise, if it's your wish, you shall marry none but me," he declared fervently.

"Then we must start out at once," Becky told him.

" . . . Start out?" Paul repeated in an uncertain tone.

"Before they catch us," Becky said. Paul's honest brown eyes grew large and round as she continued, "We shall run to Gretna Green and be married before they stop us. Then they'll see where all their farradiddle about marrying me off to a nob has led them."

"Who is this Gretna Green?"

"Gretna Green's a town, not a person," Becky explained. "It's on the border with Scotland."

"Scotland?" Paul exclaimed as if she had said they were to set out for China.

"Well, yes, that's where all star-crossed lovers go."

Paul gave his love a confused look. "Star-crossed?"

"Yes," Becky explained. "It's where they run when their evil parents won't let them wed."

"Evil parents!" Paul was astounded. "Becky, girl, my parents are good church-going Christians!"

"That's not the point!" Becky said with some little asperity at her lover's lack of perception.

"Becky," Paul responded patiently. "You know we can't just up and run away."

"But we must," Becky responded. "After what has happened we have no choice!"

Paul stared at the vision of loveliness who had besotted his senses for months on end. "We can't just up and run," he repeated, reassuring himself she had not truly heard his words.

"We can and I shall," she informed her admirer in ringing accents. "With you or alone I shall run off! I will never go back to my father," she cried impatiently.

There was a pause in which Paul took in Becky's words and in which Becky waited for Paul's capitulation. Which never came.

"You may up and run away, Becky Beal, but if you do, you'll be doing it alone," Paul responded. "You're a regular out and outer and I'm daft about you, as I told your father, but I shan't stir one step without it all being right and proper and your parents coming round to see our side. I told your father we'd be married fair and square—I gave my word and that's that."

"I thought you loved me!" Becky responded in dramatic tones.

Paul spoke fervently. "As God is my eternal witness, I do and I always will. But I won't do what's wrong, Becky, for you would think the less of me in the end."

"I never would."

"I would myself," Paul told her. "So you could not help it. Mind you, I won't squeak to them no matter what you decide. But if you choose to go off alone, Becky Beal, you must be dicked in the nob. You'll never find another who loves you as I do. You must be sensible and see you're headed straight for grief. I could never run off with my pa needing me in the shop and my ma worriting herself sick with fear for us. Have you thought of them? Or your own family?"

Becky rose to her feet. Grasping his hands, she looked the soul of despondency. "We have no choice—if we do not flee my father will marry me to Lord Andrew and I'll be carted off to London and we'll never see each other again."

"You'll not be carted off by anyone but me, Becky Beal. I told your father and I'll tell this lord, you're to be wed to none but me."

Paul felt the pull of the blonde beauty's allure as she stepped closer, still holding his hands. Becky was caught up in the romance of intrigue and danger, her eyes large, her soft voice pleading with the tall country lad.

"If you truly love me, you'll see we have no choice but to race away," Becky said in tremulous tones. "It's one thing to say you love me—"

"But I do!"

"And you've seen my father—you know how set he is upon his course," Becky said in dramatic accents. "You know he'll not listen to reason. Our only hope is elopement."

"I shall make him listen. My prospects are as good as any's and he himself told my pa we were cut from the same cloth, only he was city-bred and us country. You must not worrit your head with nonsensical ideas about running away and Gretna Greens. Your father was upset and taken by surprise but when he's had a chance to think on it he'll see we've the right of it and he'll come around."

Becky Beal felt the steel behind her beau's words, her heart turning leaden as she realised her one hope of escape seemed unwilling to do his part in the tragic romance she had been envisioning. Paul was altogether much too practical. "You professed your undying love and devotion," she told him in stricken tones. "I have given you my heart and now you desert me in my hour of need!"

"Never would I desert you! You are the dearest girl in all the world and I'm not deserting you, not a bit of it. I'll never let your father come between us, nor any others, I swear it. And I'll make everything come out right. You're my girl, Becky-my-love, and will be my wife and none will make any mistake about it."

"Papa will never accept your suit," Becky told her lover, breaking off their embrace to clasp her hands against the bodice of her sadly-crushed yellow pelisse, her once-white gloves transferring grass stains to her clothing. As he turned away Paul could see the glint of tears in the moonlight that came and went, playing hide and seek with the clouds.

"And why ever not?" Paul demanded stoutly.

"Because you have no title," Becky responded.

"Stuff and nonsense."

"You may think it so," she told Paul, turning back to face him. "But my father is quite persuaded he will have nothing but titles for Ally and me. Why do you think he invited Lord Marleigh?"

"The whole village talks of naught else," Paul answered slowly, his brow furrowed into puzzled lines.

"Oh, Paul," Becky threw herself back against his chest, seeking the comfort of his strong work-hardened arms. Her words came out in a piteous little wail. "You have not saved me! I shall be shackled forever to that odious creature, if you do not help me escape!"

Paul held the trembling girl close, digesting this newest information. "But Lady Agatha made your father promise nothing would be decided until we could talk in private!"

"You believe that? My father will lock me in my chambers and will never let me out until I'm wed to Lord Marleigh. I cannot go back!"

"By Gad, he can't be so cruel as to intend to make you marry that nob you've only just clapped eyes on and nary a soft feeling for him when he knows how we feel about each other."

"He'll hear of nothing but titles and it's to be Ally the same after me, shackled to some old tyrant for the rest of her days." Becky clung to her swain tearfully.

The sounds of dogs barking nearby startled the young lovers. Becky drew back, listening intently. Soon the calls of the dogs' handlers could be heard. "They're searching already," Becky breathed the words. "We must hurry!"

"Even if I were to agree we could not go far without a bit of mint sauce, Becky," Paul said practically. "It's a very great distance to the border and wherever this Gretna Green is and inns and post coaches in between to pay for. I've no wages from the shop, only what I earn from odd bits of work around-about."

"I've got plenty of blunt," Becky told him in a fierce whisper, omitting to mention that she had not thought to bring it with her. "We must not be caught out before we have the chance to escape," Becky continued. "You love me, do you not?"

He grabbed for her waist, bringing her near. "Becky Beal, I love you past enduring and well you know it. Haven't I proved it already this night?" He kissed her with a fine disregard for pursuers, dogs, fathers and all else.

Becky pulled back away from his lips, breathless and more than ever in love with Paul. Beckoning her lover forward, her hand was within his. "We must be away—" Becky began to run towards the river's edge. "Perhaps there is a rowboat—"

But there was none and the men and dogs were coming closer through the foggy dark. The yaps and calls came louder as the search party neared the fleeing couple.

Becky halted her headlong race, Paul bumping into her from behind. She turned downriver and then up, heating approaching footsteps and the howling dogs from each direction in turn. Finally, she pulled Paul back up the gently-sloping hill.

"This is the way to the abbey, they'll catch us for sure!" Paul protested.

"They'll not think to look at home, they'll think we're long gone. Then we can run whichever direction they've already been," Becky reasoned between gasps of breath as she ran upwards, pulling Paul along. "Besides, I've got to get to my room—I forgot my reticule."

This announcement cast the butcher's son into a torrent of mixed emotions including disbelief and exasperation at the ways of womankind but as he was being hauled up the hill at the time, he had no time to voice them.

They had almost reached the hidden abbey door when something blocked their way. Shimmering into view in the vague half-light from the pale cloud-speckled moon, the apparition slowly took shape. Their steps slowed as they came nearer.

"What—what is that?" Paul asked cautiously.

But Becky was not answering. She stared, open-mouthed, at the vague figure of a full-grown and well-proportioned man who obstructed their path.

"So there you are, you little vixen," the vision thundered.

"—Paul?" Becky called, staring at the ghost.

In the same moment that Sir Harry the Ghost realised the young chit could hear him he also realised he was safely outdoors.

"By Gad, what the devil's happening?" he demanded in only slightly less thunderous accents. "I've not been able to hie myself outside these past three years!"

"Who—who are you?" Becky wailed as Paul pulled her back from the ghostly figure and shoved her ahead of him down the terrace steps and out across the western lawns.

"Run, my girl, run!" Paul urged but Becky was rooted to the spot.

"It's a sign!" Becky said in a breathless voice. She sank to her knees on the cold terrace stones. "Oh, please, don't hurt him, he didn't mean to do anything wrong. It's all my fault!"

"It usually is," Sir Harry replied rather tartly.

"Run, girl, run!" Paul pulled her to her feet and propelled her forward, around the abbey and into the stables. They ran, as fast as their young legs would carry them, the searchers forgotten in their headlong flight from the angry vision on the terrace.

Behind them Sir Harry grumbled to himself as he watched them go. "Bloody fools, these younger generations. No sense at all. I don't know what the world is coming to. Never happened in my time, I can tell you," he said with more fervour than accuracy.

Since none were there to hear Sir Harry's comments, he faded back through the walls. But there was a decidedly self-satisfied expression upon his face. "I must have done something right, although I've no idea what," he told himself. "Because I got through the abbey walls. Next time I'll make it to the gatehouse," he promised the winds that whipped around the abbey's stones.

"I know not what that was," Paul said as he crouched along the stable wall, shielding Becky behind him. "But you had the right of it after all. We'll make for the shop where there's no deviltry that will harm you until we can make off for your Gretna Green!"

"Wonderful!" Becky forgot to worry about the vision they had just escaped and the money that was secreted in her bed-chamber far away from her grasp.

The butcher shop was in the center of Wooster, which was to say it was between the small church and the even tinier inn. The single street was silent and empty in the dawn hours, the good citizens of Wooster safely in their beds. In the distance the abbey could be seen, still glowing with light atop its hill, the servants going about the business of clearing away the party food and drink and dowsing the candles.

Paul opened the door of the shop, shushing Becky and whispering that his parents were asleep. "We must be very quiet and hide until first light."

"What will happen at first light?" Becky asked, her eyes aglow with the romance of her adventure.

"Why, the morning post coach arrives and we can book passage north."

"Oh."

" . . . Becky?" Paul questioned.

"I'm perfectly fine," Becky told her lover.

They were deep inside the butcher shop, Becky stumbling over a box of sawdust and earning more shushes from Paul. He stopped where he was, Becky seeing his attention go to the ceiling and finding her own eyes riveted to it as creaking sounds came from overhead. She held her breath until they stopped and Paul whispered for her to go forward.

"Is he coming below-stairs?" Becky asked in a quiet whisper.

"I don't think so," Paul answered.

Becky heard her beloved's tone and leaned closer to try and see his face in the gloom of the dark shop. The smells of meat and soap were all around them, making Becky's nose wrinkle. "Is something wrong?" she asked.

Paul took his time answering, his voice troubled when he spoke. "I don't like this above half," he admitted. "Sneaking out on my parents and my work. But if it must be done to get you safe then get you safe we will. They'll all have to understand once we're back."

"Oh, I hope so," Becky said.

"How far away is this Gretna Green and how much will it cost?"

"I'm not exactly sure," Becky admitted.

Paul frowned in the darkness. "How are we to know if you have enough purse to get us there and back? We can't be stranded in a foreign country with none to voucher us home."

"I might have to go back to the abbey," Becky admitted. "Just for a minute," she amended when she felt Paul stiffen.

"Becky Beal, what are you saying?" Paul asked just as a shaft of light fell across the shop from the rough-hewn wooden steps that led from the butcher shop to the apartment above.

At Becky's sharp intake of breath the light swung towards the sound and outlined the two runaways against the counter. Becky looked upwards, blinking, towards the light but saw first the carcasses hung on hooks over her head. The outlines of rabbits, poultry and mutton were back lighted by the lamplight. "Oh, my!" she gasped.

Paul's arms went around Becky as the light picked them out in the gloom.

"And what's this?" Tom Beecher bellowed. He stomped down the stairs as the young couple blanched and moved backwards, away from the light that was coming straight for them. "What's this, I say?" Paul's father demanded. "It's my Paul but who's the wench and what are you doing bringing some lightskirt to your home, I want to know!"

Paul straightened up. "She's no lightskirt, she's my Becky and she's to be my wife!"

"Miss Beal!" The elder Beecher sounded both surprised and scandalized. "Paul Beecher! What have you done, bringing her here?"

"Naught that's wrong, I swear it. Becky is to be my wife and her father shan't marry her off to some nob she'd never clapped eyes on until now."

"And who are you to tell a father what he can and can't do?" Tom Beecher thundered.

"Tom?" Molly Beecher's sleepy voice came from the stairwell. "Is it robbers then or what?"

"It's 'or what' with a vengeance, that's what it is," Tom Beecher told his wife. "You'd best come down and chaperone Miss Beal until I can get to the abbey."

"No!" Becky burst out.

"You mustn't!" Paul beseeched.

"The abbey?" Molly Beecher queried.

Before any could answer or argue further there was a loud pounding at the door and George Beal's voice shouting. "Open up in there."

- 13 -

GEORGE BEAL WITHERED Paul Beecher with one glance and marched his daughter out of the butcher's shop as Paul's father tried to express his distress and chagrin. George shoved Becky into the abbey gig, sitting in silence until they arrived home. Once there he pulled his weeping daughter up the stairs, past her mother, incensed to think she could disobey his wishes so wantonly. He paced the length of the room as he spoke. "Young lady, I will not hear another word."

"But Papa," Becky began tearfully. "I love him."

"Stop where you are," her father thundered. "I have been too lenient by half, just as your mother has said. Now you have made us laughing-stocks. Well, I cannot change what's been done, but I can certainly change my future course. And from you, young lady, I will brook no further speech."

"But I love Paul and he loves me!"

"Love as you will, after the scene you've treated us to this night you shall not marry that boy as long as there's life left in me and that's flat. You have ruined your chances for a proper marriage as well I know, but I shall send you to a convent before I allow you to run roughshod over my wishes."

"Mr. Beal," his wife protested, only to be stopped by his upraised hand.

"I shall decide what's to be done with the ungrateful chit when I have had the time to think on all sides of it," he said in portentous tones. With dignity George Beal turned away from his daughter and his wife, walked to the door and paused to look meaningfully at his wife. "Mrs. Beal, I shall await you without!"

As the key turned in the heavy iron lock, Mary drew her

child to her bosom. "But you must see, Becky, dear, your papa knows what's best for all of us and we must do as he says."

"Bother what he says!" Becky burst forth.

"Becky! You must not talk so. Your father has done us proud, look what all you and Ally have. You have wanted for nary a thing, not once in your life. How can you have been so ungrateful as to turn aside his request for you to marry the man of his choice and run off with another man?"

"Because I am in love with the other man!" Becky burst out, her mother's face blanching at the words.

"In love? What do you know of love?" Mary Beal's horrified tones brought Becky to look into her mother's worried eyes. "My child, what are you saying?"

"I love Paul," Becky replied but in less strident tones. She saw her mother's stricken expression and continued more slowly. "It's not as if we've done anything wrong."

"Done nothing wrong? How can I have raised such a rebellious child? I swear I taught you the difference between right and wrong, I don't know what's to become of—"

"Mother—" Becky tried to stop her mother's words but only succeeded in stemming them for a moment.

"I won't hear excuses!" Mary Beal insisted. "My child tells me she is a wanton. She runs off with a man who makes scenes in front of one and all—a dastardly man who would consent to be an innocent young girl's secret lover—who would make her a laughing-stock in front of all the county—and she has not the grace to blush for her lost reputation let alone for the calumny her actions have heaped upon her family!"

"Mother!" Becky remonstrated in more strident accents. "You go too far!"

"No my dear," Mary rounded on her daughter. "It is you I fear who have gone too far!"

Becky straightened herself to her full height, which was sorely lacking in inches, but she strove to make up in backbone what she lacked in address. "I will not hear aspersions cast upon my character or his."

"That's as may be, but the truth is no man who has a female's best interests at heart would have compromised his lady in such a fashion."

"He didn't compromise me, I compromised him!"

"What he did at the ball is beyond the pale!"

"Mother! He had no choice."

You may mother me as much as you like but the truth is the truth," Mary told her child tartly. "He ruined your chances for a proper marriage with his precipitous actions, he ruined your father's plans and he ruined your party."

"I don't give a fig for proper marriages or plans or parties," the recalcitrant Becky told her long-suffering mother. "We love each other excessively and there's nothing to be done about it!" Becky nearly shouted.

To her daughter's horror Mary looked in immediate danger of collapsing.

"Mother!" Becky came to her mother's aid, grabbing her about the waist and handling the older woman to the nearest chair. If she had seen her mother's grimace at the rough treatment she might have wondered if her mother was quite as done up as she seemed. As it was however, Becky was busy with getting her mother seated and was thoroughly chastened and very afraid she had given her mother a fatal shock. "Mother, please, say something—" Becky begged.

No answer was forthcoming but after a moment low moans issued from Mary Beal's mouth.

"I shall go for help," Becky told her mother breathlessly, only to be stopped by her mother's hand grabbing her arm.

"Do not leave me," Mary said in a failing voice.

"But I know not what to do to help—"

"There is no help," Mary Beal replied weakly. "I've been easy to a fault and have ruined my daughter's chances in life. It is all my fault, as your father says."

"Nonsense," her daughter said bracingly.

Mary Beal allowed herself a tremulous sigh. "Your father shall disown us all."

"Why ever should he be upset with you or Ally? It's me that's thwarting his will."

"Thwarting his will. How he will wish it were only that,"

Mary Beal said in tragic accents. "Instead of . . . the truth."
She shuddered over her last words.

"What truth?"

"How can you ask, you ungrateful girl?" Mary replied
piteously. "You tell me you have been intimate with a man
alone!" She shuddered. "We shall all be ruined. Poor Alice
will never be wed, the stigma will attach itself to her and
she shall be drowned in your misbehaviour—"

"Fiddle!" Becky exclaimed but her mother continued
onwards.

"And it's all my fault, letting you run as wild as grass.
Thinking I could trust you."

"But you *can* trust me!" Becky interrupted.

"How can you say so?" her mother cried. "Trust a girl
who's ruined herself?" Mary's voice took on considerable
strength.

Becky straightened up from her mother, her concern
turning to indignation. "I've not ruined myself!"

"Meeting some strange man and getting herself into trouble—"

"I did *not* meet some strange man!" Becky defended.
"Paul is good and honest and true!"

Mary Beal took a little hope from this last declaration.
"You said in plain English you were in love."

"And so we are!" Becky declared with a stubborn tilt of
her chin. "We've been seeing each other for weeks."

"You've been meeting him alone as the whole countryside now knows!" her mother said in horrified accents.

"It's none of the countrysides business. Just because Papa
bought the abbey does not mean they own us! Besides, I've
loved Paul for ever and ever and Paul and I have been as
proper as proper can be." A look of guilt crossed her face
when she thought of their stolen kisses and her mother
saw it.

"You're not telling me the truth," Mary declared.

Becky blushed scarlet and turned away, trying to hide
her reddened cheeks. "We've done nothing wrong," she
repeated a little defiantly. "We're in love," she added again
for good measure.

"My dear girl, you have no clue as to what love is and neither does Paul or he would never have compromised you as he did last night."

Becky turned back to her suddenly recovered mother, her face a study in despair. "But we do know what love is! You've no way of understanding what it is like to have found your very own love and then be asked to marry another."

As Becky spoke the words she felt a little stir of the air, as if a window had suddenly opened. But a swift glance showed that all windows were locked shut and snug against the chill early morning air.

"You have been taken advantage of, Rebecca Beal, and you have been foolish and wanton enough to allow it."

Becky had never heard her mother speak in such stern accents. She sank to her bed looking woeful and dejected.

"You've always taken my side," Becky said in wounded tones.

"That's my mistake and I shall correct it as of now," her mother replied. So saying, she stood up and swept past her recalcitrant daughter. "Your father will not unlock this door until you promise to behave and if he finds Paul trying to reach you he will probably kill him with his own bare hands."

"He can't kill him, I love him! I ran off to be with him but he wouldn't elope. He wanted to bring Papa around."

"It's worse than I thought," Mary said. "You surely can't expect me to tell your father that you *willingly* went to an assignation after he threw the upstart out of the abbey."

Becky bit at her lip, unable to give any answers that her mother would accept. Mary watched her daughter for some long moments before speaking again. "I don't scruple to tell you, Rebecca, that you have pushed your father to the farthest extreme and he will stand for no more rebellion. What's to become of us all I just don't know."

"I'll marry no one but Paul," Becky declared.

"And him without a penny to his name." Mary Beal saw the look that crossed her daughter's face and pressed her advantage home. "You, my girl, have no sense and that's a plain fact. Your father will make him see he can't take advantage of you."

"But he's not, he loves me!" Becky told her mother. "Mama, please, he is a good man and he truly loves me. You must help me."

Mary looked deep into her daughter's eyes. "You must tell me all. Everything. Then I shall decide."

Becky came rushing to her mother's side, sinking to her knees by her mother's chair. Her face glowing, she began to talk of her wonderful Paul.

Almost half an hour later Mary Beal called to her husband to unlock the bed-chamber door and left her daughter to ponder her future alone.

"Well?" George Beal demanded of his wife. "I hope you've put the fear of God into her."

Mary Beal sighed. "So do I," she said fervently. "And you and I must talk. But first I want to make sure Alice is all right."

"Now there's a good biddable girl," George said approvingly. "It's a mystery to me why Becky has never taken a leaf from Ally's book." As he spoke, George became more and more incensed. "I won't have any more of this bobbery, Mrs. Beal! I won't have Becky defying me, I won't have her running off and I *surely* won't have her marrying that butcher's son!"

"But her heart is set upon him."

"Then she will end up her days a spinster! I won't stand for any more disobedience."

Sir Harry appeared from the attic stairs, his expression twice as irritated as George Beal's. "Nor shall I stand to have my meditations interrupted by such comings and goings and shoutings!"

"I'll only be a moment with Alice," Mary told her husband soothingly.

Sir Harry glowered at the unseeing humans and hied himself through the wall to Becky's room.

"What with your parents brangling out there and you weeping and wailing in here, there's altogether too much noise in this establishment, young lady. Now what's all this I heard about you being torn from your true love."

"What—" Becky Beal stuttered as she looked up through tear-stained eyes at the ghost hovering at the end of her bed. "It's you! What—what are you?"

"I knew the youth of this nation were wanting in imagination but I did not think you had sunk to so low a level of intelligence to ask a question such as that!"

"Are you—a—ghost? The Abbey Ghost? What *are* you?" she wailed again.

"Thunderation, you mean *who* are you, not what, girl, have you no manners at all? I am Sir Harry."

"You look exactly as they say the Abbey Ghost should look."

"And what else should I look like? If truth be told, I'd rather not be in such an inconvenient state, but since none asked for my permission before putting me thus I have no choice."

"How does one go about becoming a ghost?" Becky asked the spectre hovering before her eyes, her own worries lost in the surprise of the moment.

"I haven't the foggiest," Sir Harry replied.

"But how could you get to be a ghost without knowing how to do so?"

"As far as I can tell I was wounded and fell asleep and damn and blast if this wasn't how I woke up." The ghost sounded rather indignant on the subject.

"Do you think I might fall asleep and wake up a ghost?"

"At the rate you are going, anything is possible," he replied dryly. "More to the point, what's all this about your true love?"

"He is!"

"Yes, yes, I know," Sir Harry said in quite testy tones. "But which one is he? Paul or Andrew?"

"Wha—what? I mean, how do you know their names? And why do you ask?"

"God's eyebrows! How could any live within these walls and not hear the names of your beaux? I ask because my salvation depends upon helping the course of true love run smooth. Although how I am to tell which is true love and how it can run smooth at the present rate is completely beyond my ken."

Becky heard the word help and forgot fear and all else as hope began to well up within her bosom. She gave the ghost her most winning smile. "Oh, Sir Harry, if you only could! You are going to have the most awful problems with my Papa but if you can only help Paul and me, I shall be eternally in your debt!"

"Don't go bandying about eternity, my girl. One day you might be forced to live up to your words."

"But I would, sir, willingly, if you could only find a way for me to be with Paul."

"You're quite sure you're not the least in love with Andrew," Harry queried.

"Quite, *quite* sure," Becky confirmed.

"This is a puzzlement," Harry told the girl. "For he can see me and only true lovers can see and hear me."

"But Ally has seen you," Becky interjected.

"Yes," Sir Harry the Ghost agreed. "That's part of the puzzlement. The wrong people—and too many of them—seem to be seeing me. I don't know what's to come of all this."

Becky's eyes lit up. "Do you think perhaps you might be able to haunt Papa until he gives up the idea of making me a titled lady?"

"I would hope we could find a quicker solution than one that involves changing your parent's mind since it seems to be something he does most infrequently. And, my girl, there are worse things you could be than a lady, I can tell you that." Sir Harry looked a mite affronted.

"Oh, I'm sure I've nothing against nobs—I suppose that's what you were—are—were—"

"Whatever," the ghost interjected in a testy tone.

"Yes, well, I've naught against you," Becky told him. "Even if you are a nob and a ghost at that! It's just that my heart lies in another direction and I could not agree to marry his lordship no matter what Papa said."

"You seem to have forestalled any hopes in that direction

already," Sir Harry told her matter-of-factly.

"You may think so, but you don't know Papa. He may still try to make the match stick."

"Your father, it would seem, is capable of almost anything but I daresay the earl will never allow the match now no matter what else is involved. He's a high stickler even if a low gambler and he will never condone this night's activities."

"Oh, are you sure?" Becky asked hopefully.

"You'd best wipe that smile from your face, Miss Beal," Sir Harry told the girl. "For even if your father can't force your marriage to Lord Andrew, he can still keep you from wedding Paul."

"But that makes no sense!"

"It does to your father," Sir Harry interjected.

"And all because Paul has no money, which we have no need of whatsoever. It is exceedingly irritating of Papa to insist on a title or money. I have no need of either since the title will never change who I am and I've plenty of money of my own."

"Not if your father leaves it elsewhere," Harry reminded her.

Becky looked glum. "That's what Paul said. We are in a fair pickle, Sir Harry. What can we do?"

"No. You are in a fair pickle," Sir Harry corrected. "I am about to retire."

"But you can't! You can't sleep at a time like this!"

"I can and I shall. I find I do much of my best thinking in a prone position. And this pretty mess will take a great deal of thinking upon," he said. As he spoke he began to fade from view.

"Will you come back?" Becky asked quickly. But he was already gone.

Next door Becky's mother was just leaving Alice's room when she cocked her head towards the wall. "Did you hear Becky talking to someone?"

"No, Mama," Alice replied.

"There's a good girl, then," Mary beamed at her younger

daughter. "We've all had such little sleep you'd best take to your bed for a few hours of rest."

"Yes, Mama." Alice looked up at her mother with serious eyes. She was sitting at a small cherrywood writing table near her draped and locked windows. "I just want to finish this one little poem."

"You and your writing," her mother said indulgently. "Only a few minutes then."

"I promise, Mama." Alice bent back over her pen and paper as her mother left the room. Intent upon the words she was carefully printing she didn't at first hear the scratchings behind her. When the scratchings became a rough thump she jumped up with a startled oath and stared at her drapes. The thump came again and then the muffled sound of Becky's voice as she called her sister's name.

"Becky?" Alice asked, her eyes going to the wall between their rooms and then back to the sounds behind her drapes. Finally she grabbed for the edge of the thick blue velvet and pulled it aside. Becky made a face through the glass at her sister. Alice unlocked the window, letting her sister inside. "What are you doing out there? You'll catch your death. You're not to be out of your room."

Becky jumped down and headed directly for the fireplace. "Shut that window before we both catch our death," were Becky's first words through chattering teeth. "You must be going deaf, it took you forever to hear me."

"I was concentrating on my poem."

Becky moved to the fire in the grate. "What are you writing about, true love?"

Alice gave her sister a sidelong look. "Yes."

Becky rubbed her hands together, warming them before the fire. "It's much easier writing a poem about it than feeling it, I can tell you that."

Alice bit her lip and came closer to the fire. "Mother thought she heard you talking to someone in your room."

"I was. That was why I had to see you. Alice," Becky announced in portentous tones, "I've seen your ghost."

"He's not *my* ghost," Alice demurred.

Becky gave an impatient shake of her head. "Yours,

mine, ours, I *saw* him. He said his name is Sir Harry, did he tell you?"

" . . . Yes, he did."

"What's the matter? Ally, I'm telling you I've seen your ghost. You're not crazed."

"Perhaps were both touched in the head."

"Alice Beal, you are such a ninny-hammer. We are perfectly fine and we happen to own a ghost, that's all."

"A ghost you did not believe in," Alice pointed out. "Besides, how can one own a ghost?"

"Because Papa bought him with the house," Becky said firmly. "*And* he's going to help me marry Paul."

Alice stared at her sister. "How?"

"He's not quite sure yet. But he did promise. Now, you must listen, because he says he's here to help lovers and only lovers can see and hear him. But Alice, you saw him before I did and you're not in love with anyone, are you? You don't still have a *tendre* for Tim, do you?"

Alice's expression went through several changes, from surprise at her sister's first words through guilt at her secret thoughts to disdain at the last. "I was a child of fifteen and I thought him the best horseman I'd ever seen when we arrived. But then, I'd never seen any horsemen, so I was easily swayed."

"I didn't think you would be in love with Tim but I couldn't think of any other possibilities. I mean you don't know anyone else. Do you?"

Alice's cheeks bloomed. "No. Of course not."

Becky shook her head. "The ghost was so positive it makes me worry about his other prognostications."

"If Sir Harry said he could accomplish the impossible, then accomplish it he will," Alice said firmly.

Becky did not look convinced. "Papa is sure to be a most difficult fly in the ointment. Do you truly think the ghost can help?"

"Yes."

"Why?" Becky asked her sister.

Alice hugged herself, her pink night robe wrapped around

her slender frame. "Because his mission is to help the course of true love run smooth."

"Lord, what an assignment that is," Becky said before she slipped back to her own chamber.

Alice shut the window behind her sister before getting into bed. She puffed her covers up and sank back against the cool pillows. The candle on her nightstand was guttering away as she closed her eyes.

"Please, Sir Ghost," Alice whispered. "Please find a way to help the course of true love run smooth." None answered as she drifted off into an uneasy sleep.

At Hargrave House the Earl of Marleigh was closeted with his son and heir. Andrew leaned against the green marble mantle of the parlour fireplace as his father paced up and down the small room.

"Mother may be strident, but she is correct in saying this situation has degenerated into an impossible connexion. Surely you can see that, Father."

The Earl of Marleigh stopped his perambulation about the room long enough to meet his son's sombre gaze. "If you do not marry Becky Beal, we are lost."

"I cannot, I *must* not!" Andrew burst out.

"And why must you not?" the earl asked his son.

"Philip—" The countess's voice interrupted from the doorway. "You have a caller." She spoke the words as if they were distasteful.

"At this hour?" the earl responded.

"George Beal," his wife elucidated in acid tones as if the name explained all. "I shall be indisposed," she said as George Beal himself came towards the doorway and reached for the countess's hand. She withdrew quickly.

"Feeling a touch out of it, no doubt," George Beal said.

"I beg your pardon?" the earl replied in glacial accents.

"Your wife looked poorly. As, I own, does mine. What a stew my daughter has created."

"Quite," the earl replied stiffly.

"No need for high horses, Marleigh." George Beal gave a smile towards Andrew. "I have the solution."

The Earl of Marleigh gave the commoner a withering glance. "Permit me to doubt that," he said.

"Doubt all you like but listen first."

The earl raised his hand to stop George Beal's words. "You must realize your daughter has gone beyond the pale."

"I agree."

"My wife feels our son would be a veritable laughingstock if he were to agree to a match such as you had proposed."

George Beal took a minute to answer. "Unfortunately," he said, a muscle working in his rather corpulent jaw, "I have to agree. The match is now totally unsuitable."

The earl stood up. "Then this interview is at an end."

"Not quite."

"There is nothing more to be said," the earl told the merchant.

"Ah, but there is," George said. He looked towards Andrew. "I have a counter-proposal."

The earl stared at the man and then glanced at his son before asking the inevitable. "What are you saying?"

"I am saying I agree Andrew cannot now marry Becky."

The earl nodded. "I am glad we agree."

"But," said George Beal, "there is no reason he cannot marry Alice."

Andrew and his father stared at George Beal, trying to assimilate the words the man had just uttered. Andrew spoke first, albeit with a strangled voice. "Alice?" he repeated.

"Let me be frank," George Beal said.

"By all means," Andrew said faintly.

"My girls need respectability. Am I right?"

The Earl of Marleigh stared at the man of business. "One could hardly argue the point."

"Exactly," George replied. "And you, Marleigh, still need money." He ignored the earl's fit of coughing and went on. "Your gambling debts have not disappeared, nor do you want news of them bandied about London and your family name held up to ridicule. Not to mention the possibility of debtor's prison."

"Sir! You go too far!"

"No, sir, it is you who have gone too far. Too far into the pockets of gambling hall owners who care not a fig whether you are titled or not if your word is not good and your money not forthcoming." George turned towards Andrew. "I am a plain-speaking man."

"As I can see," Andrew answered coolly.

"Your estate is entailed, my lawyers tell me, and your competence virtually nil. Spent on fancy clothes for your mother and gambling away by your father. You shall inherit a destitute title, houses and county seats gone to wrack and ruin and lands stripped of all wealth unless you can turn the tide soon and re-invest in your lands, your equipment and your establishments."

Andrew spoke in cold accents, his stance rigid. "I hardly need your reminders on that score, sir. It is the reason I acquiesced to my father's requests. However, my family name has value in its own right and I cannot compromise it."

"Exactly my point, boy, exactly my point!" Alice's father said jovially. "And I have the solution! You marry Alice instead of Becky! Alice is a good girl, biddable and smart. I grant she is not the beauty that her sister is but she has her own charms." George Beal looked towards young Andrew and saw his surly expression. Taking it to be one of regret at losing the hope of Becky, he went on bracingly. "There is much to be said on Alice's behalf—"

"Enough!" the earl nearly shouted, disconcerting George Beal and surprising Andrew. "I have had enough of this mercantile mentality!" He looked towards his son. "Your mother has had the right of it from the beginning," Philip Marleigh told his son. "I should never have thought of bargaining away our family name for a few pieces of silver—"

"A few pieces of silver!" George Beal remonstrated. "We are talking about a near fortune in *gold*!"

"My title and my son's inheritance are above mere gold," the earl replied.

"A fine time to tell me, after I've paid off half your

debts," George Beal replied in sour tones.

"I shall repay you!" the earl exclaimed.

"How?" his son asked.

"How indeed," George Beal repeated.

Philip, Earl of Marleigh, eyed his son. "You've castigated me for weeks about this arrangement, as has your mother. I now agree. It is over and done with. Surely you are not arguing against your freedom from marrying Becky Beal!"

"We are not discussing Rebecca," Andrew interjected. "We are discussing Alice."

"Exactly!" George Beal interjected.

"Andrew?" his father questioned, "What are you saying?"

Andrew looked from his perplexed father to the intent George Beal. "I am saying I am in love with Miss Alice Beal." At his words both fathers stared at him in shock. Andrew looked from the earl's face to George Beal's. "And if she is willing to be my wife, I will be the happiest man in the kingdom."

"I CANNOT CREDIT it! How could you do this to me?" She paced the length of her bed-chamber, wringing her hands. "First you foist Becky upon the poor man and now you plan to force me upon him. I won't have it!"

George Beal's patience had long since been expended upon Becky's peccadillos. He had none left for Alice.

"You'll do as you're told, and no sass about it! I know you have no experience of the opposite sex but the boy is besotted with you and you *will* learn to love him!"

Alice turned away from the storm clouds out beyond the windows. Rain began to beat against the abbey's stone walls. "What did you say?" Alice asked her father.

"I said he told me he loves you. How you managed to gain his attention I have no idea, but gain it you did and you should be properly thankful instead of prosing on about rights and wrongs!"

"He said he loves me?"

"And his father there to hear it, as surprised as I."

"I must hear the truth from Andrew himself. And Papa, you must let me speak to Becky."

George Beal, hopeful Alice would acquiesce to his wishes, agreed to let the sisters talk. But he relocked the door when he left Becky's chamber.

Becky sat on a stone window seat, her knees tucked up under her chin. She looked towards Alice then turned back to her perusal of the gloomy countryside. "If they've sent you to coax me to eat, I won't do it."

"I've come to tell you the news."

"Of Paul?" Becky looked hopeful until she heard the news was of Andrew whereupon her face fell, only to be revived into wonder when Alice told of their father's visit. "You? You and Andrew?"

"You don't need to sound quite so surprised."

"But he can't possibly love you."

"And why not?"

"He's hardly talked to you," Becky pointed out.

"It would seem we've talked enough. And he's kissed me." Alice saw Becky's surprise and hurried on, blushing. "And we've talked of history and literature and religion and danced."

"But when did you do all this?" Becky objected.

"While you were busy planning trysts with Paul."

"I had no idea," Becky told her sister. "Ally, are you positive you're not doing this for Papa or for me? No matter what Andrew feels, can you honestly say you care for him?"

Alice considered the question carefully. "I would venture to say that whatever he feels pales by comparison to how much I love him."

"Oh, my," Becky said.

"Exactly," Alice reached to embrace her sister. "Becky, you always said I was never meant to become a spinster and you were absolutely right."

Becky puffed a long face. "That's wonderful for you but what is to happen to me? Papa will not hear of my even talking to Paul. And I'll marry none else!" she burst out passionately and then trailed off into sadness. "So there's nothing to be done," she finally admitted.

"There's always something to be done," Alice said.

"Not always," Becky replied.

"Always," Alice repeated. "One must only find the way."

"And how can that be done?"

Alice smiled. "I have just the answer."

" . . . What? I don't understand."

Alice grinned. "Sir Harry our Ghost," she replied.

Becky regarded her sister carefully. "Are you sure you feel quite well?"

"His mission is to bring true lovers together."

"You may find it rather hard to order a ghost around," Becky told her younger sister.

"Not necessarily." Alice smiled encouragingly. "Besides, I have other work for him."

"Such as?"

"Such as making sure Andrew means what he says."

The sound of the key in Becky's door stopped their conversation. "Who is it?" Becky called out.

Mary Beal opened the door and smiled. She stepped aside to let Lady Agatha enter. "Becky," Mary said, "you have a visitor."

"Lady Agatha!" Becky came to her feet and crossed the room towards the dowager as Mary closed the bedroom door.

"Hold your head higher, remember what I've taught you," Lady Agatha said, watching as Becky did as she was bid. "Much better."

"Yes, but what good will it all do me?" Becky asked.

"Good manners and good posture can never fail to be of value in any situation." Lady Agatha moved to a wing-back chair near the windows. "Good day, Alice," she acknowledged.

Alice gave a pretty curtsey and smiled up at the older woman. "It is good of you to come since we must surely be in bad odour after all that has happened."

"After all I've done, you mean," Becky interjected.

"I have some experience with gossip," Lady Agatha told the girls. "And although my situation was different and long ago it would seem that gossip and the general reaction remain the same no matter the era."

"Yes," Becky replied passionately.

"In the main part of your own creation," Lady Agatha continued, earning a downwards glance and a murmured affirmative. "However now is the time to strike forward upon a new path."

The rain slapped at the window panes, Alice glancing towards the sound, transfixed. Becky was speaking to Lady Agatha, defending her position, when she saw the direction of her sister's gaze and looked towards the window behind Lady Agatha's wing-back chair.

Becky saw a very wet and bedraggled Paul Beecher on the ledge. Becky's quick intake of breath and burst of conversation did not go unnoticed by Lady Agatha. With imploring eyes Becky begged Alice to *do* something while Becky herself continued to prattle on of household problems and nonsensical comments, trying to keep Lady Agatha's attention drawn to her words.

Alice drifted closer to the window. She was behind Lady Agatha's chair, turning to shoo Paul away when Agatha, looking into Becky's worried eyes, spoke. "I would suggest you let him in, unless of course you wish him to perish of the influenza."

Alice gasped. She unlocked the window, Becky running to help drag the shamefaced Paul inside.

"What are you doing here? Papa will kill you," Becky cried.

"I had to know if it were true, what they're saying in the village. Is it true he's offered for—" He saw Lady Agatha and his words stopped, his mouth gaping open. "Oh, no."

"Oh, yes," Lady Agatha replied, standing up. Becky ran towards her.

"Lady Agatha, please don't tell Papa."

"Your father has forbidden this boy the house and yet here he stands, disobeying all."

"Have you never been in love?" Becky asked, desperately trying to find a way to Lady Agatha's heart.

But it was Alice who changed Agatha's expression from one of disapproval to something much harder to define.

"Lady Agatha," Alice said. "Can you possibly conceive of what it would be like to be forced to marry a man you do not love?"

Lady Agatha stared at the girl for a long full moment before she spoke, her tone guarded. "Go on."

"Becky loves Paul. But even now, when Father knows Becky will never marry Andrew he still will not let her marry the man her heart has chosen. Can you imagine yourself in her place?"

Agatha fought her own emotions, long-gone feelings welling up at Alice's unsuspecting words. "I well know the results of such a match," Agatha finally managed to admit.

"I thought I heard my Aggie," Sir Harry the Ghost said, coming into vague view as he spoke. Becky and Alice stared towards the ghost, Agatha turning towards the fire-place, drawn by the girls' wide-eyed stares.

"Becky—?" Paul asked. "W-what is it?"

"Are you near-sighted young man?" the ghost asked.

Paul gulped. "I'm going daft."

"Buck up, you don't have far to go," Sir Harry told the boy. Lady Agatha's sharp intake of breath brought Harry to stare at her. "Aggie? Can you finally see me?" he asked in surprise.

Lady Agatha's eyes were wide, her mouth opening to speak and then closing. As her eyes closed too, Sir Harry tried to grab her. "Help me, she's falling!"

Paul caught Agatha, laying her on Becky's chaise longue. Becky sank to her knees and chafed Lady Agatha's hands while Alice ran for smelling salts. Sir Harry hovered, look-ing pale even by ghostly standards. "You must *do* some-thing," he insisted.

"And you must go," Becky told Paul. She rose to embrace him and then gave a little push towards the windows.

"But I must know the truth of what's happening," Paul protested. Sir Harry replied in thundering tones. "The truth is I shall eat you alive if you do not give Aggie a bit of peace!"

Paul Beecher was not given to seeing ghosts. Since the apparition had first appeared he had done his best to ignore it. Now it was shouting at him.

Becky urged him forward. "Go on as he says before you are caught!"

Unwillingly Paul left through the window. Becky was back beside Lady Agatha when Alice came running with vinaigrette, followed by Fannie. Below-stairs, Cook informed Peeves of Lady Agatha's condition and Peeves went in search of Mrs. Beal.

"It can't be," Lady Agatha murmured as she revived.

"Aggie, are you all right?" Fannie asked, worried sick and forgetting all formality. "You've never fainted, never in your life."

Sir Harry stayed by Agatha's side, invisible in case he might upset her. "Aggie, I didn't mean to scare you," he whispered.

"She'll be all right," Alice assured the ghost.

"Of course she will," Fannie answered in bracing tones, thinking the girl spoke to her. "Right as rain," Fannie continued, praying the girl was right. "What happened?"

The girls looked at each other. Finally Alice spoke. "We were speaking of being forced to marry one you did not love—"

Fannie sighed. "What a sorry topic."

Alice came closer to Fannie and whispered in her ear, "Did she, I mean, was Lady Agatha forced into such a match?"

"Yes, she was, and her heart never the same for it," Fannie answered truthfully. She waved more vinaigrette beneath her mistress's nose.

"Get that horrid-smelling stuff away from my nose, and help me up," Agatha replied. Her voice was much weaker than her words.

"You'll stay where you are," Fannie told her employer.

"Help me up," Agatha insisted, slowly sitting up with Fannie's unwilling help. "I'm perfectly fine," she told her abigail and the two girls she saw watching her with widened eyes. "And you'll do me the kindness of refraining from prattling on about my momentary weakness to all and sundry."

"We never would," Alice said.

"We shall say nothing," Becky promised.

"Good." Lady Agatha forced herself to sit as straight as a ramrod. "I had a slight dizzy spell. At my age that's to be expected. Fannie, stop hovering so."

"Yes, your ladyship," Fannie said, returning to the formality of mistress and servant.

"I shall now return to the gatehouse," Agatha announced.

"I shall call for Homer and the gig," Alice replied.

"I can walk—" Agatha said but this battle was lost before it began.

"Do you think she truly is all right?" Becky asked her sister once they were alone.

"Yes," Alice replied.

"Are you quite sure?" Sir Harry's voice floated down towards the girls.

"Oh, dear, where is he now?" Becky asked, looking around herself. "It could be disconcerting in the extreme to have an unseen presence forever hovering about one and listening to all you say and do."

"It will teach you to have a care, young woman." Sir Harry materialized, worry written large across his handsome features.

Alice watched Sir Harry drift nearer. "He means no harm," she told Becky. "And, after all, he's only a ghost— it's not as if a living gentleman flitted in and out of our walls."

"I have never flitted in my life," Sir Harry said with great dignity before he stalked through the bed-chamber walls.

"Do you suppose seeing the ghost was the reason Lady Agatha fainted dead away?" Alice asked her sister.

"No. He told us himself only lovers can see him. Which now we know since you were in love all along with Andrew and none the wiser. Not even you, I'll wager," Becky said laughing. "So it wasn't so surprising that you saw the ghost after all. But Lady Agatha could not. She's too old."

"I hardly see where her age is either here nor there."

"Alice Beal, parents and widows don't feel romantic love. They're too old."

"I have a feeling you might be surprised what widows feel," Alice replied, smiling.

At the gatehouse Fannie was hovering over Lady Agatha. Once the abigail had her mistress in bed with a comforter tucked up around her, Fannie began her questions. "What truly happened up there, Aggie?"

Agatha Steadford-Smyth looked bemused. "I know this will sound as if I am in my dotage but for a moment, mind you, I know it's impossible and it was only a moment but, for one moment, I could have sworn I saw Henry. Just exactly as he once was."

Fannie eyed her mistress. "What did he look like?" Fannie asked shrewdly.

"What?" Lady Agatha regarded her serving woman. "Surely you don't take this seriously. I was obviously suffering from mental fatigue or—or—or my vision was playing tricks or the light from outside blinded me for a bit."

"What did he look like?" Fannie asked again.

"Why do you keep asking?" Lady Agatha snapped testily.

"Because I think you may have at long last seen the Abbey Ghost."

Her words were greeted with a stunned look. "There are no such things as ghosts. Especially not ghosts that are the exact image of Henry Aldworth. It is simply not possible," Agatha repeated.

"That's as may be, but if he's tall, dark, handsome and dressed in tattered velvet, then you've seen the Abbey Ghost," Fannie said in a neutral tone. "And it's about time," she added with more asperity.

"Fannie Burns, leave my room and take your fanciful notions with you," Lady Agatha replied.

"You need not bellow," Fannie said calmly.

"Go!" Lady Agatha demanded. She watched her abigail leave the room and not until she was alone did she reach into the bureau drawer beside her bed. With trembling fingers she brought out a yellowing packet of love letters, holding them close against her fast-beating heart as she closed her eyes. "It can't be you," she whispered. "Can it?" She fell asleep into troubled dreams of years and pain long gone.

- *15* -

MARY BEAL CALLED her daughter Alice into the red parlour an hour after Fannie and Lady Agatha left the abbey. In Mary's hand was a short missive written upon thick creamy paper and bearing the Marleigh crest.

"Yes, Mama?" Alice said from the doorway.

Mary took a good long look at her younger daughter before she spoke. Alice wore a gown of lemon-coloured muslin, with high waist with rounded neckline and short puffed sleeves. Masses of auburn curls were caught within a yellow riband which braided through her hair. There was a bloom on her cheeks and a sparkle in her large hazel eyes which livened up her countenance and matched the smiling lines of her mouth, as though she contained a wonderful secret.

In contrast to her daughter's happy gaze Mary Beal's lips pursed together in silent reprimand.

"Mama?" Alice asked, coming forward to search out her mother's expression. "Is something wrong?"

"I have always felt you were a good girl, Alice. Trustworthy and reliable."

"Thank you, Mama."

"Now I find you have been as wild as your sister."

"Mother!"

"I am now told the earl's son is in love with you." Mary watched her daughter blush. "You have been meeting him on the sly."

"I never did! It wasn't like that," Alice defended. "We met to talk of Becky's feelings in the spinney and we happened to be in the gallery alone but we did not plan it and we were told to dance together at the ball—"

Mary Beal did not believe a word. "You are going to begin at the beginning and tell me every single thing that has thus far transpired before I send word to allow him to come here."

Alice's eyes widened. "Come here?"

Mary waved the letter. "His lordship wishes permission to take you riding." She saw her daughter's widening smile and spoke again. "I'm waiting for the truth."

Alice happily began to recite her every thought since first she met the handsome young lord.

An hour later, her mother somewhat mollified, Alice was allowed to change into her riding clothes and Lord Andrew was given permission to call. He arrived with alacrity and within the hour Andrew and Alice rode the Dorset hills towards the purple moors. Alice drank deeply of the warm spring air, the sunlight welcome after the days of winds and rains. She wore a bottle-green riding habit trimmed with braid *à la militaire* and a saucy bottle-green hat trimmed with black irridescent *coq* feathers.

Alice cast a sidelong glance at Andrew as they cantered towards the arched gateway. He wore a coat of wine-coloured superfine and dove-grey breeches and looked exactly as she imagined a prince in a fairy tale would look, his dark hair ruffled by the warm breeze, his tall lithe body astride a great black stallion. She urged her dappled grey forward as they left the gates behind, streaking across the spring countryside with all the joy of freedom and new love.

Fields of hyacinths and crocuses stretched away around them, their sweet scents carrying on the breeze. They raced past stands of elms and oaks where bleeding hearts and wild violets clung to the sheltered spots around thick roots.

The sky was vast and blue above, wisps of snow white clouds chasing each other towards the horizon. Alice and Andrew raced towards the river's edge and then slowed, laughing, gasping for air, as they paced their steeds sedately along the riverbank.

"This day is glorious," Alice exclaimed.

"Life is glorious and you are most glorious of all," Andrew replied.

Love shone from the depths of her eyes. "Can this last? All of it? This day, these feelings, everything?"

"I would give you nothing but sunshine and happiness if it were in my power, sweet Alice. But alas it is not. What I can promise is to hold you close and keep you warm and sheltered through all of life's storms."

"Then I shall long for the cold and storms."

"Alice Beal, you are a flirt and none have ever known it."

"Nor will any but you, for ever and ever." A thought clouded Alice's eyes and Andrew saw it.

"What is it?"

"It's just I am so happy and Becky is so miserable. Papa will not allow her to see Paul and Mr. Beecher and Papa both agree Becky and Paul would never suit, but they do! Andrew, we must help them!"

Andrew looked none too sure how to go about accomplishing Alice's wish. "I would do anything you asked, but I'm not sure how we can help."

"Perhaps if you talked to Mr. Beecher," Alice ventured. "If you could persuade him, perhaps all of us could persuade Papa."

Lord Andrew looked doubtful. "Since we've never met, nor are likely to in the general course of things, I can only think Paul's father would assume me a terrific meddler."

Alice was crestfallen. "Papa is so dreadfully upset he is determined to keep them apart. Even Mama is upset with Becky for causing so much trouble and for making such a spectacle at the ball. Mama is still quite done up whenever she thinks on it."

"It was a terrific to-do," Andrew allowed, a teasing look coming into his dark blue eyes. "And even shy Alice contributed her own little lecture to the group."

Alice blushed and looked down at the dappled grey's mane, patting it and trying to control her colour. "I could not help it."

"You did not seem able to," her intended agreed.

She turned to see his expression. "Were you terribly

embarrassed? Was I dreadfully wrong to do it?"

"I would venture to say that lecturing your papa in front of an entire assemblage is not the done thing. And as to the content of your speech, I shall withhold comment since I cannot very well condone my future wife venting her spleen in public. However, as to the reason for your outburst, I must admit some sympathy. And as to the outcome, you are to be commended."

"Commended?"

"Most assuredly. You ended your father's diatribe which was very much louder and more disgraceful than your attempt to stop it."

"None of which helps Becky and Paul," Alice said, coming back to the point. "Their unhappiness casts a pall over our own joy."

Andrew reached for Alice's gloved hand, riding close beside and pressing it tight. "Then we shall contrive a way to make them happy."

The sound of fast-approaching hoofbeats heralded young Tim's approach. He reined in his brown mare as he reached Alice's side. "Begging your pardon, Miss Alice, is anything amiss?"

"No. What could be wrong?"

Tim gave a sidelong glance to the tall lord who held Alice's hand. Lord Andrew withdrew his hand from Alice's and smiled easily at the abbey retainer.

"There is nothing out of the way," Andrew reassured the young man.

"That's as may be, but I'm charged to make sure nothing goes amiss," Tim replied.

"Has my father sent you to spy?" Alice demanded, anger rising.

"No, miss," Tim replied. "Your mother sent me to see to your safety."

"Safety!"

Lord Andrew grinned. "It would seem Tim here has been commandeered to do chaperone duty."

Tim looked sheepish and Andrew laughed out loud, earning a swift glance from his fiancé.

"I do not think it humourous to be treated as a child," Alice told both young men.

"Quite right," Andrew replied. He coaxed an unwilling smile from Alice. "It seems we are not to be left alone. And she is right to worry," he proclaimed. "For I don't know how I could keep myself from ravaging you."

"Just you wait!" Tim sputtered. "I've never heard such goings-on!"

"We can out-race him," Alice offered. "That brown mare can never keep up with your stallion."

"Miss Alice!" Tim was scandalized.

"It will never serve," Lord Andrew agreed. "If we're in your parents' bad graces we shall never be able to help the course of true love run smooth."

"What did he say?" Tim asked suspiciously.

"He said we should ride back slowly and ponder what can be done," Alice replied.

Tim looked from one to the other. He watched them turn their horses around and followed a few lengths back as they moved sedately back towards the abbey hill. Every now and then they would look back to make sure he was still behind, and he could hear their laughter.

When they arrived at the abbey Andrew lifted Alice down from her mount, giving Tim a wink. "Perfectly proper," he assured the abbey retainer as Sir Harry came through the thick stone wall beside one of the large oriel windows. Perched precariously atop the sturdy stone corbel which supported the window, he looked down impatiently.

"Hurry along, I've found a solution."

"What?" Alice asked.

"Miss?" Tim asked.

Alice looked back at the boy. "You'd best take the horses to the stable."

Tim responded with alacrity. He was already moving off with the animals as Andrew and Alice drew closer to the ghost.

"Have you truly found a solution?" Alice whispered to

the ghost, afraid of Tim overhearing and turning back to find her speaking to the wall.

"Come along, both of you," Sir Harry said as he began to fade back through the wall.

"Sorry, old man," Lord Andrew said. "But you see we must use doors."

Harry's disembodied voice floated down towards them. "One of the problems of being a mere mortal. I'll be in the chapel." So saying, the ghost was gone.

Alice and Andrew were delayed by Peeves who explained that Mr. and Mrs. Beal were awaiting their arrival in the red parlour. The two young people spent several minutes with the elder Beals discussing their wedding plans. Alice realised her father was determined to have the bargain sealed and the young couple wed as soon as possible. She looked towards Andrew.

"Sir, I would be glad to say our vows today," his lordship said feelingly.

"Today!" Mary Beal interjected. "There are a hundred things to be done and the banns to be read."

"The earl has a special dispensation," her husband replied.

"But that was for Andrew and Becky."

"The names were not filled in and if Andrew is willing—"

Mary spoke firmly. "Mr. Beal, I am positive the countess will expect a grand affair."

"I should rather like a small wedding," Alice put in hopefully. "We can have receptions and parties later, Mother."

Andrew smiled politely at Mary Beal. "I am sure my mother will be content with what Alice wishes." He did not add that getting his mother to the ceremony would be enough of a challenge. The fewer people there, the easier she would be persuaded.

"Capital," George pronounced. Seeing his wife's expression, he continued, "We shall have a small ceremony here in the abbey chapel as soon as Mrs. Beal is ready."

Remembering the disrepair they had been shown in the weeks just past, Andrew ventured a question about its readiness but George waved his concerns away.

"Nonsense, my boy, a little elbow grease and a great deal
of silver coin and all will be as good as new in no time."

"Shall we go see it?" Alice asked Andrew with a mean-
ingful look, chafing to keep their appointment with the
ghost.

"We shall all go," George offered.

"No," Alice said quickly. She tugged at Andrew's sleeve.
"I think just ourselves."

"Alone?" Mary Beal objected, but her husband overrode
her concern.

"Mrs. Beal, there is no need for coyness." Andrew
bowed, allowing Alice to precede him into the hall. She
fairly danced with impatience until they reached the chapel
door and slipped inside.

"Sir Harry?"

"You certainly took long enough," he complained.

"We're sorry, but Mama and Papa called and we could
not leave. They are talking of having our wedding here."
Alice looked around the dusty, cobweb-strewn chapel. A
walnut altar with the Tudor rose carved into it was set
behind the chancel rail. A high round stained-glass window
far above poured afternoon sunlight down upon the oaken
pews and thick stone flooring. "It is truly lovely," she said
softly.

"You must be married here," the ghost informed them.

"Must?" Andrew questioned.

"I have found the solution to all the problems and it
depends on your being wed here."

Alice and Andrew eyed the ghost expectantly. "Why?"
Alice asked.

"Because then Becky and Paul can be married here too."

"Never," Alice objected. "Papa will never allow it."

"He will not know until the deed is done," Harry replied
in self-satisfied accents.

Andrew was perplexed. When he spoke it was as politely
as possible. "I realise that your—perspective—must be a
great deal different from ours but surely you can see that
such a marriage could never be accomplished without Mr.

Beal knowing about it. Particularly as it would be held under his very roof."

"That's the beauty of it," Sir Harry replied, pleased with himself for having found a solution to the knotty problem. "It will be precisely here, under his roof, so that I may interrupt any rash acts he might attempt at the very last minute."

"That's all well and good," Alice put in. "And I am sure if anyone could, you could scare my father into silence, but it still won't wash."

"I could scare the devil out of hell," Harry opined modestly. "Why won't it wash?"

"Because there are ever so many plans and needs before a wedding and you could never keep him from finding out all such was going on. Even assuming you could convince Mama and the staff to not only keep silent but to court his wrath and even dismissal from his service by helping put together a ceremony behind his back."

Sir Harry waved a ghostly hand. "No problem whatsoever my girl. They'll not know, nary a one of them. The only one you have to convince is Aggie."

"Lady Agatha?" Andrew looked blank. "I'm afraid I don't understand why she would have to be involved."

"Someone's got to teach the boy manners. He can't just run in willy-nilly as he did at the ball, he needs some help with his airs and graces."

"I should say that was an understatement," Andrew put in quietly. "Howsoever, with all the deportment in the world and assuming Lady Agatha would agree, I still don't see how you can accomplish their being wed without the entire household knowing, not to mention Mr. Beal."

Sir Harry gave the young man a self-satisfied look. "That, young man, is because you both are so daft about each other you can see nothing but yourselves. I, on the other hand, have in mind the whole picture, as it were. And I have in mind to accomplish two lovers' matches at once and thus perhaps gain my freedom from this house."

"Are you quite positive you want to leave the abbey?" Alice asked.

"Yes, I am."

"Perhaps to haunt the gatehouse instead?" Alice said.

Sir Harry grimaced. "I'd liefer be at rest than alone in this halfway measure betwixt and between. I'll not go near Aggie again for fear of doing her harm and without her presence there's little enough I want around anything which was ever owned by Ambrose Steadford." At the thought of Agatha's father Sir Harry's countenance took on a forbidding cast.

"Sir Harry," Andrew said. "Your plan of action?"

"Why, sir, the only possible plan. They must be wed when you are."

Stunned silence greeted his words. Andrew recovered the use of his voice before his fiancé. "They must be wed with us," he repeated, insuring he heard the ghost correctly.

"Of course. How else could all the preparations be done with none the wiser?" Sir Harry drifted atop one of the pews, settling himself and waiting for compliments for his perspicacity.

Alice sank to one of the ancient wooden benches. "It might be possible."

"Of course it's possible," Sir Harry said bracingly.

"There are many things that would have to be done—" Alice said.

"And many that could go wrong," Andrew pointed out.

"But it might work," Alice said. "If we can manage Lady Agatha and sneaking Paul in . . ." her voice trailed away unhappily. "There are a *great* many problems with this scheme."

"I can't think of everything," Sir Harry grimaced. "You four will have to do some of this yourselves."

16

BECKY STARED AT her sister across the length of the library, her mouth open in stunned stupefaction. "What did you say?" she asked weakly.

Alice and Andrew had agreed that Alice would speak to her sister as soon as Andrew departed. He would ride to the village and somehow contrive to see Paul and slip him a message to meet them in the spinney after all else had gone to bed.

"Are you willing to try?" Alice now asked her sister.

"But it will never work!"

Sir Harry shimmered in the wine-coloured high-backed leather wing-chair by the fire. "Alice Beal, don't coax the wench. Either she wants to marry the scoundrel or she does not."

"He's not a scoundrel," Becky burst out. "He's good and honest and true!" Becky's anger brought the fight back into her sky-blue eyes. "Alice," she asked her trusted sister. "Do you think we can truly manage to pull it off? I don't want Papa shooting Paul or stabbing him through."

"That is my department," Sir Harry the Ghost pointed out.

Alice gave her sister a supportive smile. "We are to make all haste with the ceremony, which is all to the good since it will keep Papa busy with the chapel repairs and mama busy with the food and the linens and our dresses and what all. Although you shan't have a proper wedding gown, Becky."

"I don't care a fig about a dress," Becky told her sister. "I just don't see how we're to get Paul ready and here without Papa knowing."

Sir Harry gave a decided harumph. "You've found ways to get him in and out of the abbey on the quiet before this, young woman. As to getting the boy ready, there I agree." Talking to himself of silk purses and sows' ears he melted away, leaving the girls to discuss their doubts and plans in private.

"What do we do first?" Becky asked.

Alice reached to hug her sister. "There's the spirit! First we must convince Papa you'll not run away. Then, once you can leave your room, we must visit Lady Agatha."

Becky groaned. "Bearding lions in their dens."

"Buck up now, we shall overcome the worst hurdle first and all else will be that much easier," Alice encouraged. "I confess I could never have been truly content in my happiness knowing you were pining away for a love you could not have."

"Let's go before my pluck deserts me," Becky replied faintly.

"Nonsense!" Alice said, borrowing one of Sir Harry's favorite tones of voice. "You are pluck to the backbone!"

Hoping her sister was correct, Becky prepared for her meeting with her father.

Two days later, having convinced their father Becky would obey his commands, the Beal girls arrived at the gatehouse just as Fannie and Lady Agatha finished their afternoon tea. Curious, but above listening at doors, Fannie contented herself with clearing away the dishes and going outside to cut fresh roses for the parlour. While Fannie snipped the first peach and pink blooms, Alice and Becky explained their mission to Lady Agatha.

"I am shocked," that redoubtable lady said when at last the girls finished their explanations. "How can you ask me to go against your father's wishes?"

Becky looked crestfallen. "I knew she would say no," she told her sister.

But Alice was not to be easily dissuaded. "Lady Agatha, you know a father can sometimes wish the wrong things for his children!"

A faraway look crossed Lady Agatha's dark eyes and was quickly gone. "Whether I do or not, it is one thing to disagree in principle, it is quite another to meddle into a family's private business."

"But I love Paul," Becky burst out. "And I'll marry no other, no matter how much Papa tries to buy me titles. I don't want titles, I want Paul!"

"Child we cannot always have what we want in this world," Lady Agatha told the girl.

"But ma'am," Alice put in quietly. "Have you never had a time in your life that you wished someone *would* meddle into your family's business? Would help you and give you the opportunity of hope and happiness and love?"

Agatha Steadford-Smyth turned to face her young interlocutor. "Why do you ask?"

"Because I have heard of someone who pined most dreadfully for the want of your affections."

Agatha stared into the girl's golden hazel eyes. "There is no such person," she said finally. "Nor do I appreciate such stories being bandied about."

"Alice," Becky said to her sister, her eyes filling with unhappy tears. "This is of no use."

But Alice stood her ground, ignoring her sister's pleas to leave and pressing on in spite of Lady Agatha's forbidding countenance. "Which is the worse sin, Lady Agatha. The sin of omission, of omitting to mention something *not* asked, or the sin of commission, of deciding another's future by deliberately deciding to give them no help?"

Lady Agatha watched the young woman who so reminded her of her own granddaughter Jane. "You, young lady, argue with all the circumlocutions of a wily barrister. And you have turned things topsy-turvy. The sin of commission would be in aiding and abetting a daughter's rebellion. The sin of omission would be in having no part in the scheme, in keeping silent and keeping out of the middle of a family's private business. And that much I will promise," she added. "I shall not say anything to your parents regarding this visit unless directly asked. More than that I cannot agree to." She stood up, ready to dismiss them from her presence.

Becky got to her feet but Alice sat where she was and still pressed their case. "You have already promised Mama to instruct us as much as possible in the social graces, have you not?" Alice got to her feet, coming closer to the matriarch. "And we shall need instruction for the wedding ceremony, shall we not?"

Lady Agatha regarded the determined girl. "And if so?"

Alice smiled winningly at the older woman. "Then all we ask is that you enlarge the size of your student body. By one."

"You have much cheek, Miss Alice Beal."

"It is in *such* a good cause, your ladyship."

"One would think it was your own happiness you were fighting for instead of your sister's."

"I am fighting for my own happiness, your ladyship. I am being entirely selfish for if Becky is unhappy then so shall I be and my love for Andrew will forever be overshadowed by the fact of my sister's misery."

Lady Agatha stared at the girl. "One can only admire such loyalty amongst siblings."

Becky looked more hopeful than she had since Alice had first voiced her plan. "Does that mean you will help us?"

"No," Lady Agatha said. And, seeing their crushed expressions, she continued slowly. "I cannot help or condone disobedience. However, I most heartily dislike bad manners and have already decided to continue your deportment lessons here at the gatehouse. If another should happen to benefit by my instructions I would feel it my duty not to turn them away."

"Oh, Lady Agatha!" Becky reached for the venerable matriarch and in her enthusiasm hugged her most prodigiously. Over Becky's honey curls Agatha saw the look of gratitude and love in Alice's eyes.

And so it was that Fannie Burns walked inside the small gatehouse parlour to find her mistress being embraced by Becky Beal while Alice Beal and Lady Agatha smiled at each other over Becky's head.

"Am I interrupting?" Fannie asked, shocked to the core.

"Get away with you now, child," Lady Agatha said to Becky and gave her a little push to enforce the words. "You will sadly crush your dress, not to mention mine, and you must learn to control your more—impulsive— reactions."

"Yes, ma'am," Becky replied, dipping a deep curtsey to Lady Agatha and then bobbing a curtsey to Fannie. "Thank you. *Thank* you," she said fervently, earning a look of complete incomprehension from Lady Agatha's serving woman.

Alice curtseyed to Lady Agatha and took her leave, thanking her again and, at the door, stopped to look back at the lovely Lady Agatha. Her thick silver-shot dark hair was piled atop her head, fine lines outlined her lustrous dark eyes and generous mouth, but Lady Agatha's figure was trim and erect, her waist still slim, her complexion the purest ivory. She wore a plain gown of grey silk, frilled with ivory lace and a simple cameo and pearls.

"You had no sisters, no siblings, had you?" Alice Beal asked.

Agatha took a moment, surprised at the question. "I had one brother," she answered finally.

Alice's expression went from soft to hard. "I hate him excessively," she proclaimed.

Becky stared at her sister. She was further surprised when Lady Agatha gave Alice a brief smile. "As did I," Lady Agatha said before the girls left the cottage. When she turned she stared into Fannie's disbelief. "Well?" Lady Agatha asked. "Is something wrong?"

"Are you asking that of me?" Fannie said pertly. "Or of yourself?"

Not being sure of the answer to Fannie's question, Lady Agatha made no reply.

While a bemused Lady Agatha went back to her mending at Hargrave House Andrew was ending a rather difficult interview with his mother and father.

"I simply cannot credit it," the countess told her son. "You are no longer being forced to marry into that odious clan and yet you not only go forward with such plans, you have the temerity to suggest that I countenance this impossible liaison."

"Jane, my love," the earl put in. "If he truly loves this girl—"

"Stuff and nonsense, Philip, I won't hear a bit of it. If it weren't for your own association with that impossible man, and your unfortunate gambling excesses, none of this would have come to pass. We would never have been hauled into these hinterlands and Andrew would never have met the girl!"

"And my life much the poorer," Andrew told his mother.

"Youthful fancy," his mother dismissed. "Once you are back in London you will forget all about this *misalliance*.

"Mother I assure you I shall never desert Alice. I have offered for her hand and she has accepted. We are to be married and the only question that remains is whether you will be there to wish us well." Andrew's voice took on a very stern timbre. "I have ever been the dutiful son. Do not presume upon that duty now." He looked from one parent to the other. "I agreed to sell my future, my happiness, and my title to rescue my parents and my estate from debt. I agreed to marry a woman I had not met and did not love in order to insure your security. You released me from that duty. Now you cannot have the *temerity,* as mother puts it, to ask me to forego the future I have planned for myself."

"Andrew," the earl said. "Do not talk to your mother so."

Andrew took a deep breath. "I love Alice and thankfully, she returns my love." His eyes impaled his father. "You, sir, of all people, should be relieved at this turn of events since we both know you have already accepted Mr. Beal's financial help and since we both know you have no way of repaying the debt."

"Andrew—are you doing this for me?" the earl asked, disconcerted by the news.

"No," Andrew replied firmly. "I am following my heart. But as it happens your folly has ended in some good. I leave you to discuss the situation with your wife. I warn you both, as I have ever been the dutiful son, I will expect proper courtesy toward my bride." He let his words sink in before continuing. "I shall insist upon your attendance at our wedding. It will be at the abbey chapel one week hence."

"A sennight?" The countess could not believe her son's words. "It's not possible! There are banns to be read and arrangements to be made."

The earl gave a small cough. "My dear, I arranged a special dispensation of the banns, if you remember. It was meant for Andrew and Rebecca."

"Good lord," the countess replied. "One week from this day Alice Beal will be her ladyship, the future Countess of Marleigh." Andrew turned on his heel and left.

"Andy?" Hero Hargrave called from the study. "Are you truly marrying the Beal girl?"

"Which one?" Andrew asked as Hero caught up with him.

"I beg your pardon?" Hero replied, more than a little taken aback.

Andrew shrugged. "If you are asking about Becky, then you are wet, as she is madly in love with a butcher and will not brook having me near her."

Hero Hargrave gaped. "Lord Andrew Marleigh, future Earl of Marleigh, has been thrown over for a butcher?"

"And happily so, old boy," Andrew commented. "Now, on the other hand, if you are asking about the wonderfully intelligent and ravishingly lovely Alice, then I must confess, your intelligence is correct. I am to wed Alice Beal."

"Good God," Hero managed to reply. "Your parents are demented, forcing you from one sister to the other."

"My parents are against the match. At least my mother is," Andrew told his friend.

"Are you saying you are not being coerced? That you willingly agree to this match?"

"Willingly, passionately and the sooner the better."

"Good God," Hero said again. "I can hardly credit my own ears."

"You must credit them, Hero, because you are to be my best man."

Upon this intelligence Hero Hargrave repaired to the study where his friend poured him a medicinal measure of brandy, smiling all the while.

17

THE VILLAGE OF WOOSTER was full of the news of an abbey wedding. Alice being the bride instead of Becky took the county by surprise and many conjectures floated across the countryside as to why the older girl was passed over in favour of the younger.

Leticia Merriweather tried to regain her reputation for knowing every particle of gossip by smiling a knowing smile and allowing her friends to pry out of her the facts she had obviously known all along. As all sensible people had said from the first, the Earl of Marleigh would never allow his heir to marry such a hoyden as Becky Beal.

Poor Becky, Leticia lamented, had sealed her own doom by her sorry actions. The earl had fixed upon the younger and much more sensible Alice as his son's future wife, and had kept the news a secret in order to give the young people a chance to know each other.

His strategy had worked, they had developed a *tendré* and would be immediately wed. The immediacy of the wedding was the subject of much conjecture once London heard of the coming nuptials, but although Londoners were quick to assume the worst, the county well knew that young Alice had only just clapped eyes upon the young lord. The county wisdom was that the haste for the wedding was to end Becky's embarrassment at having been passed over. Soonest over, quickest mended, was thought to be a sound remedy for such problems.

Whilst the villagers gossiped, the workmen at the abbey worked long and hard in the chapel, readying it for the ceremony. Meanwhile, Lady Agatha was instructing Alice, Becky and their young friend in the fine art of socially correct behaviour.

* * *

Two days before the wedding, Lady Agatha insisted on a rehearsal since neither the bride nor her family had any experience with the formal service the countess demanded. The skies were overcast and grey, Lady Agatha assuring Fannie it was not a portent of things to come.

"Are you quite sure?" Fannie asked. "What with Paul Beecher sneaking in through the flower beds and the—"

"Fannie Burns, you will say nothing about the flower beds," Agatha told her abigail.

"And who would I be talking to, I ask you? I'm only saying it's a wonder what's going on and what all will come of it."

"It's none of your concern," Agatha said.

"I still say it is a shame that little Becky is to be married in an old gown when a perfectly good one is going to waste in the attic above our heads."

"What did you say?"

Fannie stared her employer down. "I said there is a gown in the attic you never even look at because it reminds you of nothing but grief but that gown would be lovely for Becky if it was altered just a bit."

"Fannie Burns, you have been listening at keyholes," Lady Agatha accused.

"I have never done! It's not my fault if those young people babble at the top of their voices and the walls are thin."

"I am ashamed of you," her employer retorted.

"That's as may be, but what about poor Becky?"

Fannie watched Lady Agatha's deliberation as she thought about what all had been said. Finally Agatha turned away. "I have nothing to do with the girls' apparel," was all she said to her abigail but Fannie recognised the tone of her voice and knew her employer was not displeased. Satisfied with herself, Fannie headed up the stairwell towards the attic trunks.

At the abbey George Beal was supervising the workmen who were refurbishing the ancient chapel, doing more harm than good. The abbey was alive with activity from attics to cellars, Peeves seeing to all the myriad details that were needed to make the coming ceremony a success.

Peeves had taken the debacle at the abbey ball personally and still frowned whenever Becky Beal was in his immediate vicinity. He felt the confusion and controversy caused by Becky and the boy he referred to as "her butcher" redounded badly upon his—until now—sterling reputation. Peeves was determined to redeem his reputation by insuring that the coming nuptials would be properly impressive, pompous and totally unexceptional.

While Peeves snapped orders to his staff, and George Beal asked questions of the chapel workmen, in the village of Wooster Paul Beecher was heading out the back door of the family butcher shop. He was not precisely sneaking as he sidled past the thick wooden carving table but his mother's voice stopped him in his tracks.

"And where do you think you're going in the middle of the workday, Paul Beecher?"

"I'm to go to Hargrave House, Ma."

"Again?" She tied a wide white apron around her ample frame as she came down the stairs towards him. "And what are they wanting now?"

"More chickens—"

"More chickens! They've placed nary an order since they arrived and now they've ordered twenty in three days."

"Maybe they're partial to chicken," Paul offered.

"They must be more partial than any I've ever met."

"Ma, I'll be late."

"Late for what?" Molly Beecher asked.

"Late for delivering the chickens." He grabbed three chickens and pushed the back door open.

"You mind, they pay on delivery!" his mother said as he left.

The late spring day was blessed with warmth and sunshine, the sky cloudless as Paul headed the rough-hewn butcher's cart toward Hargrave House. Crates of live chickens cackled behind him as he worried himself sick over his lies to his parents. He did not have the temperament that allowed him to lie easily or well and now, in the midst of an intrigue, he felt guilty over every half truth. He hadn't precisely lied to his mother; Lord Andrew had ordered the poultry and had paid even though he never ate a bite of it.

Paul's love for Becky warred with his innate honesty and his impulse to tell his parents the whole of it but he knew they would never understand sneaking about to learn fancy manners, let alone a clandestine marriage to Becky Beal or anyone else.

His worries deepening frown lines into his wide forehead, he thought about all the trouble to come. It would be a rare mess and that was a fact. But she was worth it and that was a fact that would make everything come out all right in the end. He hoped.

Paul delivered the chickens to the Hargrave's cook, who muttered about the ways of the nobs, then he raced to where Andrew waited near a stand of elms. Andrew greeted the butcher with civility, riding alongside Paul's cart earning startled looks from Homer and Jake as they arrived at the abbey.

Lord Andrew handed his reins over and asked Homer to water the butcher's nag. Homer took off his cap, scratching his head as the young lord and the village lad walked towards the gatehouse.

"A lord and a butcher's boy meeting day after day . . . Something havey-cavey's going on," Homer opined.

In the little house by the arched abbey gate, a small group, congregated in the parlour, were discussing the rehearsal.

"It's absolutely impossible," Fannie Burns told the assemblage in no uncertain terms. "And too dangerous by half. If Paul tried to sneak into the chapel before the wedding and got caught then where would all this end?"

"With a funeral, considering Mr. Beal's temper," Andrew said dryly.

Paul kept silent as the others looked towards him, his own gaze turning towards Lady Agatha. That matriarch was not looking pleased.

"Lady Agatha?" Andrew prompted, earning a swift look from his hostess before she rose to her feet and paced to the windows. "You look concerned."

"Concerned is a vast understatement, I assure you," she replied. "I am afraid this mad scheme has no chance of success. Have you thought through all the possibilities of discovery and failure? And the price Paul in particular will pay if your plans fail? Not to mention if they succeed. Think of how his parents will feel, finding out about his marriage after the fact."

"But they will be there, Lady Agatha," Becky supplied happily. "It's all planned."

Lady Agatha stared at the girl. "Are you saying they know of this mad plan?"

"No," Alice replied quickly. "None know but those in this room."

"And every man-jack of the servants who've seen his lordship parading about the countryside with the butcher's son," Fannie told them tartly. "Don't think they haven't eyes in their heads and curiosity enough to drop a word here and there."

"We shall be married before they can cause us harm," Becky supplied.

"You'd best hope so," Fannie ended.

Lady Agatha regarded first Becky, then Alice. "I don't understand how you intend to arrange for Paul's parents to be at your wedding but there are many other pitfalls to be negotiated betwixt now and when you all are safely wed. And I must tell you, Andrew—and Alice—it is entirely possible that this plan will fail. And if it does you will be in no better odour than will Becky and Paul." Lady Agatha shook her head in amazement at the turn of events that had led to this meeting. "How I came to be so deeply involved in this debacle continues to mystify me." She cast a sidelong glance towards her abigail which Fannie studiously ignored. "It goes against all better judgement and sense to meddle so in other's business."

"Oh, Lady Agatha," Alice interrupted. "Don't ever say so and please, please, don't withdraw your help. We would have been lost without your own and Fannie's assistance."

"I'm not so very sure I am pleased at that thought," Agatha responded in acerbic tones.

Paul stood up. Twisting his cap in his large work-hardened hands, he spoke slowly, measuring each word. "I think Lady Agatha has the right of it. Becky and I should not have got you involved. It will be best that we call this off."

"Paul!" Becky exclaimed in horrified accents.

"Paul?" Andrew questioned. "It's a bit late for backing out now."

"I don't want to get others in trouble for trying to rescue my bacon from the fire," Paul said in a troubled voice. "And all this sneaking about can't be right."

"What are you saying?" Becky cried. She came to her feet, her hands reaching out to grasp his. "We love each other and I'll never wed another!"

"Of course you shan't," Paul responded. He looked down into eyes the colour of a spring sky and felt his heart thud as it had the first time they'd met. Blonde curls framed the lovely face that was lifted to his in supplication. He tried to smile but his eyes remained troubled. "I was wrong to get you into this and I was wrong to say no when Becky wanted to run to Gretna Green."

"Gretna Green!" Lady Agatha looked horrified. "Good grief, young man, if that is your only alternative then we must conspire away, for you shall never do such a thing to this girl's reputation. Better a surprise marriage in front of all than sneaking off alone. Do you want the poor girl to have the stigma of having to marry quickly and in secret following her for the rest of her days?" Agatha saw Paul's expression turn from resolve to confusion and pressed her point home. "When faced with appalling choices, one must brace oneself and accept the least dreadful of the alternatives. In that fight, this surreptitious plan is by far the best remedy to an impossible situation."

The room was silent around her.

"Now," Lady Agatha continued in calmer tones. "Shall we continue our instructions? Where were we?"

"About to continue Paul's education by schooling him in the fine art of the quadrille."

Paul groaned. "I'll never get the handle on such goings-on. I've two left feet and both of them stepping all over poor Becky's little slippers."

Alice stood up. "I shall offer my feet into your service, kind sir." She smiled at him. "It will be far easier, I assure you, when you have the proper music to guide your movements."

Paul looked glum. "I fear it will never be easy for the likes of me to cut figures on a dance floor."

"Nonsense," Alice said bracingly. "After all, you must lead your bride in her wedding dance, Mr. Beecher."

Paul did not look terribly convinced but he let Alice lead him forward, Andrew counting the measures as they, yet again, attempted the intricate figures of the dance.

Fannie watched the scene with failing hopes. She was very afraid Paul Beecher had the right of it and this would all end in disaster for them all. But she was not about to voice her fears since she had been so vocal in convincing Lady Agatha to join their effort. Fannie pinned her own hopes on the fact that the wedding was only three days hence. If they could manage to get through the next two days, the wedding would be upon them and all this would be over.

"Fannie, you'd best make tea," Lady Agatha told her serving woman quietly as the young people attempted to dance to unheard music. She watched Paul Beecher stumble through the instructions Becky and Alice were giving as Andrew counted time, Alice letting out little shrieks of pain when one of his thick boots trod onto her dainty halfboots of crimson jean. "I fear they will sorely need all the sustenance they can manage before tomorrow ends."

The rehearsal was scheduled for early evening, the wedding party to share a light supper beforehand. The Reverend Doctor Whipple arrived with Charlotte Summerville and her mother, Charlotte to be the second bridesmaid. The earl and Hero Hargrave arrived without the countess whose excuses were becoming as weak as Fannie's smiles. While Fannie worried, Lady Agatha carried on a lively general conversation as did Andrew and Alice. Charlotte spent the meal nodding polite disinterested assents to whatever the reverend and her mother were saying whilst maintaining a flirtation across the table with a very smitten Hero Hargrave.

After supper the wedding party walked the abbey halls to the refurbished abbey chapel, Lady Agatha enchanted with the rubbed and oiled walnut and oak and brass of the ancient room and the wall tapestries which had been cleaned and resewn. While George expounded on the work he had commissioned and told of the work on the pipe organ as well, Andrew puffed his father aside for a private chat.

"Father, I shall never forgive mother if she does not attend the ceremony."

The earl, having had the self-same conversation with his wife before riding over alone to Steadford Abbey, attempted to reassure his son that he would be able to convince the countess the next morning.

"I told her I shall be excessively displeased if she does not come up to the mark and do her duty. Your mother is a high stickler for duty and I promise you, she shall come round." The earl spoke in bolstering tones but his son felt there was a great deal of bluster and hope beneath the fortifying words. "Stop worrying, my boy," the earl continued. "It shall come out right in the end, I'm confident of it."

"I pray your confidence is warranted," Andrew replied as he thought about all the secrecy and subterfuge in which he had involved himself. If his mother knew of the plans for Becky and Paul Beecher to share their marriage vows with her son she would never appear at the ceremony.

The chapel was lit by a multitude of brass candle-branches, thin white tapirs blazing their light down upon the highly polished oak of the pews.

Lady Agatha and Fannie retreated to the refurbished pipe organ, Lady Agatha testing the pedals. "It's been a very long time since I've played," Lady Agatha said as she pulled out stops and tested the keys.

Sir Harry the Ghost drifted through the wall, staying invisible but coming near to hear her play. He perched on the end of the organ bench, watching Agatha flex her fingers and then concentrate on her chording as she began to play.

"Fannie, don't hover so. Go find something to do."

"I haven't the brass to sit down there with the others, I'm as nervous as a cat and I know I'll say the wrong thing and land us all in a kettle."

"Once committed upon a course of action—no matter how rashly conceived," Lady Agatha cast a telling look at her abigail. "One must have courage. There is naught else to be done at this point."

"And that boy hiding up—"

"Shush," Lady Agatha whispered sharply, missing a chord and stopping. She glanced down at the assemblage, giving a brief smile to the reverend who glanced up when she stopped playing. She began again and he nodded to himself at the lovely Bach chords before turning back to the young couple and the others around them.

"I'm afraid I've lost my place—let me see, oh, yes, the father of the bride will step forward—Mr. Beal—" he called out. "If you would step forward, please—"

Becky hovered beside Charlotte and Hero, near Lord Andrew and Alice, fidgeting from one foot to the other, her gaze going constantly to the choir loft.

"Becky," Mary pulled her daughter aside. "Are you feeling quite the thing? You seem all done up."

"I'm perfectly all right," Becky said and then, feeling guilty as she looked into her mother's innocent expression of concern, she kissed her mother's cheek.

Mary Beal glanced about, admiring the polished woodwork and brass and then saw Peeves watching her. She gave the man a weak smile and turned hastily away, darting toward the altar and the others.

George Beal stood with the earl just in front of the first pew, the father of the bride-to-be looked more than a little pleased with himself while the groom's father looked more than a little apprehensive. The earl thought of his prodigious arguments with his wife over attending the coming ceremony. She adamantly refused to countenance the joining of "those Beals" with her son. The thought that a vulgar cit would be the future heir's grandfather rankled past endurance. Movement caught the earl's eye and he saw the butler moving around the side, casting a sharp eye towards the organ and the choir loft.

Very aware of Peeves's constant scrutiny, Becky watched the butler, sure he was on to them. Becky drifted away from Charlotte and Hero's whispered flirting, sinking to a wooden pew and praying Peeves did not find Paul hiding in the choir loft. Her mother came to join her, Becky giving a little start when her mother leaned to whisper in her ear.

"Don't worry about Peeves," Mary said, earning another startled look from her daughter. "He casts me into the high fidgets each time I see him, but your father says he is the very best and all will go exactly as planned."

"I hope so excessively," Becky said with great feeling. She earned a pat on the hand from her mother.

"There's a good girl. I was so afraid you would be cast into gloom seeing your sister marry Andrew."

"I am pleased for them both," Becky said truthfully. "If you think I'm to be cast into the sullens to see my sister happy, you're quite out. I am glad it turned out well, for Andrew's not nearly the coxcomb I thought him to be."

Mary patted her daughter's hand. "I must tell you, your father is very impressed with your recent conduct. He says you have become a biddable young miss and he thinks much good may have come from this situation even if not in the way he planned. Alice will be a lady and a countess and you've learned to obey his wishes. And I convinced your father Alice will get on with her mother-in-law much more easily than you should ever have done. "Yes," Mary said complacently, "things are working out for the best."

Becky's sigh was profound. "Oh, I most *ardently* hope so," she said with so much emotion her mother was more than a little disconcerted.

"Ladies—" the Reverend Whipple called.

"I'm so sorry, we didn't mean to interrupt," Mary Beal said with a smile.

"We are ready to rehearse the processional, as Lady Agatha suggested." The reverend cast a look upwards in time to see Fannie staring down at him. She popped back out of sight as Lady Agatha nodded to the reverend, saying she was ready. As they spoke Peeves started up the short stairwell towards the organ and the choir loft beyond.

"If you *all* will take your places—" the reverend directed, stopping Peeves on the steps.

All obeyed the reverend's commands, the opening chords of the processional beginning and Peeves leaving the loft stairs, moving swiftly towards the back of the chapel.

Up above in the organ loft Fannie Burns took a deep breath while in the hallway beyond the wedding party organized themselves. Mary Beal watched the open doorway from her seat on the bride's side of the aisle as Charlotte and Becky entered the chapel. A few paces behind them Alice entered on her father's arm, Peeves standing at attention.

"Fine," the reverend told them as they approached. "Fine, now you'll end just here, by the altar. Do we need to rehearse the service itself?"

Becky cast her eyes up towards the organ loft and met Fannie's. They shared a silent prayer as the others concentrated on the work at hand and answered the good Reverend Whipple.

18

GEORGE BEAL HAD planned on an early breakfast alone the day before Alice's wedding but Alice was already buttering toast when he walked into the dining room. She made her announcement as he reached for his coffee.

"You did *what*?" George Beal roared.

"I invited the villagers to my wedding, Papa," Alice repeated.

Mary arrived a moment later to the sounds of her husband bellowing. "Did you hear what your daughter has done?"

Mary sighed and signalled to Martha to bring her eggs. "What has Becky done now?"

"Not Becky. Alice!"

"Alice?"

"She has invited the entire village to wedding!"

"Yes, we've arranged refreshments in the servants' hall."

"She means to the *service*!" George interrupted. "We can't invite the village and not invite the Beechers and I won't have that boy in my house!"

"Papa, Andrew and I invited them personally and Lady Agatha was pleased. She feels it will be good for our family to be better known in the county and to take over the abbey obligations to the village."

"George, dear," Mary put in meekly. "The boy will hardly create a problem at the wedding. After all it is Alice who is being wed to Lord Andrew, not Becky."

"And," Alice pressed the point home, "since he knows he is in your bad books and he still hopes to convince you to let him call on Becky, he will be as quiet as a mouse. I'm sure of it."

"Too much to be hoped for," George grumbled.

Mary Beal reached for Alice's forehead. "You look a bit feverish."

"I'm perfectly well," Alice replied, trying to stop the guilty colour from staining her cheeks.

"I think she'd go back to bed," Mary said and Alice was quick to agree, glad of the chance to be off alone.

She left her mother to placate her father and escaped the room, hastening up the stairs to Becky's room.

"Did Paul get home safely?" Alice asked her sister.

"I've no way to know," Becky replied. "I'm half-frantic but I was afraid to send Meg to find out for fear his parents would find out."

"We would have heard if anything untoward had happened," Alice said, hoping the words were true. "All will be well. He knows how to get back through the secret stairway and with so many people here tomorrow morning, none will notice one more about the grounds," Alice reassured her worried sister.

"But from the stair he must come through Papa's rooms and then all the way down through the kitchens to the back hall to the chapel—" The more she thought about the dangerous course her beloved must traverse, the more worried she became. "What if one of the servants catches him out? Peeves is behaving most strangely, peering about into every nook and cranny."

"He's checking for dust the maids have missed, not looking for hidden lovers," Alice told her sister. "You must buck up and be brave. The best thing you and I can do is keep busy and not worry about what we can't control."

"That is very much easier said than done, Ally."

While Alice was reassuring her sister, below-stairs Peeves opened the door. "Miss Burns," he said, surprised a servant had come to the front door. He tried to take the large parcel she carried.

"I need to see Miss Alice," she said sharply, keeping her bundle firmly in her own hands. "This is a present from Lady Agatha for Miss Alice's wedding trip."

Alice appeared at the head of the wide stairwell. "Miss Burns? Is anything amiss?" Becky appeared beside her sister, gazing anxiously downwards.

"Nothing I know of," Fannie replied. "I have a present for you from Lady Agatha."

The girls came down the mahogany stairs to help her with the unwieldy parcel but not until they were safe behind closed doors in Becky's bed-chamber did Fannie take a deep breath.

"I said this was for Alice, but it's from Lady Agatha for you," she told Becky. "It must be fitted and Lady Agatha said I'd best help since there's so little time."

"Ohhhh—" Becky's word was a long drawn-out breath as she saw the glorious gown unfolded. It was made of cream silk and encrusted with thick creamy lace. "It's lovely . . ."

"It was a bit old-fashioned, of course, but I've changed the waist and the sleeves and—"

"It's the most beautiful thing I've ever seen," Becky said in awed tones and Alice agreed. "Not that it's more lovely than your own gown," Becky said hastily and earned a wide smile from her sister.

"You will shine like the evening star," Alice pronounced. She turned towards Fannie with a questioning look. "Was this Lady Agatha's wedding gown?"

"Yes."

"But I couldn't take her very own gown," Becky cried.

"My dear girl, you shall hurt her no end if you do not. She wants you to have it and I've already made most of the alterations. It is our wedding present to you."

Becky found tears welling up in her eyes and she wiped them away. She came forward and reached to kiss Fannie's cheek. "I must thank her in person."

Fannie shook her head. "You'll have plenty of time for that after the ceremony. Now we must get to work."

Soon Becky was standing on a chair, wearing the wedding dress while Fannie bent to place more pins in the material. Alice was helping until her sister gave her a very speaking look. Alice watched Becky's eyes go to the window behind Fannie and saw Sir Harry.

"Oh my," Alice said.

"What's amiss?" Fannie asked, her attention on the pins.

"Nothing's amiss," Alice replied.

"Yet," Becky added.

Sir Harry came through the glass. "There's no reason for worry."

"So you say," Becky replied.

"What?" Fannie asked.

"Nothing," Alice replied, giving her sister a warning look. "Miss Burns, tell us about Lady Agatha's own wedding."

"What would you like to know? She was the loveliest bride imaginable, even if an unhappy one. So young and beautiful, she could have been a fairy princess come to life."

"Why did she marry a man she did not love?" Becky asked as she watched Fannie work.

"She had no choice, her father would hear of nothing else. I think she's helping you and your Paul because she knows better than most what it means to be forced into a loveless marriage."

Sir Harry scowled and turned away. He paced the room, his hands behind his back as the romantic Becky pressed for more information. "Was there no one to rescue her?"

"None that came," Fannie replied.

"Woman, that's not fair," Sir Harry turned round and glared at the unhearing Fannie.

Alice watched Sir Harry's troubled expression. "Was she in love with another?" Alice asked.

"Aye, and the more fool she. He caused more harm and grief to her and hers than any that ever lived," Fannie replied.

"God's teeth, woman!" With a glowering look he faded away. "A gentleman does not discuss a lady's private business," he said.

Becky and Alice shared a look over the top of Fannie's bent head, their curiosity more enlivened than ever.

"He was too handsome by half," Fannie was saying more to herself than the girls. "That's what gets most into trouble, it is. Handsome is as handsome does but none pay any heed until it's too late."

"But he did truly love her," Alice objected.

"And how would you be knowing that? It all happened years before you were born."

"I—I can't imagine a man not falling in love with her," Alice replied. "Her portrait tells how beautiful she was."

"She was beautiful and he handsome and both head over teacups in love and all that came of it was shame and grief."

"Shame?" Becky asked, avid to hear more.

Fannie realised she had said too much. "It's a long time past. Turn 'round, I need to see if I've got the pins even before I stitch up the hem."

At Hargrave House the earl and the countess were argumenting in their chamber. In the billiard room on the floor below Hero Hargrave played a desultory game of billiards with Andrew. Both politely ignored the clamour from above until Andrew thrust his cue aside.

"I say, Andy, I'm sure she'll come around."

Andrew grimaced. "I'm not convinced I want Mother at the ceremony in her present state. It will only make a complicated day that much more trying."

"Good grief, what a way to describe your wedding day." Hero made his shot and put down his cue. He watched his friend closely. "Something's got you on the high ropes. You're not having second thoughts are you?"

"About Alice? Perish the thought." Andrew smiled a very real smile for the first time in several days.

"Judging by the night of the ball she has herself a temper," Hero said noncommittally.

"Aye, she's a mort o' mettle, she is," Andrew agreed contentedly.

"Good God, Andy, you've been around that village lad too much."

"Actually my London bootblack has a much more colourful vocabulary than young Paul."

"What *are* you doing with the butcher's son? And don't try to bam me with that gardening nonsense you told your parents. I know you too well."

"I am turning over new leaves," Andrew said mildly.

"You're bloody well growing entirely new branches," Hero replied. "And some of them are mighty whisty, if you ask me."

Andrew grinned. "Then I shall thank Providence that none have asked you."

"It has to do with Alice, of that I'm sure."

"Best not bet on it."

"Then what is it?"

"A deep dark secret," Andrew said, unable to tell Hero the truth and unwilling to tell him a bouncer.

"You must tell me all."

"It's not mine to tell. If it were I should have confided in you long since, for I would have been glad of your advice and help."

"Help, advice, long since, eh? And not yours to tell. Lord, don't tell me there's some worse Beal secret you've yet to foist upon your unsuspecting mother!"

Andrew's chagrin showed but he tried to cover it with a disarming smile. "Hardly likely."

"I agree it would be hard to find anything your mother would put past the infamous *pere* and *mere* Beal. Now let me see—"

"I can't tell you and that's flat. At least not yet."

"Then when?" Hero demanded.

"Tomorrow," Andrew said, "you will know all."

"Then I shall not tell you my secret until the morrow," Hero replied. Rewarded by a quizzical stare, Hero smiled. "Ah ha, you thought yourself the only one with secrets to keep, did you? Well, you're totally wet, because I've also got private business pending. I swear I should make you wait but I can't contain myself. I'm thinking of offering for Charlotte Summerville."

Andrew was truly surprised. "Charlotte who? Oh, I remember, the Spanish-looking beauty. But she's been out for ages. You told me yourself she was firmly on the shelf."

"And that I'd know her forever but only across a crowded room, that sort of thing. And she is three years, so we never had much congress until now."

"Are you serious?" Andrew asked.

"I'm not quite sure," Hero replied. "But I find the idea intriguing. And the parents would be pleased as punch. Good family, good reputation and country-bred, a bit older and more sensible to settle me down, don't you see?"

"My Lord, I think you are serious. Well, I wish you happy, that you know."

"It might be good for me." Hero would have said more but the earl walked in, telling Andrew his mother wished to see him.

The countess watched with reproachful eyes as her son entered the chamber, the earl just behind. "Your father is determined to encourage these people to feel themselves above their station by insisting that we attend this horrid affair."

"I doubt it possible to convince George Beal that he is *below* anyone's station," Andrew said mildly.

"He is a boorish oaf who shows no sensitivity to our rank and the respect due it. He speaks to your father as if they were bosom bows and to me in such a light as he might just as well be talking to his wife or—or a washer-woman."

"He treats none better," Andrew defended.

"And is that supposed to be a recommendation?" his mother cried.

"I shall marry his daughter on the morrow," Andrew replied.

"I simply cannot feature being related to that family."

"You brought me to Dorset to make just such a match," her son reminded her.

"That was before I had met them," she said with a darkling look at his father. "And I was very much opposed to the trip from the beginning. However, I shall swallow my pride for the sake of your happiness."

"Thank you, Mother," Andrew said with sinking heart. He could not imagine what his mother's reactions would be before the ceremony was over but he very much doubted he would ever hear the end of it.

While the Countess of Marleigh was swallowing her pride and agreeing to grace the wedding with her presence Lady

Agatha sat alone in a rocking chair near her bed-chamber window in the abbey gatehouse. The packet of yellowing letters were on her lap as she looked out across the country-side, her thoughts many years away. She looked down at the letters, fingering the fading red riband. Slowly, she unravelled it, retrieving the top letter from its envelope and opening it.

"My dearest one, they would not let me near, and you do not answer my pleas."

Lady Agatha did not read further. She refolded the letter and closed her eyes. The fading daylight outside her win-dow unseen, she drifted off into dreams of the past.

In the village, the shops were closing. Molly Beecher already in the family apartment above the butcher shop was arguing with her husband.

"There's naught reason to go," her husband said.

"All are going to the wedding. We'll look bad for being the only ones not. It's not just the money they bring us, Tom, it's Lady Agatha's wish as well. Miss Burns came in to buy a joint and said her ladyship wanted us there especial."

Tom Beecher looked at his quiet son. "And you think we should go, I suppose, so you've got a chance to see the young Becky."

"I would do anything Lady Agatha asked," Paul answered truthfully.

"And anything young Becky asked too," his father retorted. "There's naught to be gained by mooning over a wench you can never woo or wed."

"I was planning on cleaning out the hen house at first light," Paul told his father. "And fixing old Belle's harness as I promised."

Molly Beecher smiled. "Now, there's a thought. We can pay our respects and no reason for young Paul to have to trek up too if he has chores to do."

"Aye, mayhap," her husband answered grudgingly. "But only for a bit, mind you, as I've got plenty of work meself."

"That's settled then," Molly said.

19

THE NEXT MORNING dawned clear and cold, the cloudless blue sky slowly warming as the morning sun rose over the abbey hill. Fires had been stoked all night in the abbey kitchens, buckets of bazing-hot water already waiting to be tipped into tin hip-baths in the upstairs bedrooms. The staff was up before dawn to insure all would be readiness for the family and the onslaught of wedding guests.

Peeves was at once ordering last minute details, his strict manner and forbidding face keeping the maids mute and the footmen in their place.

Alice woke to hear the morning cock crows in the distance, twittering birds adding their music to the spring morning. Toasty-warm beneath comforters and covers, Alice stretched lazily, a contented smile playing across her pretty face until she thought of Becky and Paul. The thought made her sit straight up, the sounds outside her closed bed-chamber door resolving themselves into individual meanings. Someone was sweeping the upper hallway, Peeves speaking in low early-morning tones to one of the footmen. All was hustle and bustle in the upper hallways which were normally silent until the family were up.

Paul Beecher was to traverse this obstacle course as early as possible this morning to avoid detection. Alice squeezed her eyes shut, offering up a prayer that he was already in the attic. If not he would never be able to get past the phalanx of troops Peeves had unwittingly placed in his path.

Paul Beecher was not in the comparative safety of the abbey attics. At the very moment Alice was offering up prayers, the young man was crouched behind a large elm tree on the west side of the abbey, a wide expanse of open lawn between where he stood and the rose bushes that hid the ancient secret door.

At the far end of the line of early-blooming peach and pink roses a gardener was cutting blooms for the wedding bouquets. In a quandary, Paul did not hear the approaching horse hooves until the animal was almost upon him. He turned, his back against the thick elm, and looked up to see Andrew reining in beside him. With a swift glance towards the gardener beyond, Andrew spoke in a low tone.

"I thought I'd best ride over early and see if my services were needed."

"Aye and I'm that glad, your lordship. I've been crouched here so long I feared my back would turn curved and never straighten out."

"Won't your parents wonder where you've got to?" Andrew asked the butcher's son.

Paul looked sheepish. "I told them I'd be off early to deliver more chicken to Hargrave House."

Andrew groaned. "More chicken."

"Aye, that's what my ma said."

"Couldn't you think of something other than chicken?" Paul regarded the young lord with honest brown eyes. "I'm not that good at telling bouncers, your lordship. I wasn't sure what else you might be wanting to eat."

"I can assure you I never want to see another chicken in my entire life. I cringe at the thought that the Hargrave cook will report my demented desire for multitudinous chicken dishes to my friends' cooks and thus seal my doom. A diet of chicken for life. Thank God this farce is soon over or I should have begun clucking for I'll tell you flat none else in the household wished to partake of the bloody little beggars after the second meal."

In the distance the gardener straightened up, his hand going to the small of his back. He glanced about as he caught sight of rider and horse stopped by the large elm.

"Stay still," Andrew warned. "He's looking our way."

"What do we do?"

"We can't stay here or he's sure to think I've rats in my upper storey. Keep pace with Goliath's hind legs until we're near the bushes. I'll distract the man as you make for the hidden door and be quick about it for we've no idea who else is about."

Suiting action to words Lord Andrew walked his huge black stallion towards the house at a sedate pace. The gardener heard the horseman approach and glanced up.

"I say," Lord Andrew called out. Determined to keep the man's eyes on his own face and not drifting off to where Paul hid alongside, Andrew spoke in a peremptory fashion.

Recognising the aristocratic tone of authority the gardener tugged at his forelock and came towards the young nobleman. "Yes, your lordship?"

"Damn and blast, he's coming this way. You'd best make for the door," Andrew spoke under his breath as he turned directly towards the gardener, putting Goliath's rump between the man and Paul. Paul slipped behind the row of thorny rose bushes, doubled over and moved as quietly as he could.

"I want to take a look 'round the gardens," Andrew said in loud tones, hoping to drown out the scrabbling sounds Paul made as he moved behind the bushes. "Please see that my bags are deposited safely inside and see to my mount."

The gardener thought the young man must be a bit deaf by the way he shouted. He reached for the reins the young lord handed over as he dismounted. Andrew assumed a properly attentive mien and bent to an inspection of the nearest bushes. The gardener stared at the bush his lordship seemed so taken with. It was a plain cabbage-rose bush like a thousand others. Muttering to himself about the ways of the gentry, the gardener walked the horse away, leaving Lord Andrew to his strange pursuits.

Andrew straightened up, saw the man was still not gone, and bent towards another bush, peering intently at the rose petals whilst the gardener disappeared around the corner of the house. Safely alone, Andrew sped towards the secret door Alice had shown him, snagging the arm of his hacking jacket as he pushed behind a bush and reached for a narrow stone slab. It gave with the pressure, the tiny narrow door opening into what looked to be a black hole. Andrew ducked inside and shoved the stone slab closed, breathing more easily once he was inside.

"Paul?" he called out in a sharp whisper.

"Aye, I'm here," Paul's muffled reply came from somewhere nearby and above.

Feeling his way, Andrew started up the narrow stone steps that wound upwards in corkscrew circles. He bumped into Paul half-way ahead.

"Let me get past and clear the way outside," Andrew said, although a moment's reflexion would have told him George Beal was likely to be as stunned by Lord Andrew stepping out of his bed-chamber wardrobe as he would be by Paul Beecher's similar appearance.

The huge oak wardrobe had been built into the wall in Tudor times for the express purpose of hiding the end of the secret stairwell. As capacious as it was, it was still cramped quarters for men the size of Andrew and Paul.

Andrew reached for the knob on the inside of the wardrobe door. Holding his breath, Andrew pushed against the wood. The door swung open, revealing the stiff dark master bed-chamber, heavy drapes drawn against the encroaching morning sunlight. The sound of snoring came from the huge carved bed across the large room, giving the two young men momentary pause.

Paul shrank back into the dank dark stairwell but Andrew reached for his arm and propelled him forward. They made it to the sitting room and paused at the hall door regaining their held breath and listening.

Andrew told himself they could not stay where they were, nor go back, so they'd best go forward. He took a deep breath and opened the door. A startled maid stopped her dusting across the wide hall. Seeing the master's door opening so early she averted her eyes and scurried towards the servants' stairs and the kitchens below to alert them Mr. Beal was rising early.

Motioning Paul forward, Andrew moved with hurried steps to the servants' stairs and up to the unoccupied third floor nurseries and schoolrooms and the door to the attic stairs. Paul kept close behind Andrew as they reached the attic.

In whispered tones Andrew told Paul to make quick work of donning his wedding finery. They looked about to find the parcel of clothes Andrew had sent to the abbey.

Sir Harry wafted up the stairwell, a grimace plain across his ghostly face. "Stop banging about. You'll have the entire household up here."

Paul Beecher's brown eyes widened into saucers. "It's him I'm seeing again," he said to Andrew.

"I see you've already met Sir Harry," Andrew replied.

Paul was looking from the ghost to Andrew. "Sir Harry?" he questioned.

"Yes?" Harry answered, staring into the young man's frightened eyes.

Paul gulped. "It has a name, then, and all—"

"He does indeed," Andrew agreed.

"I've not gone barmy with worriting about all this then."

"I should say not," Andrew replied.

Sir Harry glowered. "No more so than he ever was at any rate." The ghost drifted towards a trunk. "They put his mish and the rest in this one," he pointed with a ghostly white finger. "I shall stay and advise him on his appearance whilst you, young lord, had best hie yourself back to where you are supposed to be before any catch you out."

Paul Beecher was set to argue but Andrew explained the sense of the ghost's instructions. As Andrew left the attic Sir Harry was impatiently coming to Paul's sartorial rescue. "No, no, that's a cummerbund, *this* is your cravat!"

"I know which is which but I'll be stuck in the nitch if I know how to nabble a starched neck cloth and get it about me the proper way."

Sir Harry gave forth a deep, heartfelt and ghostly sigh. "I can see this will take even longer than I expected."

Andrew heard no more as he closed the attic door and started towards the servants' stairs. Behind him Mary Beal reached the top of the front stairs and saw the tall figure headed away. "Who goes there?" she called, startling Andrew. "Lord Andrew?" she exclaimed when he turned around to face her, a weak smile upon his lips.

"Please," he came swiftly towards the little woman, "Mrs. Beal, since I am to be your son-in-law, I insist you call me Andrew." His hand to her elbow, he propelled her back towards the front stairwell.

"Thank you, Andrew. I was just going to see if I could find a box of gloves in the attic—"

"Ah, but you can't! That is to say," Andrew prevaricated, thinking furiously fast, "you see, ah, Becky needs help with her dress and I was sent to fetch you."

Mary Beal's eyes widened. "*You* were sent to fetch me?"

They reached the next floor, almost running into Peeves as he came up the stairs to check on the linens.

Peeves stared at the young man. "My Lord, I was not aware you had arrived."

"I, ah, came early to examine the, ah, gardens."

"The gardens?" Peeves repeated. "Of course, your lordship." He cast a glance towards the upper floor. "What were you looking for upstairs," Mary asked innocently. "There's naught there but the old schoolrooms and nurseries. And the attics."

"Just so," Andrew said. "I am designing new nurseries for Marleigh House—and gardens," he added hastily.

Mary Beal blushed. "It's not delicate to speak of such things as yet."

"Must always be prepared," Andrew said bracingly. "That's my family motto."

"How very practical of you," Mary managed to say.

"The girls shouldn't have sent you, that's quite too fresh of them even if we are to be made family today." She stopped in her tracks, looking alarmed. "You haven't seen Alice this morning, have you? It's bad luck."

"No, I have not," Andrew answered truthfully.

"Good. It's best if you don't wander about up here so as to accidently run into each other," Mary said as they paused outside Becky's bed-chamber.

Alice was helping Becky into Lady Agatha's wedding dress. When they heard their mother and Andrew. "Go away," called Alice. "Andrew mustn't see me!"

Andrew grabbed Mary Beal's arm as she reached for the door. "What are you doing?" Mary asked.

"Alice. I—I'm not to see Alice—"

Mary Beal disentangled her arm from the hand that attempted to pull her back from the door. "Andrew," she said in firm accents, "there is no reason I should not see my daughter and you yourself said Becky had sent to fetch me. Alice," Mary called, "I am coming in."

Andrew, try as hard as he might, could not think of a reply in the time it took for Mary Beal to open the door. Casting his eyes heavenwards he turned and moved towards the stairs. Peeves watched, his face a study in quickly masked confusion.

"Would you care for something, your lordship?" Peeves asked in neutral tones.

"Tea," Andrew affirmed. "*Strong* tea," he amended as he followed the butler towards the ground floor and the dining rooms beyond.

Becky was covered from toes to chin by bedcovers when their mother walked in, asking why they had sent for her.

"Sent for you?" Alice repeated blankly.

"Andrew said he was sent to fetch me," Mary Beal told her daughter. "But he vowed he had not seen you."

"Oh, no," Alice quickly agreed. "He had not."

"Becky, why are you still abed?" Mary asked coming near.

Becky cast an imploring glance towards her sister and Alice gulped and began to speak. "It's on that head that we called for you, Mama," Alice paused and then rushed on dramatically, "We're frightened for her health!"

"Her health?"

Becky tried to look ill as her sister continued to speak. "Yes, Mama, she'll not be able to attend the ceremony."

"Nonsense," Mary said calmly. "You girls do get such notions."

At this Becky began to moan. Her startled mother felt her forehead. "She does seem a bit feverish, but she was right as rain when I woke her."

"It came on quickly," Alice fibbed. "Getting up and walking about must have done it. She'll never be able to be a bridesmaid this day. Will you, Becky?"

Becky moaned again and closed her eyes.

"Oh, dear, I hope this doesn't mean things will all start to go awry. Peeves will be ever so upset." She felt her daughter's forehead again. "She does feel feverish."

"She feels simply dreadful," Alice said hopefully. Becky emitted another little groan and looked properly woebegone. "And the ceremony shall be perfectly all right," Alice continued. "Charlotte shall still be my bridesmaid, so we really don't need Becky and all is well," she ended brightly.

"Alice Elizabeth Beal," her mother remonstrated, "I have never heard you so lacking in fellow-feeling."

"I mean for Peeves," Alice said quickly.

"Mama," Becky said quickly, "Ally's got the right of it. I shall feel ever so much better knowing everything is going forward with the wedding and me not fainting or something in the middle of it. You must go right now and see to every little detail so that all will be well. I'll feel ever so much better if I'm just left alone to suffer in peace."

"Doing it too brown," Alice said in an undertone but Becky merely batted her long eyelashes at her sister and then looked towards her mother with a pitiful expression on her lovely face.

"I truly would like to be alone," Becky repeated.

"I suppose it's the best thing," Mary said doubtfully. As she spoke she reached to check Alice's forehead. "Are you feeling quite well?"

"I'm fine," Alice told her mother. She drew her away from Becky's bed and towards the door. "But I need your help with my bridal toilette. Margaret is all thumbs today and young Meg worse than useless. Besides, we don't want to catch whatever Becky's got and give it to the earl and the countess and everyone."

At that horrible thought Mary Beal allowed herself to be drawn out of Becky's room. Alice gave her sister a wink as she closed the door and followed her mother down the hall.

Becky waited until their footsteps receded before sitting up. She was rising from the bed when a tap at her door sent her diving back under the covers.

"Miss Becky?" Fannie called out softly.

"Yes, come in," Becky answered.

Fannie came through the door alone. "All this skulking about has aged me ten years. I was afraid it was Mama coming back. Am I crushed beyond repair?" she asked as she came around the bed towards Fannie and the pier glass.

Fannie muttered to herself about meddling relatives as she shook out the organdy and silk folds and attempted to repair the damage.

The sounds of arriving guests wafted up the abbey stairwells towards the attics high above.

"You are as ready as you are likely to be," Sir Harry told Paul Beecher. "I must say, you clean up tolerably well, young man, when put in proper clothes. I own I never thought you could possibly cut such an elegant figure."

Uncomfortable in the borrowed formal attire, Paul glanced down at himself. "Are you sure I look as I ought?"

"Actually you look quite *comme il faut*," the ghost replied honestly.

A look of panic met Sir Harry's words. "What's wrong with it?" Paul asked.

Sir Harry grimaced. "Nothing," he replied. "That was a compliment."

"I'd rather have them in English so that I can understand the meaning," Paul told the ghost.

"You're not likely to get many in life so you'd best be grateful for any that do come your way," was Sir Harry's considered opinion. "In whatever language."

"This day is bound to end up a bloody disaster," Paul said gloomily.

"You may think what you like," the ghost replied, "but I am determined the wedding ceremony will be a success."

"And what good will that do when my pa is sure to kill me as soon as he claps eyes on his son dressed up like a dandy and finds out the truth of it all. My ma will most likely burst into tears and the five girls will throw fits because their ma is crying."

"Five girls?" Sir Harry asked.

"Me sisters. From two to twelve, and me the only boy."

"I should think your father would cry tears of joy to see some of Beal's silver and gold come into the family coffers at the thought of five dowries to be gotten up."

"I've no notion about getting dowries for the girls," Paul answered. "I just hope they're not along to see all this and start whooping and yelling when they see me. They've been at my grandmurm's for one got the measles and all others followed. Mayhap they're not well yet and won't come, if I'm lucky." A new idea made him look a little happier. "Mayhap the wee ones are still so sick me ma will have to stay with them. If she does, Pa won't come alone, he never wanted to come from the first of it." Another thought made his happiness turn back into sombre reflexion. "Even so and even if we've the luck to get away with it and be well and truly married, Mr. Beal will likely have me drawn and quartered."

"Very likely," the ghost agreed.

"Or mayhap a firing squad," Paul continued, cast into gloom by the future that lay ahead of him.

"One can always run," Sir Harry offered. "If one is a coward."

Nettled, Paul cast a glance towards the apparition he tried to avoid looking directly upon. "None's ever called a Beecher coward."

"Good, that's settled then," Sir Harry replied. "Follow me."

Paul started after the ghost only to stop as Harry drifted through the wall. "I can't go through there," Paul objected in a louder whisper than the one in which he had been carrying on their conversation. "It's a wall."

Sir Harry reappeared and pointed. "Use the door."

Looking sheepish, Paul moved towards the steps, awkward in ill-fitting highly polished, black leather boots. Paul and Andrew were of a similar size but Paul's feet were enough broader that Andrew's boots pinched.

Paul made the next floor without incident and nearly made it down the next flight of the servants' stairs before the sound of a maid rising up the narrow stairwell came towards him. Harry motioned Paul back up and into a servant's room just before the maid passed by.

"How far is it from here to the chapel?" Paul whispered.

"Too bloody far," the ghost replied as he passed through the wooden door and made sure their path was once again clear.

20

THE GUESTS WERE all in place, aristocrats rubbing elbows with villagers much to the chagrin of each.

Leticia Merriweather spied Margaret Summerville across the aisle and stood up, excusing her way back out from her seat and crossing the aisle to plunk herself down beside Charlotte's mother.

"I hope I'm not crowding you, Margaret, dear," the plump and aging widow said as she crowded in beside the unwelcoming elder Summerville. "But I simply had to have a small word with you. I've heard tell your lovely Charlotte has been enjoying the attention of the young Lord Hargrave." Letty looked around them and dropped her voice to a conspiratorial whisper. "I must warn you, my dear, it is bruited about in the best circles that young Hero has a most unsavoury reputation. A word to the wise, as it were."

Margaret Summerville's head rose. Even seated she was a good half-foot taller than her companion and she made the most of her stature, staring down her acquiline nose at Leticia, her voice icy. "I have no wish to hear gossip about the dear boy."

"I was merely trying to help," Leticia replied in angelic tones.

"Thank you," Margaret replied acidly. "But although I have allowed interference in the past Charlotte is still unmarried and beggars can no longer be choosers. I wish to hear no more gossip, Mrs. Merriweather." Having completed her put-down, Margaret Summerville turned away and deliberately ignored the little widow. Leticia Merriweather was not of a sensitive temperament. She slipped out of her seat and made her way back across the aisle to tell her seat companions Hero Hargrave was on the very verge of offering for dear Charlotte Summerville and him so much younger.

Another ripple of gossip enlivened the Tudor chapel when Molly and Tom Beecher entered and checked on the threshold. With them were Paul's five young sisters who stared around themselves in open-mouthed awe but Paul himself was not with the small entourage. Stories of the abbey ball made their way around the room together with conjectures about the reason for Paul's absence, the consensus being George Beal would not allow the boy in his house and more's the pity since Paul Beecher was such a fine upstanding young man. If anything was havey-cavey between Paul and Becky Beal the villagers knew who to blame and it was the hoyden Becky, not the honest young Paul.

Lady Agatha came through the doorway, followed by Fannie. Lady Agatha greeted the Beechers with a smile as they paused on the threshold, the girls pushing to move forward, the parents looking as if they might turn and flee, dragging the girls with them. Lady Agatha spoke with Molly and Tom, ushering them to seats very near the altar. Fannie came behind, helping to herd the awestruck girls forward. They'd never seen the inside of the abbey before nor such a stained glass window as the one high above their heads where the Archangel Michael with widespread arms protected a very much smaller than himself village and abbey. In flowing white robes and with feathery golden wings, the angel stretched out across the azure sky, rainbows radiating from his arms and falling towards the green of the village and the silver of the abbey.

Fannie gave the last girl a little push into her seat on the pew beside her parent before following Lady Agatha on up the side aisle towards the short flight of steps to the organ and choir lofts.

Tom Beecher leaned towards his wife and spoke in gruff low tones. "Why'd she put us so near the front?"

His wife's answer was tart. "Her ladyship probably wanted to keep you in your seat instead of letting you sneak out the back when none were looking. Now sit up and smile unless you want the county to be asking why Tom Beecher isn't man enough to face a few gossipy females."

"I'll show you man enough, Mrs. Beecher," Tom told his wife.

"You'd just better," she told her big bear of a husband. "For Lady Agatha saw to our comfort and none others, so you'd best be on your good behaviour."

The Reverend Mr. Whipple arrived in the chapel, taking his place in front of the altar. An acolyte in a starched white surplice followed behind the reverend, looking properly solemn for the grand occasion. The reverend gentleman glanced towards the closed chapel doors and nodded to Peeves. Then he looked upward towards where Fannie Burns was peering anxiously over the organ loft railing. At his nod Fannie whispered to Lady Agatha and the dulcet yet strangely melancholy chords of pipe organ music began to reverberate throughout the chapel and to the halls and rooms beyond.

In the empty choir loft, uncomfortable in borrowed finery, Paul Beecher crouched out of sight of the assembled throng and prayed all would go well. When he opened his eyes he saw the ghost at the edge of the choir loft, watching Lady Agatha with loving eyes as she played the Bach strains that signalled the beginning of the processional.

Fannie Burns sat on a narrow wood chair behind Lady Agatha, her attention never leaving her mistress. Not daring to look towards the choir loft where she knew Paul should be hiding, Fannie kept her eyes on the pipe organ and Lady Agatha's dexterous hands as the late morning sun streamed thorough the high stained glass window and rained its rainbows down upon the guests in the oaken pews below.

The Countess of Marleigh leaned towards the elder Lord Hargrave, just last night arrived from London to join his son and guests. "Giles, I am dreadfully sorry to drag you to such a spectacle."

Giles Hargrave, father of Hero and well-known London raconteur, smiled. "Nonsense. Must do our duty to the county after all." He lifted his quizzing glass to one bland blue eye and then stared rather obviously at the assemblage around him. "By Gad, are all these rustics relatives of the bride?"

Her answer was precluded as Andrew and Hero came from the vestry and took their places directly beside the Reverend Whipple. As they stood waiting for the arrival of the bride Hero gave his oldest friend a sidelong look and spoke in a whisper.

"Holding up, old man?"

"Never better," Andrew replied in an equally low voice. "You must try this one day."

"I just might do that," Hero replied. You never told me what you thought of Charlotte Summerville."

Andrew shot an appraising glance at his friend. "Are you seriously dangling after her? I think she's a bit long in the tooth for you," he saw Hero frown and grinned. "But winsome," Andrew continued, seeing Hero's expression changing. "Very winsome."

The music changed, Charlotte Summerville herself appearing at the open chapel doors. Dressed in cherry-coloured silk, her sleeves shot at the shoulders with long silver ribands that fluttered out around her, she walked sedately towards the altar. After a moment Andrew saw his very own Alice coming towards him upon her father's arm and he smiled wide, all else but his bride forgotten.

No matter her many heartfelt reservations concerning the Beal family, the Countess of Marleigh had to own to herself that Alice herself was truly beautiful in a snow white gown of gauze and lace. One of the Marleigh family heirloom coronets winked diamond starlight from amongst her auburn curls.

Alice clung to her father's beefy arm, her eyes full of stars as she looked into Andrew's loving gaze. With all eyes on the bride and groom below none saw Paul Beecher as his head shot up over the choir loft railing.

"You silly son of a gut merchant," Sir Harry's whisper was loud in Paul's ear, "Do you want to ruin the work of a lifetime? Deathtime. Whatever. This may be the deed that sets me free if I can pull it off and you bouncing about like a jack-in-the-box!" Sir Harry ended more irritated than when he began.

While bride and groom looked expectantly at Mr. Whipple, while Sir Harry glowered at young Paul, Lady Agatha was speaking in a hurried whisper to her abigail. "You'd best go below."

Fannie Burns heard the words with sinking heart. She stood up, moving slowly down the short narrow stairwell and slipping out along the side aisle towards the doors to the hall. As she moved the Countess of Marleigh noticed movement in the comer of her eye and glanced towards the aisle and then the choir loft. "Is someone bobbing about in the loft?" she asked her husband.

"Shush," her husband replied as the Reverend Whipple intoned the solemn words that would make Alice his son's wife.

Across the aisle, on the bride's side of the church, Mary Beal watched her daughter with such love and happiness that tears were streaming down her cheeks as Alice and Andrew exchanged their vows of never-ending fidelity in front of God and the entire assemblage.

"I now pronounce you man and wife," Mr. Whipple intoned in solemn measure. Andrew, still holding Alice's hand squeezed it gently as the clergyman gave the benediction.

The recessional music began, the assemblage waiting for the bride and groom to turn away from the altar. Instead, Andrew gave his bride a quick kiss on the cheek and left her at the altar, walking alone down the aisle.

His startled viewers looked from his rapid departure to his smiling but obviously nervous bride who put her hand on the minister's arm and whispered frantically into his ear. He seemed ready to depart but paused to stare towards the back of the chapel.

"What is it?" George asked his wife as she turned in her seat in the front pew and peered towards the back of the chapel.

"Who on earth is *that*?" Hero's father asked, his voice carrying across the chapel. At his lordship's startled cry all eyes turned towards the aisle where Fannie was slowly walking forward, a bouquet of roses in her hands, her eyes riveted to the floor. Behind her Lord Andrew escorted Becky who seemed timid for the first time in anyone's memory. Dressed in ivory lace, with roses in her honey-coloured curls, she looked to be an angel come down to earth. They moved slowly down the aisle, the pipe organ accompanying their progress. As they moved forward Andrew pressed the hand Becky had upon his arm.

"Courage," Andrew said in firm undertones. "You don't want to let your poor besotted Paul down, now do you? He'll never recover. Nor probably ever leave that blasted loft. Doomed to haunt it forever, waiting for his bride to come down the aisle."

Andrew earned a small smile from Becky and then they were in front of the Reverend Mr. Whipple and Alice was leaning to kiss her sister's cheeks.

"What is happening?" Charlotte asked in querulous tones when Fannie took her place as a bridesmaid, Hero repeating the same question in lower tones.

"Hang in there just a bit, old man," Andrew told Hero. "And you will have a story of fireworks to tell your grandchildren about in the years to come."

Hero stared at his friend as Lord Andrew looked up towards the stairs from the loft.

In the loft, lost from view, Sir Harry urged Paul Beecher forward. "Damn and blast, we've not gone to all this trouble to see you the ruin of it. Get you down there lad!"

"I can't—my knees have turned to cheese."

"Cheese or not, you'll go down those stairs if I have to push you down them," Sir Harry said in no uncertain tones. "I've not languished as a ghost for all these years, waiting for my release, just to have a young scapegrace such as you end all my hopes!"

Paul was backing away from the ghost who encroached ever so slowly forward, inch by inch, until Paul was on the steps and a great gasp went up from the assemblage.

Once committed, the clatter of his feet overcame the organ music for a few brief moments and then Lady Agatha reasserted the power of Bach, drowning out Paul's awkward steps as the assembled guests watched the butcher's son, in formal wedding attire, move to stand beside Hero Hargrave.

Hero gave the young man a long questioning look. "I say, old chap, have we met?"

Andrew gently shoved Paul to his place beside Becky and in front of the Reverend Whipple as Tom Beecher realised the young man in formal finery was his son. Tom called out Paul's name, George hearing it in the same moment that he realised the boy was beside Becky and in front of the priest.

Andrew heard the muttered oaths behind them and pressed the special licence Lady Agatha had procured into the man's hand. "Hurry, man!"

"I don't understand what you are expecting to do," the reverend told the small knot of young people. "This is highly irregular."

"You *must* marry them *immediately*," Alice said urgently. "*Lives* are at stake!"

Mr. Whipple misinterpreted the words of urgency. He frowned, balancing his sense of morals against his duty as a man of God. Andrew grabbed back the paper and unfolded it. It's a special licence. Lady Agatha used her influence to obtain it."

"This is most unusual," the clergyman said again but he turned towards the assemblage and said. "Who gives this bride away?"

There was dead silence in the church and then a clear, firm voice spoke out. "I, her brother-in-law, do," Andrew replied.

Andrew's mother rose from her seat, the earl standing as his wife arose. "My God, now my son plans to be related to the butcher!" Her words rang out across the small stone chapel as she raised one pale hand to her eyes and fainted dead away. She fell back against her husband, her body moving inelegantly even in a swoon as she slipped into his arms and down to the oaken pew.

"Wait just one minute there!" George Beal bellowed, coming out of his shock and very vocal as he started forward. Not to be outdone, Tom Beecher stood up and started forward towards the young couple.

Sir Harry was above the two fathers waiting for them to make their moves. He reached for the bronze candelabrum hanging above their heads and ordered the brass links that held it to its perch to melt. Pleased with their swift reaction to his concentration, he watched the links dissolve, the huge and heavy brass holder slamming down to the stone floor immediately in front of George Beal's feet and nearly upon his head. Thrown back against Tom Beecher, they both lost their balance and went crashing to the floor.

As they tried to scramble to their feet shouts of surprise came up from all around them as something huge and black came swooping down from the rafters.

Andrew urged the priest to continue as pandemonium began to reign all around the tiny group at the altar. Sir Harry, spreading his black velvet cloak wide, rushed down upon the men, emitting fierce sounds which they did not hear. But the dark apparition, very much like a huge bat, made a sound as if storm winds were roaring through the chapel, the sound almost deafening.

Fannie Burns looked from the hesitant clergyman to the forestalled fathers. Grasping the situation at once and realising something must be done, Fannie raced away from the altar and towards the two fathers, screaming to the guests they must flee. "The Abbey Ghost is upon us! Flee for your lives!"

"Good for you, wench," Sir Harry encouraged from the ceiling above as he swooped back down. Since Fannie could not hear the ghost his encouragement did her little good but she ran forward anyway, screaming that the ghost would get them all. Confusion erupted, the villagers more openly superstitious but the aristocratic guests reacting with very near the same frenzy.

Villagers and aristocrats alike were on their feet, shoving out into the aisles and forcing their way towards the back of the chapel. The swell of humanity blocked George Beal and Tom Beecher as they tried to move forward, shoving them two steps back each time the men tried to forge forwards. Together they shoved and swore and finally George Beal struggled past the last of the onslaught and forced his way towards Reverend Whipple. Tom Beecher came close behind, his fists ready for any comers as the reverend intoned the final words, "I now pronounce you man and wife."

"No!" Tom Beecher shouted.

"You cannot marry those two!" George Beal bellowed.

"It would seem, I already have done," Mr. Whipple replied as the bride pulled her husband into her arms and kissed him long and hard.

21

THE GUESTS CONGREGATED on the lawns, milling about and once out into the sunlight feeling rather foolish. People spoke of the strange and ferocious wind in the chapel, amazed that none were hurt, the talk of a ghost better left unspoken when none could rightly say they'd seen much more than a strange shadow. A trick of light. And the wind must have gone down as fast as it came up since all was serene outside, the terraces massed with huge tables of food and drink, the vast lawns invitingly strewn with chairs. The fact that the chapel had no open windows through which a wind could have come was better left unsaid.

Stories of the Abbey Ghost were whispered amongst some of the guests on the terraces and at the refreshment tables but most preferred to ignore the unexplainable and put a more discreet label to the strange goings-on. None departed, all speaking of the shock of the double wedding and the fact that the families had still not made an appearance.

While gossip was rife outside, inside the abbey library George Beal and Tom Beecher were closeted with Mr. Whipple, irately demanding he undo what he had just done.

"Only God can undo what has been done," Mr. Whipple told the irate men. "Aside from which you certainly do not want your grandchild to be nameless." Having struck both men dumb, the reverend smiled complacently and went in search of his tea and refreshment.

In the red parlour, midst admonitions that they should not have kept such things from their mother, Mary Beal was hugging first one daughter and then the other as their new husbands looked on.

After a shy pause Mary reached to hug Andrew and then gave Paul a long searching look before finally reaching to hug him too. Mary saw Molly Beecher in the doorway, her daughters shoving close around her in the hall beyond.

"I . . . I was looking to find Mr. Beecher," Molly said hesitantly.

Mary Beal went towards Paul's mother, urging her to come inside and greet her new daughter-in-law. "Please join us," Mary said, her open heart going out to the young girls who hovered about their mother. "Shall we find you some lovely cakes?"

"Ma." Paul came towards his mother, Becky beside him. "Please give us your blessing."

"Is it my blessing you now want?" Molly asked her son. She looked from her son's happy face to his bride's glowing expression and her heart melted. "You've never kept things from me in your life."

"Nor will I again," Paul promised.

"I can't think what your father will be saying to all this," Molly said.

"You must make him see the sense of it," Andrew said, earning questioning looks from the others as he continued. "As Mr. Beal must too. After all, everyone's got what they wanted."

Paul Beecher stared at his new brother-in-law. "I don't see how you'll convince my father of that."

"Just think, all of you," Andrew included the others as he looked from one to the next. "Alice and I are in love and are married. Paul and Becky are in love and are married. Both you, Mrs. Beal, and you, Mrs. Beecher, want what's best for your children, so you must be happy for us." He saw their expressions change and pressed his point home. "You can see I have the right of it, and even your own girls, Mrs. Beecher, shall in the end profit from this day's work."

The girls, hearing themselves spoken of quieted, their eyes rounded as they listened to the tall, handsome lord in his black velvet wedding finery talk about their rosy futures. They stuffed themselves with tea cakes and reached for more of the sweet confections as the adults talked on and on.

George Beal interrupted Andrew from the doorway. "I must say I am more disappointed in you, Andrew, and Alice, than I am in the others. I expect no good sense from Becky." Becky began to protest her father's words but he continued over her protests. "She's never had any, nor do I expect any more from any fellow she could bamboozle into doing her bidding."

"You've not got the right of it, Mr. Beal," Paul put in.

George Beal's face turned even angrier. "And I'll not talk to a man who gets a good girl to traipse about behind her father's back"

"Papa!" Alice objected.

"And," George continued, "getting her into trouble!"

"I never did!" Paul defended.

"Mr. Whipple says otherwise!" George Beal shouted.

"Just a minute here," Tom Beecher came in behind Becky's father. "My son would never have clapped an eye on your Becky if she hadn't been traipsing about alone in the first place!"

"He clapped more than an eye by the looks of it," George sputtered.

"One moment, gentlemen," Andrew interjected smoothly. "Before you come to fisticuffs, might I remind you there are ladies present and that your ire is misspent in ranting against a marriage of true love."

"Nonsense," George Beal began.

"*Papa!*" Becky stamped her foot against the turkey carpet.

"Mr. Beecher," Andrew continued before any more could interrupt, "has five lovely daughters to think of and I'm sure Becky and Mrs. Beal will be a great help to him and Mrs. Beecher in seeing them well-sent-off in the world when they're ready for their first seasons. They might want to come visit us in London."

The idea of visiting London made the Beecher girls glow but their bemused mother was staring at the young lord, realising there might be a chance for all her daughters to marry as well as her son had done.

"Tom," Molly said as she reached for her husband's arm. "They're in love and it's done, so let's make our peace with it and with the young ones."

"Beecher, you're not about to stand for this!" George Beal objected.

Tom Beecher looked torn between his wife's entreaties and George Beal's outrage causing Andrew to move quickly to George's side. "But consider, Mr. Beal, you have the most of any to gain from this match."

"I? *I*?" George roared.

"You shall have your own back against society. A man of high principles without the slightest drop of prejudice in his veins, is how history will remember George Beal. His condescension impeccable whether to the village butcher or the Earl of Marleigh. None can ever say he was ashamed of his beginnings, nor his class."

"And none better!" George interjected.

Andrew smiled and continued smoothly. "Nor his class, wishing to raise his status by marrying into nobility no, no! I say, he was unconcerned about such petty matters. He never forgot the strong roots from whence he sprang. And the proof will be before all eyes his sons-in-law. One from the upper class whose snobbery George Beal would never condone, one from humbler beginnings but decent and strong and willing to work his way up in the world. What more could a father ask for his daughter?"

"George?" Mary Beal looked beseechingly towards her husband. "They are so in love."

"Papa?" Becky entreated, coming nearer her father, her sky-blue eyes sparkling with tears.

"Then too," Andrew added in seeming innocence. "Can you just imagine what a nettle all this will be in my mother's side?"

George Beal stared into Andrew's eyes, the memory of the countess fainting dead away fresh before his mind's eye. A small smile tugged at the corners of George's mouth no matter how he tried to stop it. "She's bound to make us all pay the very devil for this turn of events," George said.

Andrew looked properly chastised. "That is the truth, sir, nor can I hide it. My mother is a snob of the first water. But," he smiled towards Alice, "she shall come round in the end. I'm sure of it for none could resist my Alice for long." Andrew reached for his bride's hands.

"Nor my Becky," Paul added stoutly. Becky smiled at her new husband, reaching to link their hands.

The two young couples faced the others in the room and waited.

Mary Beal turned towards her own husband. "George, they're that happy and we couldn't ask for more."

Molly Beecher looked up at her husband and then marched past him. She kissed her son and after a shy moment she reached to hug Becky and then turned round, her determination facing her husband and the Beals. Mary Beal made her own decision, joining her children and Molly with a resolute expression.

Molly, Mary, Becky, Alice, Paul and Andrew stood arrayed in a battle line before Tom Beecher and George Beal. The Beecher girls huddled around the tea table and watched the adults with silent awe.

George Beal looked from his wife to his children and then to Andrew. Finally he looked straight at Paul Beecher.

"I suppose I have no say in the matter, what's done is done and more talk if I try to undo it," he said finally.

Becky flew towards her father, hugging him close. "Oh, I *knew* you couldn't stay angry with us, Papa, you love us too much!" The last of her words were smothered against her father's morning coat.

"All right, all right, now," George Beal said over the lump in his throat, "that's enough there. I suppose that's the end of it, then, with your old father foxed."

"Never foxed, sir," Andrew replied.

"No and you'd best all know it," George responded. "Well, I guess all's well that ends well as the poet said. And don't you look so very surprised, young Andrew. I've done my share of reading in my time."

"Of course, sir," Andrew replied in properly impressed accents.

"Well?" George Beal looked around himself. "I suppose there's nothing left but to toast the brides and grooms."

"There's something more," Paul Beecher said quietly. He looked towards his own silent father. "I've need of a word from my father before I feel peaceable about all this."

Tom Beecher eyed his son. "And why now?"

"I always wanted your best wishes Pa, you've more sense than any three I've ever known. But there just didn't seem any way to go about getting them."

"That's no excuse to go against your ma and your pa."

"No, sir." Paul looked properly downcast.

"Then again," his father said, "it's a Beecher trait to go after what a bloke knows should be his."

Molly Beecher came towards her husband. "Tom Beecher, you hug your son before another word goes by."

Tom Beecher stood where he was. Awkwardly, he moved towards his son. He hesitated before him and then, finally, hugged him close.

While the families came to terms in the red parlour and the wedding guests milled about the terraces and lawns, enjoying the sunny day, the refreshments and their gossip about what all had transpired, the abbey chapel was silent.

Fannie Burns pushed through the thick oak doors, looking for her mistress. Whom she found sitting in a front pew and staring up towards the glorious round stained glass window high above.

"Aggie, are you ready to leave?" Fannie asked quietly.

"In a moment or two," Lady Agatha replied.

Fannie looked around herself. "I've been told I looked quite natural as a bridesmaid. Mrs. Merriweather said perhaps I'd soon be a bride myself."

"Don't let Letty Merriweather give you ideas," Agatha replied.

"Me?" Fannie queried. "And who would I be marrying, I ask you that. Let alone you could never do without me and well we both know it." Fannie thought about her words. "No, I've spent my life in your employ and the rest of my life is as set as it ever was and is here with you and well it is," Fannie ended. "I'd be lost out in the world somewhere alone and lonely."

"You never need worry about that," Agatha responded.

The two women sat in companionable silence for a bit, the sunlight patterning rainbows around them, the distant sounds of the wedding reception far away outside.

"Well, then," Fannie said as she stood up. "Shall we join the others?"

"You go on ahead," Agatha said. "I'll only be a moment."

Fannie started to protest but something stopped her and she agreed to wait outside for her mistress. Agatha stayed where she was, quiet and alone in the empty oaken pews.

"Henry?" Agatha queried. "Henry, it was you, wasn't it? Not the wind at all."

There was no answer to her words.

Agatha looked towards the stained glass window, then down to the choir loft. "They've prattled of an abbey ghost and I have told them they were foolish but it's been you, all along, hasn't it?" She waited for an answer which never came. "I saw you," she whispered.

When no answer was forthcoming Lady Agatha Steadford-Smyth slowly got to her feet. Traversing the stone slab floor of the ancient Tudor chapel, she did not stop until she reached the thick double doors that led to the abbey hall. There she hesitated. And, silent, looked back once more.

Her eyes were drawn to a point high above her head and just below the huge, round, stained glass window where the Archangel Michael reached to protect all he saw. Sir Harry shimmered into view. He hovered, half-transparent and half-visible, as he saw Aggie's eyes upon him. With all the will he could muster he could not seem to make himself appear more substantial before his beloved.

She was staring at him, her breath caught in her throat. "It *is* you. But it can't be, for you look the same. Just the same . . . I must be dreaming while awake."

"Aggie, you see me and you're not fainting away at the sight," Sir Harry breathed words Agatha could not hear.

She stared at him, transfixed. "Harry" she breathed the beloved nickname so long banished from her thoughts and her dreams. "I've grown old while you've remained the same."

"You could never grow old, Aggie my love. Not to me," Harry told her softly. "You look as beautiful as when first my eyes did eye you."

" . . . could you possibly speak to me?" Agatha was asking.

"I am speaking to you, but, dear heart, you cannot hear me," Harry drifted closer to his love.

There was movement behind Lady Agatha, the doors opening as Alice and Andrew came in search of the Lady Agatha.

"There you are!" As Alice spoke Harry faded away, Lady Agatha watching after him and then turning towards the new arrivals.

"Yes," she said quietly.

"Fannie said you were. Why are you still here when all the party is outside? We've gotten our parents to talk to each other, even Andrew's! Come along and we'll tell you how brilliant Andrew was," the young people urged, oblivious of anything but their own happiness.

Lady Agatha glanced back at the seemingly empty chapel.

"Lady Agatha? Are you coming?" Alice asked.

Agatha hesitated, looking back for sight of the man she had instantly recognised. When nothing was to be seen, she turned towards the young couple. "Yes, child . . . Yes. I'm coming."

The chapel was silent after they left. Until Sir Harry the Ghost shimmered into view near the organ. He moved towards it, touching the keys ever so lightly with his ghostly fingers. Listening to the sounds of revelry from outside the chapel walls, Harry sighed. "This is how the abbey should always have sounded, full of happy people and the shouts of the young. And you, Aggie my love, as beautiful as ever."

Sir Harry smiled to himself. "And you saw me. Finally and at long last, you saw me!" Sir Harry placed his hands upon the organ keys, willing them to create their sweet and melancholy sounds. The music welled up through the chapel, carrying out of the abbey and across the grounds.

"Ah, Aggie my love, we've made fine progress. Finally you can see me, dear heart. And soon I'll find a way to make you hear me. And when you do—when you do Agatha Steadford—we'll never be apart again."

Outside Becky and Paul, Alice and Andrew, were accepting congratulations while the music drifted across the late spring afternoon. The guests partook of the wedding largess and enjoyed the organ melodies. Only the family were surprised, glancing towards each other as the sounds drifted across the late spring afternoon.

"But who can be playing?" Becky asked the others. "Lady Agatha is here. Lady Agatha," Becky waited for the lady in question to turn towards her from the banquet table, "who is playing the abbey organ?"

Agatha Steadford-Smyth smiled, a gentle curve to her lips, a soft light in her eyes. "An old friend, I think," Agatha replied. "An old, old friend," she repeated quietly to herself. Only Fannie heard the strange tone in her mistress's voice.

"Aggie, are you all right?"

"Better than in many, many years, Fannie. Better than in years."

They all saw Lady Agatha's soft smile. But none saw Sir Harry's smile as he sat alone at the chapel organ and dreamt of things to come.

**ACCLAIMED AUTHOR OF THE NATIONAL
BESTSELLER *DESERT SUNRISE***

CALICO

Raine Cantrell

Maggie vowed to open the New Mexico
mines she inherited and run them as well as
any man. Especially McCready, the one
man who stood in her way. He was a
thieving scoundrel, a land-hungry snake
who could cheat the sun from the sky. She
despised him—and yet she was bound to him
in a stormy marriage of convenience. And
McCready was determined to win this battle
of the sexes. But first he had to tame the
wildest heart in the West...

___1-55773-913-7/$4.99